Hearts Divided
(The Founders 5)

by

Robert Vaughan

Print Edition
© Copyright 2017 (as revised) Robert Vaughan

Wolfpack Publishing
P.O. Box 620427
Las Vegas, NV 89162

All rights reserved. No part of this book may be reproduced by any means without the prior written consent of the publisher, other than brief quotes for reviews.

ISBN 978-1-62918-813-3

This book is dedicated to Richard Gallen, modern day warrior of the code. The battles aren't as bloody, but it still pays to have a good man on your side.

Chapter 1

DAN O'LEE SHIFTED in his seat, the better to restore the circulation in his sore and cramped legs, and pulled the curtain back to peer through the stagecoach window. The snow, which had started as a light powder when they boarded this morning in Springfield, Missouri, was now coming down in large, heavy flakes. It was falling so steadily that the line of woods to either side of the road was all but obscured.

It was January 23, 1862, and Dan was twenty- three-days out of San Francisco, with just two more days to go before he reached St. Louis. Twenty-three days of bone-jarring stages, high mountain passes, wide-open spaces, and now the woods and hills of Missouri. He had come nearly two thousand miles since saying goodbye to Lady Pamela Buttle-Jones.

If Dan had learned one thing in the last twenty-three days, it was the best way to get comfortable in the cramped confines of the stage. He stretched his long legs out, folded his arms across his chest, pulled his hat low over his eyes, and cast his thoughts back . . . back to New Year's Eve, and the going-away dinner Pamela had given him.

"I really feel I should stay," Dan had told her.
"Whatever for?" Pamela asked.
Dan laughed. "I don't know. Maybe it's just that I feel that

I'm deserting you in your hour of need."

This time it was Pamela's time to laugh. "My dear boy, it is not my hour of need we are concerned with here. It is yours. You are the one who suffered a broken heart."

"It wasn't broken," Dan insisted. "It was only bent. Besides, you've helped me to get over it quite nicely."

"Dan," Pamela said gently, placing her hand on Dan's cheek. "I am flattered that you would find me desirable enough to assuage the hurt you felt. But I am also much older than you." "That means nothing," Dan insisted.

"Shh," Pamela said, putting her finger to her lips. "Hear me. I am much too vain a woman to sit by gracefully, should your eyes ever wander to a younger woman."

"Pamela, how could you suggest..."

"Shhh," Pamela said again, still smiling. "Perhaps you're right. Perhaps your eyes never would wander. But mine might. Don't you see, darling? I love you, I truly do, but I don't want the responsibility of your heart on my hands.

That's why I think it is best that you go to St. Louis."

Dan took Pamela's hands in both his, and held them tightly for a moment. Finally he spoke, surrendering to her logic. "You're right," he agreed. "There are too many memories here." "Exactly," Pamela said. "If you go to St Louis, soon all the unpleasant memories will fade, and there will be only the pleasant ones. I want to be remembered fondly, Dan, not lost in the morass of bitter reminders."

"So I'll go to St. Louis," Dan agreed, smiling at her persuasiveness.

"Wonderful. And I have some news for you. I've had some detective work done by my friend Allen Pinkerton. Your brother is currently employed by the Mississippi Transportation Company, as a loading foreman. He's working on the levee in St. Louis.

"You've located Burke?" Dan asked, surprised. "Located him yes, and written to him as well, though I've received no answer to my letter as yet. But that doesn't matter. What matters is we've found him. How long has it been?"

Dan ran his hand through his thick, reddish-brown hair as he thought. He looked up. "It's been twelve years," he said. "He was a ten-year-old kid when I left him with my aunt and uncle—to come out to California to make my fortune, you know." He grinned ironically. "Well, came to California, anyway."

"That will make him twenty-two now. Do you think you'll recognize him?" Lady Pamela asked.

"I ... I really don't know," Dan shrugged. "Fact is, I'm not sure if he would want to see me again. He was pretty upset by my leaving him there. He couldn't seem to understand that a twenty-one-year-old had no business raising the little tyke he was. At least that's what I told myself. But I've often wondered if I wasn't just being selfish. I could have kept him with me if I had worked at it. Maybe I should have."

"Never mind that now," Pamela said. "That's water under the bridge. It's only important that you're going to see him again."

"Guess you're right," Dan said. He smiled. "Damn, I do believe I'm looking forward to this."

"As well you should," Pamela said. She slid her arms around his neck, then leaned into him and brought her lips just a kiss away from his. "And I, my handsome young traveler, am looking forward to telling you goodbye, and wishing you a happy new year, in a very special way."

"What about you?" someone asked Dan. The memories suddenly popped out of Dan's mind as if someone had burst a balloon, and he realized that he was on the stage, being spoken to.

Dan slid his hat back and looked into the face of a red-faced, fat-cheeked drummer by the name of Quimby. He'd met the salesman just that morning; he was in cookware.

"Beg your pardon," Dan said. "Did you say something to me?"

"Yes. I said this here war is all but over, but these fellas

Hearts Divided

don't seem to agree."

"I'm afraid I haven't been following the news as closely as I should. I'm only recently arrived from California."

"Well, I'll tell you what I know," the drummer said. He leaned forward confidentially, as if sharing a war secret with Dan and the other two passengers, one a Union army officer, the other a preacher. "I was in General Halleck's office myself last week, and I seen dispatches that said that the Federal troops were pushing the Secesh all over the place. Why, General Thomas run them plumb outta Mill Springs, Kentucky where they fought a battle, and the Rebel general, a fella named Zollicoffer, he was kilt."

"Zollicoffer was an amateur," the Union officer said. "He had no more business in a uniform than you do."

Dan and the preacher laughed.

"Just 'cause you got that soldier's suit on, that don't make you no military expert, sonny," Quimby said, piqued. "I'm tellin' you the Secesh don't have no officers worth a tinker's dam." "What about Beauregard, and Albert Sidney Johnston?" the Union officer asked.

"Or Sterling Price, Jeff Thompson, or even Quantrill?" the preacher added.

"Beauregard and Johnston are cowards," the drummer said resolutely. "Price, Thompson, and Quantrill? Incompetents, hardly worth mentioning."

"If I see Quantrill I'll tell him of your high regard for him, sir," the preacher said.

The Union officer smiled, then peered through the window again, for perhaps the hundredth time since they'd left St. Joseph. At first Dan had thought the officer was concerned with the weather, but there was a nervousness in his manner now not brought on by the snow. Dan watched him curiously, but without question.

Quimby went on, a bit angrily. "You fellas are talking like a couple of Secesh. It's a good thing you're a wearin' that blue uniform, elsewise I might wonder just whose side you're on.

'N I could ask the same thing of you, preacher." "I'm a man of the cloth, sir," the preacher said, smiling. "I will preach the word of the Lord to whoever shall heed it, be he Union or Confederate."

"That's a dangerous position to take in Missouri," the drummer said. "You've got to assort yourself here. Elsewise in this state, nobody will know who is for what."

"On the contrary," the preacher replied wryly. "I would say that this is the safest position to take in a border state."

"And you, sir? You've just arrived from California. How stands that state?"

"I can only speak for myself, not for California," Dan said. "Me, I sure don't want to see the Union dissolved. But I've no wish to take up arms against my fellow countrymen either. I still have hopes of a peaceful solution."

"All such hopes are gone, I fear," the Union officer said. "The drummer is at least right on that point. By the way, we haven't met. My name is Thomas Ward. I'm a lieutenant in the regular army."

"Dan O'Lee," Dan said, taking the hand offered him. It was a firm and friendly handshake. "Are you on leave?"

"No. I'm on special orders," Ward said. "I'll be joining General Halleck's staff in St. Louis. Is St. Louis your destination as well?"

"Yes," Dan said. "I've a brother there whom L haven't seen in many years. And I've a bit of business to attend to."

Dan was truthful in telling the officer he had business in St. Louis. Lady Pamela Buttle-Jones had given him a bank draft for ten thousand dollars, with instructions to buy a piece of land. The land was owned by Hiram Dempster, an old acquaintance of Lady Pamela's, and he had promised to sell it to her if the ten thousand dollars was "personally delivered" to his hands.

"If I can be of any assistance in any way," Ward said, "please look me up."

"Thanks for your offer, lieutenant," Dan said. The

Hearts Divided

conversation died down, each man seemingly lost in his own thoughts. Outside the stage slipped and slid through the blinding snowstorm, its forward motion now reduced to a speed no faster than a man could walk.

Chapter 2

UNDER A CLUSTER of trees near the stage pike, a group of horsemen waited. They wore sheepskin coats, and scarfs wrapped around their necks, and hats, which were brimful of snow.

"I don't think he'll be a-comin' out in this kind of weather," one of the men said. He squirted a stream of tobacco juice toward the snowbank, where it browned for just a moment, then was quickly buried by new snow so that it wasn't visible.

"The chief said it would be here, it'll be here," another answered.

"You think the chief cain't do nothin' wrong," the first said. "What's he got for you, boy? A pocket full o' sugar titties?"

The boy who had defended his chief unbuttoned his coat, and faced his taunter. The man's gun hand was clearly visible, and the boy moved his hand to hover menacingly over it.

"Pull your gun, you son of a bitch, or ride out of here," the boy said.

"Jesse, come on, he didn't mean nothin' by it," one of the other men said..

"I said pull your gun," Jesse said again, looking at the man with cold, calm, blue eyes.

A third man moved in between the two. "Dingus, we got us enough Yankees to kill, without havin' to shoot up our own," he complained. He was using Jesse's nickname as a placating gesture, but Jesse wasn't put off by it.

"Burke, get out of the way," the boy said coldly. "I don't want to shoot you."

"Then call this thing off," Burke said. "Leastwise 'till we get somewhere where you two can settle it between yourselves without putting the rest of us in danger. Frank, talk to your brother."

Frank James rode over to his younger brother and put his hand on Jesse's arm. "Close up your coat, Dingus," he said. "You're gonna catch your death with a chill."

There was a tense moment, then Jesse relented. "Sure, Frank," he said. "Whatever you say." He buttoned his coat back up, then stuck his hands in his pockets to warm them.

"I don't know why he got so mad. All I said was . . ." the other man started, but the rider nearest him, the one called Burke, twisted in his saddle and cuffed him on the jaw, stopping him in mid-sentence.

"Hey, what'd you do that for?" the man asked.

"Figured I'd save your life, you damn fool," Burke said. "We don't want to hear what you said. Just shut up, and listen for the stage." Burke O'Lee settled back in his saddle and tried to fight off the cold. He had made a decision to support the South and had joined up with the guerilla William Clarke Quantrill because he thought that was the quickest way to get into the war. Quantrill, who often used the alias Charley Hart, was thus called Charley, had the deadliest gang of cutthroats and brigands ever assembled in one company. Burke O'Lee could hold his own with most men, had in fact been in a few duels in his young life, and the fact that he was still around attested to his success in them. But men like Frank and Jesse James and Jim, Bob, and Cole Younger were little more than cold-blooded killers and thieves, and Burke was becoming disaffected with his association with them.

Quantrill wasn't with them for this mission. He had left Frank James in charge. It was a relatively simple mission. They were to stop a stage and recover a document, which was being carried by a Yankee courier.

"Listen up," Frank suddenly called, holding a hand high. "I think I hear 'em comin'."

Burke strained to hear. In the softness of the snowfall, he could hear the driver whistling and shouting at his team to urge them on.

"Burke, you ride out into the road and try'n stop the driver. Tell him you want to buy passage to the next town, and you aim to tie your horse on back. Well have the drop on him that way, and we might can pull this off without any gunplay."

"It would be simpler just to shoot him," Jesse said easily.

"Well try it my way," Frank insisted.

The rest of the gang melted back into the woods to wait for Burke to do his job. Burke rode out onto the road and stood there with his hand raised.

The plan may have worked, but the rider who had been braced by Jesse earlier got a little nervous and dashed out of the woods too quickly. The driver saw him out of the corner of his eye, and, realizing something was up, raised his rifle and shot Burke.

Burke felt a searing pain tearing into his shoulder, and his breath left him as the bullet knocked him off his horse. Almost as soon as he fell into the snow, he heard the guns of the others open up. He saw the driver pitch off the high seat, then land spread-eagled in the snow, his blood staining red on the pristine white.

From Burke's vantage point on the ground, he saw, despite his pain, a peculiar thing. The rider who had compromised their position suddenly tumbled out of his saddle, shot dead, though not one bullet had been fired from the stage.

The riders reined up alongside the stage, their horses

prancing about in excitement and breathing clouds of steam into the cold air.

"You folks in the stage, climb down outta there," Frank shouted.

Cole Younger rode over to where Burke lay in the snow and looked down at him.

"Help me onto my horse, Cole," Burke said, keeping his voice calm. He wasn't sure but that they might shoot him if they thought he was hurt badly enough to slow them down, so he was underplaying his wound as much as possible.

"Are you bad hit?"

"No," Burke said. 'It's just a flesh wound." The bullet was in fact buried deep in his shoulder. He could feel the weight of it and the heat of it, as if someone were holding a hot poker to his flesh.

Burke followed the action near the stage as best he could, while Cole helped him mount. Four men stepped out of the coach.

"Boy, am I glad to see you gentlemen of the South," the drummer said nervously. "I've been expressing my Southern sentiments to these fellas, but they are all Union to the core, and they've given me a pretty rough time of it."

Frank laughed. "Is that true, Charley? Have you fellas been giving this Southern patriot a hard time?"

The preacher stroked his Vandyke beard for just a moment, then smiled and removed his long, black coat. Beneath it he wore the gray and gold tunic of a Confederate captain. "Oh, yes," he said. "We've really been giving him a rough time."

"You!" the drummer said, his face reflecting his fear. "You're a Rebel!"

"Gentlemen, my name is William Clarke Quantrill, at your service," the man said, smiling at them. He dropped the black coat and wrapped himself in a grey officer's coat, provided him by one of his men who also brought up a spare horse. "I regret the inconvenience, but it is a necessity of war.

Lieutenant Ward, I do believe you have a dispatch which would interest us."

"I have nothing of the sort," Ward said stiffly. "Please, just give it to us and we'll be on our way," Quantrill said. "I don't want to have to shoot you."

"I don't know what you are talking about," Ward said again.

"I'm sorry, lieutenant. You are a brave man, and it is a shame to have to kill you," Quantrill said. He signaled to the young, beardless boy, and the boy raised his gun and fired without a second's hesitation.

There was a loud, unexpected boom. The impact of the heavy .44 caliber bullet slammed Lieutenant Ward against the wheel of the stage. Then he slid down to the ground, holding his hand over the wound in his chest. Blood spilled over his fingers and ran down the front of his coat.

"Search him," Quantrill ordered, and two of the riders swung off their horses and began stripping the lieutenant. Within moments the young officer was lying naked in the snow, his body already turning blue, the blood from his wound coagulating in the cold.

"There ain't nothin' on him, Charley," one of the searchers said.

"Are you positive?"

"Well, hell, look for yourself. There ain't nothin' in his clothes, 'n he's as nekkid as the day he come into the world. Where would it be at?"

"Damn," Quantrill swore, striking his fist into his hand. "We must have been given the wrong information. Well, mount up. We've got us a long ride ahead."

"May I attend to the lieutenant now?" Dan asked.

"Yeah," one of the riders said. He was the one who had shot Ward. "But he's gonna die, 'cause I shot him in the heart. You can try'n get him warm if you want."

One of the other riders laughed. "Dingus, I allus did say your heart was too soft for serious killin'."

"I do my job," Jesse replied.

Quantrill shouted an order and the riders rode away into the snowstorm. Dan noticed that one of them was wavering in the saddle, obviously seriously wounded.

Dan took the coat Quantrill had discarded and used it and Lieutenant Ward's own coat to try and make the lieutenant comfortable.

The lieutenant barely had the strength to raise his hand to his mouth. He pointed, then opened his mouth and raised his tongue. Dan saw a rolled-up piece of white paper in his mouth, and, realizing that the lieutenant wanted him to get it, reached in and pulled it out.

"I'll get this to General Halleck for you:," Dan promised.

"Liberty," the lieutenant said, the word barely audible.

"What? What did you say?"

The lieutenant coughed, and the spasms shook his body so that he had difficulty breathing. Finally, he was able to speak again. "Liberty," he said, struggling to get the word out. Then his head rolled to one side, and a final, rasping breath escaped from his mouth.

"He's dead," Dan said.

"What was he sayin'?" the drummer asked. "Sounded like liberty."

"Yes," Dan said, standing up and looking down at the dead officer.

"The poor fella must'a been delirious," the drummer suggested. "I guess he was tryin to tell us that he died for liberty."

"I guess so," Dan said. "Come on, help me get him into the coach."

"What? You mean he's gonna ride inside with us?"

"He's going to ride inside with you," Dan said. "He, and the driver both. I've got to drive this thing. I'll be on top."

"I don't want to ride inside with a couple of dead men," the drummer complained. "Why'nt we just leave 'em out here 'n send somebody back for 'em? They're dead now. It won't make no never mind to them."

"I have a better idea," Dan said.

"What?"

"I'll leave you here, and send someone back for you."

"No," the drummer said. "I don't want to stay out here all alone."

"You won't be alone," Dan suggested. "You'll have him for company." He pointed at the dead guerilla, lying perhaps twenty yards from the stage, his body now nearly covered with snow.

"You wouldn't really leave me out here, would you?"

"I'm considering it, if you don't help me get these two inside," Dan said. "We'll leave him for whoever wants him," he added, pointing to the raider's body.

The drummer complained mightily, but he helped Dan load the bodies of the driver and the lieutenant. Then he got inside with them, and Dan climbed up on the high seat to take the reins of the horses.

It was a fifteen-mile run to the next way station. Though the snow finally quit falling, it still took them the better part of three hours to make it. When they got there, Dan was relieved to see a detachment of Federal troops also at the station, and he turned both bodies over to them.

Dan considered surrendering the paper he had taken from Lieutenant Ward's mouth to them as well, but at the last minute, he decided to keep it himself and deliver it personally to General Halleck. After all, he was going to St. Louis anyway. This way he would be satisfied that Lieutenant Ward's mission, whatever it was, would be completed.

Chapter 3

THE TERRIBLE PAIN stopped and a warming numbness set in. It was that numbness which allowed Burke to keep up with the others on their mad ride away from the scene of the holdup. But with the numbness came also a weakness from loss of blood, and by the time they rode into Rolla, Missouri just before dawn the next morning, Burke was staying in his saddle only by supreme effort of will.

"Hey, chief, Burke's about to keel over here," Jesse called. Jesse had taken it on himself to ride beside Burke, and for the last three hours it had been he who held the reins to Burke's horse, while Burke used both hands on the pommel, just to stay up.

How like Jesse James that was, Burke managed to think, despite the befuddling haze of pain he was in. Dingus, who could kill a man without blinking an eye, could also be moved to acts of extreme kindness and gentleness. By far the youngest of Quantrill's band, he was clearly the most fascinating.

"I know a doctor in this town who'll patch him up," Quantrill said.

"Do we have the time?" one of the other riders asked.

"We won't wait for him. We'll just drop him off and ride on our way."

"What if the sawbones turns him into the Yankees?" Jesse asked.

"We'll pay him enough to buy his silence," Quantrill said. "Dingus, you and Burke come with me. Frank, you and thee rest of the boys ride down to that farmhouse there. It belongs to a fella name of Matthew Poe. Tell him you're with Charles Hart and that we've come to Rolla to buy cattle. He'll have his woman fix you some hot grub. Me'n Dingus'll take breakfast at the doc's house."

"Let's go boys," Frank said.

As they left, Quantrill, Jesse and Burke headed for the doctor's house. Though it was still pre-dawn dark, the snow on the ground made it appear light. As the three rode through the street, they could see squares of golden light on the snow, cast there through the windows of the houses where early risers were already beginning to set to breakfast.

Quantrill halted them when they reached the end of the street.

"What is it, chief?" Jesse asked.

"That's the house down there," Quantrill said, pointing to a low, single-story building which sat nearly half a block away from the others. A wisp of wood smoke rose from the chimney, carrying with it the aroma of frying bacon. "I just want to make sure there's no one around."

The saddle squeaked as Jesse twisted in it to look around. Burke held on, telling himself there was only a short time left and then he could lay down and rest in a warm house.

"It looks clear," Jesse said calmly.

Quantrill clicked to his horse, and the three of them slowly crossed the distance. They stopped just in front of the doctor's house.

SAM COYLE, M.D., the sign read by the door. Quantrill didn't bother to knock; he just pushed it open. Then he and Jesse half-carried, half-supported Burke inside.

"What the—? What is this?" the surprised doctor asked, looking up from his breakfast table. His wife was standing at the stove frying bacon, and she looked around in alarm as well.

"Don't get fretted none, doc," Quantrill said quietly. "It's just me. One of my men got hisself shot up yesterday afternoon. He needs some doctorin'."

The doctor moved quickly to the door and looked around nervously before he shut it. "Did anyone see you bring him here?" he asked anxiously.

"No," Quantrill said. "We know it ain't healthy to be Secesh in this town."

Jesse lay Burke on the bed. Doctor Coyle sat beside him and opened his coat, then his shirt.

"He's lucky," he said. "The cold stopped the bleeding, and I don't think there's any festering. But the bullet is going to have to come out."

Quantrill sat at the breakfast table without asking and began helping himself. Jesse stood by the bed for a moment longer, then, when the doctor's wife invited him to breakfast, he too sat at the table.

"Here's a little laudanum," Dr. Coyle said to Burke, handing him a small bottle. "Take it. You'll need it when I start probing for the bullet."

Doctor Coyle's wife assisted him. They removed Burke's shirt and then the doctor began digging into the wound for the bullet. Quantrill and Jesse ate their breakfast as if totally unconcerned with what was going on over on the bed. A few minutes later, when Coyle announced that he had the bullet and then dropped it with a clink into the pan of warm water, neither of the two made a comment.

"Can he ride out with us now?" Quantrill asked, when he and Jesse finished their breakfast.

"Are you serious? I should say not. It'll be a few hours before he'll even wake up." Quantrill tugged at his beard for a moment, then reached into his coat pocket and pulled out a gold coin. "Here, doc, this is for fixin' up the boy and feedin' us breakfast. Tell Burke he's on his own when he wakes up. We can't wait around for him."

"I can't keep him here," Doctor Coyle protested.

"You don't have to keep him here. Send him on his way."

"He should have at least a day's rest," Doctor Coyle said.

"Then give it to him," Quantrill said. "You've been paid handsomely enough. Come on, Dingus, we've got to be on our way."

Quantrill and Jesse left the small house, and Coyle and his wife stood there, looking at the door as if unable to believe what had happened to them this morning. They waited for a moment, and when they heard the horses leave, Doctor Coyle walked over to look through the window to make sure they had gone.

"Sam, you knew those people?" Coyle's wife said. She brushed a wisp of errant brown hair out of her eyes, and looked at the young man who lay on their bed, bare from the waist up and now sleeping peacefully.

"That was Quantrill," Doctor Coyle said.

"Quantrill! The murderer?"

"Molly," Dr. Coyle said from the window. "If anyone comes by today, you tell them I was called to Jefferson City, do you have that? I'm going to Jefferson City."

"What for?"

"Unless I miss my guess, there'll be a reward out for this man. I aim to bring a couple of soldiers back with me."

"Sam, you're going to leave me with him, alone?" Molly asked, surprised by his statement and frightened by the prospect.

"Don't worry none. He'll mostly be out of it for the next twelve hours, and I figure to be back by nightfall. If anyone asks who he is, why, you just tell them he's your nephew, wounded in the war."

"Sam, what will they do to him?" Molly asked, looking at Burke.

"Hang him, most likely."

"Hang him? But he's just a boy."

"That ain't none of our concern, Molly," the doctor said,

already slipping into his coat. "You just do like I told you, and I'll see you tomorrow mornin'." He smiled. "Countin' the gold piece old Quantrill gave me, 'n the reward this boy's sure to bring, why this'll be a pretty profitable day, don't you think?"

Molly put the "doctor out of town" sign on the front door after Coyle left, then cleaned up the breakfast dishes, and then the house. But throughout the morning, her eyes kept wandering over to the boy on the bed. His hair was blond, and he had a thin, blond mustache over lips which were almost too full for a man's. There was a dimple in his chin. His chest, though adorned with only the sparsest blond hair, was full and muscular. The skin was clear and smooth.

Whenever Molly caught herself looking at him, she would scold herself mentally, and look away. After all, the boy couldn't have been much over twenty, and she was thirty-eight years old ... a married woman who had no right to think about how handsome a man might be.

But she couldn't keep the disturbing thoughts of him from creeping into her mind, and before she knew it, she would be looking at him again.

Molly stoked up the fire in the fireplace, not because it was cold in the house—in fact, it was quite warm—but just to keep herself occupied so that she wouldn't look at him.

But it didn't work. Once more she turned to see him, and this time as she stared she could feel a warmth in her body which wasn't brought on entirely by the fire she had built. She took off her sweater. She felt some respite from the increased temperature but no relief from the heat building within. The heat drove her to unbutton the top six buttons of her dress, and she folded the collar back, almost all the way down to the swell of her breasts. She knew it was a scandalous move, but as she was alone, she didn't care.

No, she thought, she wasn't alone. The young man on the bed was with her. But he's sleeping, she decided, thus justifying her scandalous action.

Molly walked over to the stove and poured a kettle of hot

water into a basin, then carried the basin over to the bed and sat on it. She began giving the young man a bath. She was doing no more than administering to a patient, she told herself. But her breathing began to be more labored, and felt such a churning within that it could scarcely be contained.

The man's eyes opened.

He started to sit up, but so abrupt was his movement that it sent a searing stab of pain into his shoulder, and he fell back down on the bed.

"Lie still, sir, and you will be more comfortable," Molly instructed.

"Who are you?" Burke asked. He looked around. "What is this place?"

"Don't you remember coming here, earlier this morning?"

Burke looked into the face of the woman who was bathing him. It was a pleasantly attractive face, he decided, and it eased some of the fear which shot through him.

"No," he finally said. "I remember only the cold. The cold, and the riding. Where am I?"

"This is the house of Dr. Coyle in Rolla."

"Where are the others?"

"Your friends have gone," Molly said. "They left you here to mend."

Burke looked up at the ceiling. Molly thought she had never seen eyes so clear a blue. They looked like the afternoon sky on the sharpest, sunlit day.

"Where is the doctor?" Burke asked.

"He's ... gone ... on business," Molly said. "There are just the two of us here."

As Molly talked, she continued to bathe Burke, and now the cloth was on Burke's stomach. The action caused Molly to bend over and as she did her unbuttoned dress fell forward slightly, exposing the curve of her breast. She felt a heat there, then looked up to see that Burke was staring at the scene she had thus presented.

"I . . . I'm sorry," she mumbled, and she reached up to

Hearts Divided

close the buttons.

"No," Burke said, putting his hand on her gently. "You don't have to close the buttons if you don't want to."

"I'm a silly old woman," she said. She turned her head away from him, closing her eyes tightly and biting her lower lip.

"You are a lovely woman, without age," Burke said easily. He reached down and unfastened his breeches, then pushed them down and guided her hand, the hand which was now mindlessly bathing in a circle on his stomach, down further, until she felt his bulging manhood.

"No," she said, "please no." She was trembling now, like a frightened bird. Tears streamed down her face. "Help me to fight this evil want that's come over me."

Burke put his hand behind her neck, then gently pulled her head down to his, pressing her lips to his.

She let out a small whimper, and returned his kiss with surprising ardor. Her skin was incredibly warm, and he could feel the pulse in her neck beating rapidly. Finally, with a gasp of breath, she sat up. "I beg of you," she said. "Don't you know what you are doing to me?"

Burke smiled, and pulled her back to him for another kiss. This time he began unbuttoning the remaining buttons. Without mind or will of her own, Molly helped him, so that within a moment, she lay beside him on the bed . . . the bed she shared with her husband ... as naked as was this beautiful young man.

Molly tried to fight against the terrible need, which was consuming her body, but she was too weak, too invested with desire, to be effective. The warmth spread through her with dizzying speed, and she surrendered herself to it, no longer putting up the pretense of fighting.

Burke tried to change positions, to move over her, but the pain in his shoulder stabbed at him again. When Molly saw that, she smiled gently, put her cool fingers on his shoulders to indicate that he should stay where he was, and moved over him, taking him into her, orchestrating the unfolding events on her own.

Molly felt Burke beneath her, thrusting up against her, helping her as she continued to make love to him.' Then, finally, she felt the jolts of rapture which racked her body and caused her to fall across him with a groan of ecstasy, even as he was spending himself in her in final, convulsive shudders.

They lay that way for several moments, with Molly on top, allowing the pleasure to drain from her body slowly, like heat leaving an iron. Finally, she got up and looked down at him.

Burke smiled at her. "Your husband is a lucky man, madam," he said.

Molly gasped and put her hand to her mouth. "Oh," she said. "I nearly forgot. You can't stay here, you have to leave."

"Why? Are you afraid he can see it in our faces?" Burke asked.

"No, it isn't that at all," she said. "But my husband has gone after the Union soldiers. He intends to turn you in for the reward money."

Burke sat up, and felt a wave of dizziness and nausea overtake him. He sat on the edge of the bed for several moments until the feeling passed. "How much time do I have?" he asked.

"He said he wouldn't be back until tonight, but if he finds soldiers between here and Jefferson City, he'll be back much sooner than that. I really can't say when he'll be back."

Burke reached for his pants. "Help me get dressed," he asked, and Molly, still naked herself, bent down beside him to help him into his clothes.

After Burke was dressed, Molly dressed quickly, then made him several sandwiches and wrapped them in a cloth to give to him. "Here's lunch and dinner," she said.

"Thanks," Burke replied, taking the proffered package. "Is my horse still here?"

"Yes, Sam took him to the barn."

"Still saddled?"

"I'm sure it is. He didn't stay out there long enough to unsaddle it."

"That's bad for ole' Poke," he said. "But good for me. I don't know if I could get him saddled myself."

With Molly's help, he put his coat on, then started out the back door. Just before he opened it, he looked at her and smiled. "Thanks," he said.

Molly kissed him goodbye, then watched him walk through the snow to the small lean-to, which served as a barn. When Burke swung onto his horse and rode away, his last sight was of Molly standing in the doorway watching him.

Chapter 4

DAN O'LEE STOOD at the window of the Federal Building in St. Louis, waiting to talk to General Halleck. From where he stood he could see the Mississippi River as it flowed by. Chunks of ice joined the other debris which floated downstream. The cobblestone levee, where several boats were tied up, was slick with winter ice, and there were several men working there, loading and unloading the boats.

Burke O'Lee, Dan's brother, wasn't one of the men. That was the first place Dan went to when he reached St. Louis, thinking his reunion with his brother should take precedence over all else. But the reunion didn't take place, for the simple reason that Burke no longer worked on the riverfront, and no one could give Dan a hint as to where he had gone.

"Mr. O'Lee, General Halleck will see you now," a staff officer said. Dan thanked him and followed him into the general's office. This was the second place Dan had come to after reaching St. Louis, feeling that the message he took from the dead lieutenant would be of great importance.

General Halleck greeted Dan with a smile of welcome. The general had a very high forehead, bushy, nearly white, mutton-chop whiskers, dark eyebrows, and large, rather pleasant looking eyes. He was known as a man of brilliance: a

West Point graduate who once resigned his commission to study law and enter into mining in California, but returned to the military at the outbreak of war due to his devotion to the Union cause.

"General, it was good of you to see me," Dan said.

"You said that you were a friend of Lady Pamela Buttle-Jones," General Halleck said. "I have a great deal of respect and admiration for that lady, and any friend of hers is certainly worth a few moments of my time. Tell me, how is she?"

"She is very well, General. In fact, one of my reasons for coming to St. Louis is to fulfill an errand for her."

"Oh? And how may I help?"

"General, my asking to see you has nothing to do with that errand," Dan said. "But rather with an incident which occurred on the stage while enroute to St. Louis."

General Halleck offered a seat to Dan, which Dan accepted gratefully, then told of the stage being waylaid by Quantrill's gang. He told of the driver being killed, and of the lieutenant's brave death.

General Halleck pinched the bridge of his nose as Dan finished the story. "Ah, such a fine young man," he said sadly. "It is always tragic for me to have to write the parents of our boys who are killed, but it will be particularly so for me to write to Tom's parents, for I have known them a long, long time."

"General, there is more to the story," Dan said, taking the paper from his pocket. He handed it to the general. "Lieutenant Wade somehow managed to conceal this in his mouth just before he got out of the stage. The bushwhackers overlooked it."

"What is it?" General Halleck asked.

"Well, I . . . I really don't know. I was hoping you would. It is obviously important, since the lieutenant died protecting it."

General Halleck unrolled the paper and looked at it. "It's in code," he said. He picked up a bell on his desk and shook it, summoning the same officer who had escorted Dan into the general's office. "Have this decoded and returned to me immediately," the general said. "Right away, sir," the officer replied.

"Tell me about Lady Pamela," Halleck said, as they were waiting for the decoding of the message. "Is she still as beautiful as ever?"

"Amazingly so," Dan replied.

"You may be interested in an amusing, and somewhat ironic incident which occurred just before I left California," Halleck said. "I was pleasantly surprised one morning to find in my mail an invitation to one of Lady Pamela's dinner parties. To be honest, I was quite busy, and had another engagement, but one doesn't spurn the opportunity to attend one of Lady Pamela's celebrated dinners, so I rearranged my schedule to allow me to go. When I arrived there, I saw an old friend of mine had also been invited. We had known each other for many years, though we had drifted apart somewhat after I left the army. We had a most entertaining visit that evening, recalling old times, catching each other up with the latest news in our own lives." Halleck chuckled. "Do you know who that old friend was?"

"No, sir," Dan said. "Though I do recall the party you are speaking of. I was out of town that evening, I believe."

"That old friend was Albert Sidney Johnston. Now I am Commanding General of the Union Army of the West, and General Johnston is Commanding General of the Confederate Army of the West. So here we have two old friends facing each other."

"General, here is the decoded message," the officer said, returning at that moment.

"Good, good," Halleck said. He opened the drawer to his desk and pulled out a pair of wire-rim spectacles, then put them on, hooking them carefully, one ear at a time. He used his forefinger to slide them up his nose, then read the decoded message.

"Well, Mr. O'Lee, you'll be interested in knowing that you have indeed brought us a message of great importance."

"I am glad, sir."

"Have you ever heard of a place called Sikeston?"

"Sikeston? No, sir, I'm afraid not."

"Well, there's no reason you should, really. It's so tiny that it isn't even on most of the maps. But it could be a crucial spot for us now. You see, there is a railroad, which runs from Bird's Point on the Mississippi River to the tiny town of Sikeston. There, the railroad ends. But from Sikeston to New Madrid, there is a fine plank road, over which we could transport men and material through the swamps. The Rebels realized the importance of Sikeston as well, and they put several pieces of artillery there to defend the railhead. But, according to this message, Jeff Thompson has pulled his guns away from Sikeston and turned them over to General McCown to use in fortifying Island Number Ten, at New Madrid."

"And that is good news to you?" Dan asked.

"That is very good news to me," Halleck replied. He smiled, and put his hand on Dan's shoulder. "And it is all thanks to you."

"No, sir," Dan replied. "It is thanks to Lieutenant Ward. It is a shame he had to die to get the information to you, though."

"Yes it is," Halleck agreed. "But when one must die, it is at least good to have one's death be meaningful. Tom Ward didn't die uselessly. He died for liberty."

Suddenly the lieutenant's dying word came back to Dan. He started to say something, thinking it ironic that General Halleck would express the same sentiment. But General Halleck was already starting for the door to summon the next in a long line of visitors, and Dan, knowing that the general's time was valuable, let the thought die before giving it tongue.

Dan was glad that this mission had been successful. Earlier, he had failed in trying to find his brother. That left only his business for Lady Pamela to accomplish, and in that, at least, he was reasonably certain of success.

Dan took a room in the Boatman's Hotel and later waited in the lobby, having sent a message to Hiram Dempster that he was at his disposal. While waiting, he read the *St. Louis Democrat.* Though the major papers of the east were already beginning to talk of the war as a phony war, with little significant action thus far, all over Missouri, Kentucky, Tennessee and Arkansas, men were fighting and dying, and the paper had one entire column listing casualties in the Western skirmishes.

Dan was about to put the paper down, when, as it sometimes will, a word seemed to leap from the page to arrest his attention. The word was liberty.

LIBERTY SPEAKS FOR LIBERTY, the head of one of the articles stated.

> Miss Liberty Welles is well noted for her ability to hold sway over a crowd by the power of her elocution, but never was she in better form than she was last night when she told of the bravery of Verity Eternal.
>
> Verity Eternal's resolute course and trying ordeal have given this sturdy lady of color a strong hold upon public attention. She is welcomed in the loyal States with a degree of warmth consonant with her own sanguine temperament.
>
> One day a crowd in Tennessee threatened to tear down the Stars and Stripes which flew in front of her house, she being a free woman and able to have a home of her own. But, like a lioness in defense of her lair, Miss Eternal threatened to shoot the first man to touch her flag.
>
> "Miss, you won't shoot, will you?" asked the leader.
>
> "You had better try the experiment," said

>Verity Eternal.
>
>"Go on, go on!" shouted the crowd. "She daren't shoot."
>
>With that, Miss Eternal instantly drew from her pocket one of Colt's revolvers and, cocking it, leveled it at the man's head.
>
>"Never mind her, she's but a colored woman," cried the mob.
>
>"My God! Look at her eye!" responded the man. He made a bow, scraped the ground and toddled off, followed by the whole crowd.
>
>This story was related before a meeting of the St. Louis Abolitionist Society by Miss Liberty Welles, and so well was it told by the beautiful lady that she was often interrupted by hurrahs and cheers, and afterwards warmly applauded.

There was that word liberty again, Dan thought, folding the paper and laying it to one side. At that precise moment, he was approached by a uniformed bellboy.

"Mr. O'Lee, there is a gentleman in the bar who wishes me to escort you to him," the bellboy said. "He says you summoned him for a meeting."

"Ah, yes," Dan said, standing. "That would be Hiram Dempster. Please, lead on," he added, handing the boy a coin.

The bar was crowded with uniformed men and well-dressed women. St. Louis was a military city, and most of her men wore uniforms, whether of the regular army or fighting reserves, or even the colorful 'Home Guards', whose gaudiness of uniform was inversely proportional to the likelihood of their ever seeing action.

The bellboy pushed through them with the self-appointed importance of being on a hotel errand, and introduced Dan to a man who sat at a table near the rear.

The man was tall and thin, with a drooping handlebar mustache and dark bags under pale blue eyes. He smiled a greeting, but his eyes did not, and his handshake was like a dead fish. Dan was placed on immediate guard with him.

"So, Mr. O'Lee, what can I do for you?" Dempster asked.

Dan reached into his inside jacket pocket and removed the envelope containing the bank draft. "I represent Lady Pamela," he said. "She wishes to buy the piece of land you have offered, and has adhered to the requirements of the deal, namely that ten thousand dollars be delivered to you by hand."

Dempster waved the money away. "The deal was that it be delivered by *her* hand," he said. "It is not acceptable, coming from you."

"You did not so stipulate in your agreement, sir," Dan said.

"It was implied," Dempster said.

Dan sighed and returned the draft to his inside pocket. "I'm sorry," he said. "It would appear that my trip for Lady Pamela has been in vain. I will send her a telegram to that effect, and ask further instructions."

"I remember Lady Pamela . . . from the old days," Dempster said. His eyes grew deep, and were glazed with a lustful tint. "I would like to see her again. Tell her that if she wants this property, she must come to St. Louis personally, and ask pie for it."

"No, Mr. Dempster, I don't think I will do that," Dan said. "Lady Pamela is most happy in California, I assure you. Besides, with the unsettled conditions of the war, I would protest vigorously should she even consider it."

"You would protest? By what right would you protest?" Dempster asked.

"By the right of one who has been, and is still, very close to her."

"Close?" Dempster said. "What do you mean close? Are you her lover?"

The corners of Dan's mouth drew back into a tight line, and a vein on his temple throbbed in anger. He forced himself to remain quiet for a moment before he spoke, and when he did, his words fell like ice.

"Mr. Dempster, there was a time when I would have killed you for that remark. The relationship between the lady in question and myself is none of your business."

"Lady?" Dempster snarled. "She's a lady in name only. If you ask me, she's a . ."

Dempster was unable to finish his sentence, because Dan suddenly whipped a vicious backhand slap across his face, bringing blood to the corner of Dempster's mouth. The sound popped loud, even over the noise of the crowded room, and many turned to look at the table, anxious to see what happened and what would happen next.

Dan was nearly as surprised by his action as the others in the room were. He had acted in a flash of anger, without thinking, and now had to prepare himself for anything Dempster might try.

Dempster jerked the tablecloth from the table, tipping over his drink and the centerpiece and sending them crashing to the floor. He patted the tablecloth against the cut on his lip, and looked at Dan. He smiled a small, wicked smile. "You will rue the day you met me, Mr. O'Lee," he said.

"I already count meeting you as one of my more unpleasant experiences," Dan replied evenly.

"Good day to you, sir," Dempster said, moving quickly through the crowd.

After Dempster left, Dan took a seat at the table and sat there for a moment while a waiter replaced the cloth and centerpiece. The crowd, seeing that the excitement had ended, returned to their own conversations, leaving Dan alone.

"Mr. O'Lee, may I join you, sir? I come bearing beer, as you can see," a man said.

Dan looked up to see a man dressed in a Union officer's uniform, carrying a mug of beer in each hand. One of them he set before Dan.

"Thank you," Dan said, blowing away the foam and taking several welcome swallows. Finally, he put the mug down, wiped his mouth with the back of his hand, and looked across the table at the officer who had joined him.

"Who are you?" Dan asked.

"I am Captain Andrew Todd. The gentleman you have just angered, Hiram Dempster, is a most influential man."

"Is he a friend of yours?"

Todd laughed. "Hardly, as I am a Union officer, and he is one of the biggest firebrands for the Secesh in St. Louis."

"He's a Rebel?"

"No, Mr. O'Lee. He's a bigot. He backs his prejudices with money. Rebels back their sentiments with blood. Whether you can agree with them or not, you can at least respect a man who has enough strength of conviction to fight for what he believes in."

"I'm glad to see that you confirm my first impression of the man, " Dan said.

"What was your business with him, Mr. O'Lee?"

"I was going to buy a piece of property for... just a minute, what business is it of yours anyway? And how do you know my name?"

"Oh, I know a great deal about you, sir. You arrived in St. Louis this morning from California, where, among other things, you were a mining engineer."

"Prospector," Dan corrected him.

"But with enough experience in mining procedures to qualify as a mining engineer," Captain Todd said. "You are thirty-three years old, your parents died when you were twenty-one, leaving you with a ten-year-old brother to care for. You deposited your brother with Dr. and Mrs. Jebediah Homung, of this city, both now deceased, and you proceeded to the California gold fields. Your brother's name is Burke, and you haven't seen him in twelve years. You hoped to find him this morning, but you were disappointed."

Dan looked at Captain Todd, first with amused interest, and then with disquieting concern. Finally, as Todd finished his dissertation, Dan spoke.

"Todd, what the hell is all this? How do you know so much about me, and why?"

"Oh, believe me, Mr. O'Lee, I know even more than I have told you," Todd said easily. "It is my business to find out about people. Especially people we feel may be helpful to us."

"Helpful? Helpful to who?"

"Why, to the Union cause, of course," Todd said easily.

"I'm not interested," Dan said, dismissing him with another swallow of his beer. "Right now my only concern is in finding my brother."

"We are both interested in finding your brother, Mr. O'Lee. Perhaps we can help each other."

"What do you mean? Why do you want to find him?"

"Mr. O'Lee, the last word we had about your brother put him with Quantrill."

"What? Impossible."

"Why do you think it's impossible? Because you didn't see him when Quantrill and his men stopped the stage? Tell me, Mr. O'Lee, would you have recognized him?"

"I... I don't know," Dan said.

"Then it isn't impossible that he was with Quantrill, is it?"

"I guess not," Dan said. "But why should I help you find him?"

"You are a good citizen, Mr. O'Lee. If you weren't, you would never have delivered Lieutenant Ward's message. You'll tell us if you hear from your brother, because it is your duty."

"What about duty to my brother? Don't I have a duty to him as well?" Dan asked.

"You should have asked yourself that question twelve years ago, Mr. O'Lee," Captain Todd replied. "Oh, by the way. Did Lieutenant Ward say anything to you before he died?"

"Like what?"

"I don't know. His mission was supposed to be secret. Somehow it was compromised. He may have realized that, and tried to tell you. Did he mention a name?"

Dan thought a moment, then decided that he would not mention the lieutenant's dying words. "Uh, no," he said. "I don't think so."

"Think very hard, Mr. O'Lee," Captain Todd insisted. "The least thing might be significant."

"I can't think of anything," Dan lied. "Besides, if your intelligence is all that good, why don't you find out who the drummer on the coach with us was, and ask him?"

"His name was Orville Quimby," Captain Todd said. "And I'm afraid he is unable to tell us anything. We found him murdered this morning, his throat having been cut."

Chapter 5

DAN HAD TAKEN the address from the newspaper, and now he checked it against the number on the building. Satisfied that it was the same, he climbed the concrete steps and went inside. A sign stood on the easel in the entry hall of the building, inviting interested guests to Room 104 to hear the "eloquent and instructive Liberty Welles."

Dan proceeded to the room, and stood in the hallway, looking through the double doors. There were several people seated inside. Their attention was being held by a woman speaker who stood in front of the room. Dan caught his breath when he saw her. He had read in the newspaper article that she was beautiful, but he had thought that was standard newspaper rhetoric. The woman he was looking at now was one of the most beautiful he had ever seen.

"If you care to hear the lecture, sir, I'm afraid it will cost you ten cents."

So entranced was Dan by the unexpected good looks of the lady in front of the room that he didn't hear the question the first time, and it had to be repeated.

Dan looked at the questioner, a small, nearly bald man, wearing wire-rim glasses. "Oh, uh, yes," Dan said. "Tell me, is that Miss Liberty Welles?"

"Yes it is," the man said, smiling proudly. "We are proud to have her as a member of our Society. The lecture will cost ten cents, I'm afraid."

"Ten cents?"

"The money goes to further the goals of our abolitionist society," the man explained.

"And what are those goals?" Dan asked, pulling the money from his pocket.

"Why, to see every man, woman, and child in this country be free," the man answered.

Dan took a printed program from the man, then stepped inside and settled into a chair. Liberty Welles was just finishing a poem:

"And not unblessed they come; their brows

Were kissed by saintly mothers;

Fond wives will for their husbands pray,

And sisters for their brothers.

Then speed them forward! they shall write

Our country's proudest story,

Or, if they die, their falling place

Will be the field of glory!"

Liberty finished the poem on a grand scale, and the audience applauded and cheered enthusiastically.

Liberty bowed, then raised up, smiling at her reception. She had flashing green eyes, ringlets of dark brown hair, rosy cheeks, and white, evenly spaced teeth. She wore a green ribbon tied in a bow around her neck, and a white and green dress, the green in both cases seeming to pick up the color of her eyes.

"Thank you," Liberty said. "That poem was written by Marian Douglas of Boston, and I feel it best expresses the way we feel about our brave soldiers in this war. Thank you so much for coming tonight, and for your generous donations to our cause. Good night."

The audience applauded again, then stood as one as Liberty took her final bows. Finally, the applause died, and the audience started for the door, but Dan remained in his seat. Soon everyone was gone except the man who had collected his money, and that man began to sweep the room.

"Sir, are you angry because I collected the fee and she was just finishing?" the man asked Dan.

"No, I'm not angry," Dan said.

"Then why are you still here?"

"I want to see Miss Welles," he said. "I must talk to her."

"I'm afraid she's already gone," the man said. .

"Gone? How could she leave? I've been sitting right here all the time?"

"She left through another door, I'm afraid. I'm sorry, I'm afraid you've missed her."

"Do you know where she lives?" Dan asked.

"I'm afraid I don't," the man said.

Dan cursed his luck, and got up from his chair and walked outside, slowly, angrily. Then, just as he reached the street, he saw her getting into a carriage.

"Wait!" he called, starting toward the carriage on the run. "Miss Welles, wait a minute, won't you?"

Liberty looked at him with a puzzled expression on her face, but waited as Dan requested.

Dan ran up to the carriage, then stopped, breathing a little harder from the exertion.

"Yes?" Liberty asked. "What can I do for you?"

Dan felt like a fool. He had yelled for her to stop, and yet he had no idea what he would say to her. He couldn't ask her if the last word on a dying man's lips had been her name. What could he say?"

"It was an inspiring speech," he finally said, foolishly, self-consciously.

Liberty laughed. "How do you know? You didn't arrive until the last two stanzas of the poem. In fact, I thought you were accosting me to return your money."

"You... you noticed me?" Dan asked, amazed that she had.

"Of course. The audience wasn't that large, and you did come in at the very last."

"I had a difficult time finding the place," Dan said. "I'm new to the city and don't know my way around."

Liberty looked at him, as if studying him. "You say you are new to the city?"

"Yes."

"That's funny. I feel that we've met before; Have we met?"

"No," Dan said. He smiled. "If we had met, Miss Welles, I would not have forgotten it, I'm certain of that. Oh, please forgive me for not introducing myself. My name is Dan O'Lee."

"O'Lee?" Liberty asked rather sharply.

"Yes. Why, is something wrong?"

Liberty smiled. "No, of course not. It's just an unusual name, that's all. You don't hear it too often."

"No, I don't suppose you do," Dan said. "Though I have a brother here in St. Louis, named Burke O'Lee. Or rather, I did have. He seems to have disappeared."

"Disappeared?"

"In a manner of speaking" Dan said. "I wanted to see him when I reached the city, but when I inquired after him where he worked, I was told he was gone."

"I'm sorry to hear that," Liberty said. She reached into her reticule and pulled out a small card. "Mr. O'Lee, I shall be giving another lecture here tomorrow night. Please return, as my guest. I feel it unfair that you arrived too late tonight."

Dan put the card in his jacket pocket. "Thanks," he said, smiling broadly. "I'll be here ... you can count on that."

Liberty smiled and waved goodbye to Dan, then climbed into the carriage and settled against the seat for the ride back to the boarding house where she lived. She thought of the man she had just met as the carriage rolled along. Perhaps she should have told him that she knew Burke. It's funny that Burke had never mentioned him. Maybe he wasn't really

Burke's brother. Maybe he was just pretending to be, in order to get information on Burke. But no, she reasoned. He was Burke's brother, she could look at him and tell that. That was why she thought she had seen him before. But on the other hand, in this war where nobody knew where the other person stood, one couldn't be too careful.

When Liberty reached the rooming house and paid the driver, she climbed the dark steps which led up to her private entrance. Once inside her room, she found a match and lit the lantern which was mounted on the wall just inside the door. She turned it up, spreading a soft, yellow light through the room.

"Hello, Liberty girl," a man said quietly.

Liberty gasped, then spun around toward the sound of the voice. There, sitting on the edge of her bed, was Burke O'Lee. His shirt was off, and he had a bandage around one shoulder. The bandage was soaked red with blood.

"Burke! What are you doing here?" she asked.

"I had to come somewhere, Liberty girl. I got myself shot up a couple of days ago." Burke winced, and put his hand up to his wound.

"Have you seen a doctor?" Liberty asked, moving to him and looking at the bandage.

Burke smiled, the wry, boyish grin which had won Liberty over so many months ago. "Yeah, I saw one," he said. "He got the bullet out, then decided to sell me to the highest bidder. I had to leave. I guess the ridin' busted open the wound again."

"Oh, Burke, that dressing has to be changed," Liberty said. "You lie down. I'll make a new bandage."

"Thanks," Burke said. He lay back on the bed, heaving a sigh of contentment.

"Is it hurting much?"

"A little," Burke admitted. He lay there, unprotesting, as Liberty cut the old bandage off, washed the wound, then started tearing strips from a petticoat to make a new dressing. "Your friend was killed," he finally said.

"Who?"

"Lieutenant Ward. Quantrill had him killed."

"Oh, no, Burke, why? What happened?" Liberty cried. "Did something go wrong?"

"No," Burke said. "He just refused to part with the paper, so Quantrill had him shot."

"You didn't do it, did you?" she asked quickly.

"No," Burke replied, wincing as she wrapped the bandage. "I was lying on my butt in the snow. Jesse James shot him. It's probably just as well, Liberty girl. Pretty soon he would have been able to put two and two together, and figure out that you were the only one he told about the courier mission. When he figured that out he would have come for you."

"I was prepared to cross that bridge when I came to it," Liberty said. She finished the dressing. "There," she said, "now if you don't go out and break it open again, that should hold you for a while."

"Are you upset because Ward was killed?" Burke asked.

"Of course I'm upset. If I had known he would be killed, I would never have sent Quantrill to intercept the message."

"Liberty girl, there's a war on," Burke said. "Folks get killed in a war, and when you give away confidential information, you contribute to it."

"It's different when it is in battle. There, everyone faces equal danger. But to set someone up, especially a nice young man like Tom Ward, that's very different, and it bothers me. It bothers me a great deal."

"I thought you said all you and Ward did was have dinner together a few times," Burke said. "You're talking like maybe there was something more."

"Nothing more happened," Liberty insisted. "And if I had known he was going to be killed, I would have never met with him in the first place."

"I have to admit, Liberty, that I find it difficult to understand you."

"Why?"

"Well, here you are, making speeches at the abolitionist society, being friends with Verity Eternal, and yet all the time you've been spying for the South."

"I'm a southerner by birth," Liberty replied. "The Welles family is one of the oldest families in Mississippi. I feel a deep sense of loyalty to my state, and to the new nation it has joined. But I am against slavery and always have been. Slavery isn't the central issue of this war, states' rights are. Slavery has just been made so by the agitators up north. In fact, after the South has won her independence, we shall move to abolish the peculiar institution of slavery."

"Doesn't it bother you that most of your fellow southerners are bigots?" Burke asked.

"Bigotry is not an exclusive franchise of the South," Liberty reminded him. "I give you Hiram Dempster as a case in point. He is northern born, but supports the South for no reason, other than his hatred of Negroes. And you. You aren't a southerner by birth, yet you have espoused our cause. Why?"

"Why indeed?" Burke replied, smiling at her. "Could *it* be because I have fallen for the charms of a delightful, if not to say, delicious temptress?"

"You mean you have no true allegiance to the South?" Liberty asked.

"Liberty girl, if you wanted me to fight for the Mexicans, I would," Burke said, laughing. And in that statement, Burke was truthful, for he had been inspired to enter into the fray by his sheer zest for adventure, and the genuine love he felt for Liberty. If she asked him now to switch sides and fight for the North, he would cheerfully comply.

"You have no allegiances, and no loyalties," Liberty said. "Do you have any family?"

"Nope."

"No one? Not even a sister or a brother?" she asked, trying to find out about the man who had identified himself as Dan O'Lee.

"I guess I have a brother," Burke said.

"Really? You've never mentioned him. Why?"

The smile left Burke's face, and he lay back on the pillow again, looking up at the ceiling. "I've got a brother, all right. His name is Danny O'Lee. Our parents died in a riverboat accident when I was a child. Danny was older and didn't want to be saddled with me, so he dumped me off with my aunt and uncle and went to California to the gold fields."

"Do you blame him, Burke? After all, you were probably quite a responsibility for a young fellow to take on."

"Yeah, I blame him," Burke said. "You see, Uncle Jebediah wasn't that enthused over having me either. He was a doctor." Burke gave a short, bitter laugh. "But the only medicine he knew for me was a dose of the whip."

"Oh, Burke, you mean he beat you?"

"Yeah, he beat me. Every day, until I grew big enough to take the whip away from him and give him a taste of his own medicine. I hated him, and I hated Danny for leaving me with him." Burke suddenly smiled. "But let's not talk about Danny," he said. "Let's talk about me."

Liberty grinned. "You don't want to talk, Burke O'Lee." She lay her cool palms on Burke's chest, feeling his smooth muscles, and experiencing a warm shiver in her body. She leaned over to kiss him with moist lips, feeling herself grow weak as the kiss deepened.

It was always like this with Burke O'Lee, she thought. From the moment she had first seen him, sitting in the back row of a lecture hall, listening to her give a speech against the evils of slavery, she had been attracted to his easy, boyish charm. Later, as they became friends, and then lovers, she discovered that he was able to bring her to heights of passion that she had not thought possible, and she was unable to deny him her bed, anytime he sought her favors.

She even fancied that she loved him. But Burke was a rash young man, given to outbursts of temper, and quick to fight, and she felt that he was just too immature for her to even consider marriage. Sometimes she laughed when she thought of that, for though she considered him immature, he was in fact, at twenty-two, two years older than she.

The musings fled from Liberty's mind, and she lost touch with time and space as she felt herself being loved by her handsome young warrior. He was a man of great strength and surprising tenderness, caressing her without subtleties but with great passion. Finally, Liberty could feel Burke's tightly muscled thigh against the smooth skin of her own naked legs, and she could see him above her, moving down to her. After that all sights, sounds and textures blended together, to carry her to rapture's door.

They lay in each other's arms after they had made love, and Liberty studied the shadows cast on the wall by the flickering gold light of the lantern. Finally she spoke.

"Burke, I don't want you to go back to Quantrill."

"All right," Burke said easily. "But Quantrill won't care much for that. He doesn't like deserters."

"Go somewhere else. Go where he can't find you," Liberty suggested.

"Do you have any ideas?"

"How about Jeff Thompson?" Liberty suggested. "He's down in southeast Missouri, and what he's doing is important to our cause, Burke. He's keeping the Yankees from using the river to strike into the heart of the South."

"I might prefer fighting against soldiers instead of bank clerks and stage guards at that," Burke said. "Besides, I hear there's a big battle shaping up down there. It might prove to be the crucial battle of the war and I'd hate to miss out on it just because I was chasing around in Kansas or someplace with Quantrill."

"I'll make the necessary arrangements tomorrow," Liberty said.

"Are you that anxious to get rid of me, Liberty girl?" Burke teased.

"Of course not," Liberty replied. "But darling, every day you stay here increases the danger for you. What if you are discovered? Especially wearing that Confederate uniform."

"I thought about taking it off," Burke said. "But I figured it would be better to be captured as a Confederate soldier than be shot as a Rebel spy."

At the mention of the word spy, Liberty flinched, and Burke, seeing the quick spasm of fear cross her face, quickly put his arms around her to comfort her.

"I'm sorry Liberty girl," Burke said, hugging her tightly. "I wasn't thinking when I made such an unkind remark."

"I knew the risks I was taking when I started," Liberty said, still trembling. "It's just that I try and keep them out of my mind, because it's too late to turn back now."

Chapter 6

DAN USED THE pass Liberty had given him and attended the lecture the next night. On this night Liberty shared the dais with Verity Eternal, and in truth, Dan was hard pressed to say which of the two ladies had made the more inspired talk.

Or for that matter, which of the two was more beautiful.

Liberty's beauty had been striking enough to cause Dan to think of her often in the last twenty-four hours. He had committed her brown hair, green eyes, and glowing pink skin to his memory. But now he felt himself, inexplicably just as taken with the loveliness of Verity Eternal.

When Verity was introduced, she glided to the podium with a movement that was as graceful as a swan on the water. She was slender as a lily, with long, blue-black hair and large, liquid brown eyes. Her skin was the color of creamed coffee, and so clear and lovely that Dan wanted to just touch it.

Finally, Verity's talk was concluded, and she and Liberty received the applause of the audience then retired backstage. This time as the crowd started to leave, however, the man who had taken Dan's ticket the night before came over to speak to him.

"Are you Mr. O'Lee?" he asked.

"Yes, I am."

"Miss Welles asks if you will come backstage to see her."

"Yes, yes of course I will," Dan said, smiling at the unexpected invitation. "How do I get there?"

"Follow me, please," the man said, leading the way.

A moment later Dan was standing outside a door as the man knocked. "Miss Welles, I have the gentleman here with me," he said.

The door opened and Liberty stood there, smiling broadly. "Thank you, John, that was nice of you. Won't you please come in, Mr. O'Lee?"

Dan stepped into the room and saw that it was occupied not only by Liberty, but Verity Eternal as well. Liberty introduced them.

"I must say, Miss Eternal," Dan said, after the introductions were made. "Your talk tonight was absolutely inspiring."

Liberty laughed. "And you can believe him tonight," she said. "For he was here the entire time. Last night I managed to inspire him with but two stanzas of *Our Mountain Soldiers.*"

"I'm sorry," Dan apologized. "I did want to meet you, and I couldn't think of anything else to say last night. I must confess, however, that events tonight have borne me out. You are an inspiring speaker."

"You flatter me, sir," Liberty said.

"I have taken the liberty of reserving a table for us for dinner," Dan invited. "I hope you'll do me the honor?"

"Why, I would be delighted to join you for dinner," Liberty replied.

"And, Miss Eternal. You will join us as well, I trust?"

Verity smiled, a slow, sad smile. "That's most kind of you Mr. Lee. But I would not be welcome at such a place."

"Of course you would be welcome," Dan said not understanding her meaning.

"Verity means she would not be welcome by the establishment of the restaurant," Liberty explained.

"Why not?" Dan asked. Then, realizing what he was

saying, he put his hand to his mouth. "Oh, forgive me," he said. "For a moment I forgot that... uh ... I forgot."

"That I am colored?" Verity asked.

"Uh, yes," Dan said. "I'm sorry."

"Oh, don't be sorry, Mr. O'Lee. I'm not in the least sorry that I am black. I hope the day comes when everyone can be proud of their color. Pride, without prejudice. That is a worthy goal, don't you believe?"

"Yes, of course I do," Dan said. "I didn't mean to imply that I was sorry about your color. I just meant that I was sorry I was so awkward."

Verity smiled. "Now it's my time to apologize, Mr. O'Lee. I knew what you meant, but I just used it to make a point. Won't you forgive me?"

"Of course, though I feel there is nothing to forgive."

"Liberty, I like your gentleman friend," Verity said, touching Dan lightly on the hand. "Treat him well."

"I promise I will," Liberty said. "Would you get my wrap, please?" she asked, looking at Dan.

Dan left to get Liberty's coat, and when he returned, Verity had already left.

"She is a beautiful lady, isn't she?" Liberty asked.

"Yes," Dan said. "Strikingly so."

"I'm glad you like her. And I'm glad you came tonight. I wasn't sure you would."

Dan laughed. "I came down almost an hour early, just to make sure I would be on time. I waited in a tavern across the street until the others started arriving, because I didn't want to come in first."

Dan hailed a hack, and fitted the lap robe around the two of them as they drove off. The closeness of the seat, and the use of the lap robe necessitated that they sit very close, and he could feel the heat of her body, even through their clothes. It was a somewhat giddy feeling, and he enjoyed it while he could, even finding excuse to press more tightly against her whenever the hack made a turn.

"Here we are, sir," the driver called back a few moments later.

"That's a shame," Dan said quietly, thinking that the excuse to be close to Liberty was now removed. Liberty looked at him with a quick smile, which told him she knew what he was thinking about, and that shared intimacy warmed Dan.

They spoke in generalities at dinner, then, over dessert, Dan asked Liberty how she became involved in abolitionist work.

"I was born into it," Liberty said. "What I mean was, I was born on a slave-holding plantation, and I saw with my own eyes the misery one human being can visit on another. Husbands and wives were separated, children torn from their mother's arms—there was a complete stripping away of dignity. Not on my father's plantation, for he was at least a good-hearted man and long ago set our people free. Oh, they still live and work on Trailback Plantation, but they are there now of their own free will."

"Is that in Missouri?" Dan asked.

"No," Liberty said. "It is in Corinth, Mississippi."

"Then the freedom they now enjoy is a matter of degree, isn't it?"

"You might say that," Liberty replied. "Anyway, it made an abolitionist of me, and I swore to pursue that goal until slavery was ended."

"But why did you choose St. Louis?"

"Because St. Louis is the largest city of any slave-holding state. And because the abolitionists are active in St. Louis. And because the Dred Scott trial happened here, and was a setback for the abolitionist movement."

"This is an indelicate question," Dan said. "But do you feel like a traitor to your own people?"

"Because I'm an abolitionist?" Liberty replied. "No, I don't feel like a traitor. There are others in the South who feel just as I do."

"Oh? I would have thought that such a feeling would be

very rare among southerners."

"Not as rare as it would seem," Liberty said. "But most of those who share my point of view have no voice. The monied factions, and the politicians who speak out the loudest for the South are strong proponents of slavery. Therefore the official position of the South is proslavery. But, I hope that changes one day."

"It will change, as soon as this war is over," Dan said. "Once the North shows the South that they can't pull out of the Union at their own whim, it will establish the supremacy of the federal government once and for all, and the slave question can be settled in Washington as it should be."

Dan thought he saw a look of disagreement flash across Liberty's face. Not her face, really, but a subtle change of her eyes. Whatever it was, it happened so quickly and was so soon controlled that he couldn't be sure. Liberty smiled then, as if in total agreement, and answered: "It would make this awful war worthwhile. Though, with so many young men being killed, I sometimes wonder if it wouldn't be better to let the South go in peace."

"Speaking of young men being killed," Dan said, "I had a rather tragic circumstance happen to me on the way to St. Louis." He went on to relate the story of Quantrill's raid on the stage, and told of the murder of the driver and the young Union officer. "His name was Ward," Dan said. "Lieutenant Thomas Ward. Did you know him by any chance?"

"Know him?" Liberty replied. "No, I don't think I did. Why? Did he speak of me?"

"Not exactly," Dan said. "Though he mentioned your name."

"He mentioned my name?" Liberty asked, this time showing some concern.

"Yes," Dan said, purposely not going into detail as to how her name was mentioned, or even if it really had been her name Ward spoke.

"Thomas Ward, you say? I'm sorry, Mr. O'Lee, but I don't

believe I knew the young man. Though, it some vanity I must confess that it would not be all that unusual for my name to be mentioned. I am often written about in the newspapers of this city, and I have given lectures for more than one year now. I have achieved a modest degree of fame."

"And well-earned too," Dan said. He signaled for the check. "Miss Welles, do you have a previous engagement for Friday evening?"

"I ... I don't think so," Liberty replied.

"General Halleck is giving a dinner for his staff officers, and I have been invited for some reason. It would be a pleasure to go if you went as my guest."

"With General Halleck, you say?" Liberty asked, smiling broadly. "My, you have moved up quickly since arriving in St. Louis. He is the Commanding General for the entire Department of the West."

"I assure you, it is not due to any achievement of my own," Dan said. "The general and I have a mutual acquaintance, and I feel he is anxious to hear more news of her."

"Her? My, this is getting more interesting. Who is this mysterious her, Burke?"

The sound of his brother s name hit Dan like a slap in the face, and he stared at Liberty in total shock. For her part, Liberty looked down quickly and flushed a deep red. The silence grew longer and more awkward. Finally Dan spoke. "What did you call me?"

"I... I must have called you Burt. I'm sorry, he's an old beau of mine. It's terribly embarrassing, I can't tell you how sorry I am. Please, you must tell me you forgive me."

Dan was silent for several seconds before he spoke. He smiled easily. "Of course," he said. "But only if you agree to come to the general's dinner with me."

"Of course I will go with you," Liberty said. "If only to make up for my *faux pas.*"

"Good, good. Oh, and the next time you see Burt, you must thank him for me."

"Thank him?"

"Certainly. By saying his name, you felt obligated to accept my invitation."

Liberty laughed good-naturedly and quickly changed the subject, pointing to the chandelier, which hung in the foyer of the restaurant, and commenting that a similar fixture was in the dining room of her home in Corinth.

Dan gracefully allowed the subject to be changed, and followed her lead in conversation as they rode in the hired carriage to return Liberty to her home.

"It's getting late," Liberty said, when the carriage stopped on the street in front of her boarding house. "You'd better take this carriage on back to your hotel while you can, for at this hour there are few hacks in this neighborhood."

"The lady's right, sir," the driver said, hoping to double his fare by taking Dan back with him.

"Very well," Dan said. He stepped out of the carriage and helped Liberty to alight.

Liberty looked up at the driver and saw that he was watching them. "Driver, would you kindly look to your horse?" she said.

"Yes, ma'am." The driver responded, looking away quickly.

Liberty looked up at Dan, smiled, and then planted a cool kiss on his lips. Dan was surprised by her action and suddenly started to put his arms around her. But she backed away daintily, smiling at him, then shook her finger in mock disapproval.

"Mr. O'Lee, I feel I have already overstepped my bounds as it is. Please do not compromise me with my neighbors." Even as she spoke, though, her flashing eyes told Dan that under other circumstances she would not have disapproved of his move. „

"Uh . . . no, of course not," Dan said. "Then it's goodnight, I suppose."

"Goodnight . . . Dan," Liberty said. She turned quickly

and started up the sidewalk toward the stairs, which led to her apartment.

Dan stood by the carriage and watched her until she reached her door. She turned and waved to him, then stepped inside, and Dan got back into the carriage and signaled the driver on. He leaned back to be with his own thoughts. Liberty was on his mind.

Chapter 7

WITH LIBERTY AT General Halleck's dinner party, Dan was keenly aware of being the envy of nearly everyone present, and he was also cognizant of the possessive way she clung to his arm when he offered it to her as they went into the dining room.

It was a small party, with no more than ten guests, so they were able to sit around one long table and listen to General Halleck as he told them how the war should be fought. Halleck was well known as a military theorist. He had taught at West Point for several years, and had written a highly regarded textbook on military strategy, which was being used not only by the United States Army but by European armies as well.

"My biggest fear," Halleck said, as he spread butter on a roll, "is that the Eastern press will get too impatient and force us into a large, set- piece battle with the Rebels. That would be a great mistake."

"Why is that, general?" a reporter for one of the St. Louis newspapers asked. "Surely you don't believe the Rebels can stand up to us in a classic battle?"

"Oh, but they can, sir," Halleck replied. "In fact, that is their only chance for victory. If they could engage us in a few large battles, the casualties would be so high on both sides that the mood of the public would quickly turn to one of peace at any cost... even if that cost was the disunion of our nation."

"Then how do you propose this war be fought, if not in the classic manner?"

"We must obtain several strategic positions and hold them," Halleck said. "Right now, for example, there is a position on the Mississippi River which is vital to us. It is an island in the river, just at the bottom of the New Madrid bend. The Confederates hold that island now. With it, they are maintaining tenuous control of the river. We must take that island, and when we do, we will have the Mississippi River, all the way to Memphis. That leaves only Memphis and Vicksburg to prevent us from controlling the entire Mississippi. Thanks to General Grant, we already have the Cumberland and the Tennessee. With the waterways under our control, I propose to start dismembering the South's railway system, so that all means of transportation is effectively shut off. Blockading the seaports means that no supplies can come in, and we'll have the Confederacy trapped in a bag. All we have to do is close the neck, and hold it until the South quits struggling."

As Halleck spoke, he demonstrated with a napkin, forming it into a sack, then drawing the neck tight and squeezing it.

"General, the plan you propose is a brilliant one, to be sure," Liberty said. "But what about people like Johnston, Beauregard, Lee, and Longstreet? Do you think they haven't considered the very thing you are speaking of?"

Most of the other dinner guests looked at Liberty, surprised that she would offer any comment at all in this, a strictly male conversation, and shocked that her comment would seem to be one which questioned the great general.

Halleck laughed easily. "I'm certain they have thought of it," he said. "Indeed, I would be upset if they hadn't, because this is just the type of concept I have preached in my lectures and advocated in my books. I would hope I have had some influence on them. But the trick, my dear lady, is to accomplish this, while they know it, but can do nothing about it. And to do that, we must avoid a set-piece battle at all costs."

"At all costs, general? Even if it means fleeing to avoid a battle?" the reporter asked.

"Yes," Halleck said. "Though in this case I wouldn't say we are fleeing to avoid the battle. I prefer to say we are merely strategically repositioning our. forces."

'What is your next objective after Island Number Ten?" the reporter asked.

"There is one very strategic railroad junction which should be taken out," Halleck said. "If we control it, we have cut off all transportation between Memphis and Charleston, and from Mobile to the Ohio. In fact, within a triangle of about twenty miles, we can totally disrupt nearly one third of the South's railway system. That will be our next objective."

"Where is that, general?"

Halleck laughed. "That is information which I am sure Beauregard would like to have as well. Better that I keep it to myself for now."

The general conversation continued in a military vein for a while longer, but as Dan was not a military man, he didn't participate in it. He was amused to see that Liberty was a spirited participant, and amazed at her grasp not only of the situation but of military concepts. He mentioned it to her as they left the dinner that night.

"I have to stay abreast of all the war news, because of my speaking engagements," Liberty explained. "I know it may not be considered a 'woman's place,' but the cause of abolition recognizes no sexual lines."

"Liberty, if it isn't too presumptuous of me, could I invite you to my room for a quiet drink?"

"To your room?" Liberty asked.

"I'm sorry," Dan said. "It was presumptuous of me. But it would be unseemly to go to your room, as you might be embarrassed before your neighbors. In my hotel, however, such things are frequently done, and done in innocence, so you need have no fear for your reputation. And I very much want to spend some time with you.'[3]

Liberty smiled. "It's sweet of you to concern yourself for my reputation, Dan. But the truth is, I fear I jeopardized my reputation long ago, when I began speaking out on behalf of abolition. Yes, I will join you in your room, though 1 don't wish to drink."

Liberty's voice had been throaty, almost husky, as she accepted the invitation, and it sent a small shiver of anticipation coursing through Dan. Was her voice a promise of something? Maybe so, he thought. It would certainly be worth exploring. He leaned forward to inform the driver of their destination.

The Boatman Hotel was equipped with Mr. Otis's elevators, and as the doors closed to take them up to Dan's fourth floor room, Dan was aware of Liberty's perfume. It was subtle, though effective enough to titillate his senses. He moved a step closer to her, and when she felt him move she looked up at him and smiled, Their gaze held for just a moment, then, a sudden, almost overpowering feeling made Dan want to take her in his arms and kiss her. Only the presence of the elevator operator prevented him from doing so. Liberty's face flushed, and Dan knew that she knew exactly what he was thinking.

"Oh, my," Liberty said as the elevator stopped on Dan's floor. "I shouldn't ride elevators. They addle my senses and make my head spin." She was covering up her own reaction, for she was as fully attracted to Dan as he was to her.

The doors were cranked open, and they stepped into the fourth floor hallway. "My, uh, room is just down here," Dan said, leading the way.

They walked quickly and silently down the hall to Dan's room, then stopped as Dan extracted his key.

"408? This is your room?" Liberty asked, the tone of her voice showing some surprise.

"Yes, why? Don't you not like the numbers 408 for some reason?" Dan asked, with a small laugh.

"No, nothing like that. I'm just making nervous conversation," Liberty said.

"There's no reason to be nervous, Liberty," Dan said easily. He opened the door and they stepped inside. Liberty didn't move on into the room; instead she stopped just inside, and when Dan closed the door and turned around, she was there before him, in as close proximity as she had been in the elevator. The overpowering urge to kiss her came over him again, and this time he did not have the restraint of the elevator operator to prevent him from doing so.

"Dan?" Liberty said softly, looking deep into his eyes and reading his very thoughts.

Dan put his arms around her and pulled her to him. It was not a hesitant kiss, soft and apologetic as it had been in the carriage the other evening, but a deep kiss, joined in with a fervor which surprised them both. Dan's hands began to move through the folds of Liberty's dress, bunching up the material of the skirt until the way was opened to give him access to her bare leg. He put his hand on her warm flesh.

"No," Liberty finally managed to say, twisting away from him suddenly. "Dan, not like this. I don't want to be some casual wartime romance ... a woman you use like a trollop."

"Do you think you are?" Dan asked, surprised by her sudden move.

"I don't know. I don't know what to think. I ... I shouldn't even be here."

"I'm sorry," Dan said. "Liberty, I don't want to hurt you."

"Please try to understand," Liberty said.

"I do understand," Dan said. "Look, if you'd rather go now, I'll take you back."

"No," Liberty said. "I don't have to go ... just yet. I just don't want you to have the wrong impression of me."

Dan smiled. "Then you'll stay?"

"For a while."

Dan kissed her again, and, as before, the kiss deepened. This time Dan's hands were in Liberty's hair, and he tilted her head back, and kissed her on the lips, the cheeks, the throat, and up to one ear.

"No," Liberty moaned deep in her throat, but even as she protested, she tightened her embrace and pressed her body against his.

Dan's hands moved from her hair down her neck, then, easily and naturally, the buttons of the high neck-dress were opened and he found the palm of his hand slipping along the smooth, incredibly warm skin until he cupped one of her breasts in his hand. It was warm and alive, and he took her hard, button-like little nipple between his thumb and forefinger.

"Oh, oh," Liberty said, almost in a whimper. She searched for Dan's mouth with her own, and when she found it, opened her lips to his deep, penetrating kiss.

Dan swept her up then, and carried her to his bed. Her protests had stopped now, and she matched his kisses, and opened her dress, offering her body to him, to use as he wished.

Dan's hands were busy, taking advantage of her assistance. He freed her breasts, then, a moment later, removed her dress, so that she lay on the bed, her naked skin pink and glowing in the soft gaslight.

As Liberty lay on the bed, feeling the silken caress of the air against her naked skin, she looked up at the man who was now removing his clothes to join her. She couldn't believe she was doing this. All sanity and reason seemed to have deserted her. It was as if he had cast some sort of spell over her. Almost from the beginning, she had known this moment would come. She knew about it and was thus forearmed . . . but still was defenseless against it.

Why? She cried out inside herself. Why was she as helpless as a kitten before him? But even as she asked the question, the answer came to her. Here was the same sensual attraction she felt in Burke . . . but in a more mature, more sensitive man. It was a combination against which she had no defense . . . and indeed, wanted none. She knew that such things were not to be enjoyed by women; in fact, some believed it was sinful even for married women to enjoy their husbands. But Liberty didn't always conduct her life in accordance with the dictates of society. She was an abolitionist among southerners, and a Confederate among abolitionists—two prime examples of contradictory, even paradoxical behavior. And add to her fight for the emancipation of slaves, the fight to emancipate women, she thought. For if it is no sin for a man to enjoy sex, then it should be no sin for a woman to enjoy it. And she was enjoying it. As she waited for him, the air sensitized her naked, splayed legs, and it was a good feeling, a grand and glorious feeling.

She felt Dan's weight come down on her, and she breathed the maleness of him. Her legs were downy soft and creamy white, beneath his muscle-hard and swarthy dark ones. When she felt him enter her, she thrust against him, feeling a pleasure so intense that she cried out from the joy of it.

Their movements established an easy rhythm, and they matched each other, move for move, until finally, with a powerful shudder, she felt an explosion of pleasure inside her that completely engulfed her, wrenching a sob of ecstasy from her throat. So lost was she in her own release that she scarcely noticed Dan's own frenzied climax.

Liberty lay beneath him for a while, feeling his weight on her, enjoying the warm and pleasant dampness that filled her. She stroked his shoulder with her hand, and he kissed her again, then rolled over and lay beside her. They were both silent, save for their breathing, which was just beginning to return to normal.

"Dan," she finally asked. "Do you think I'm an evil woman?"

Dan raised up and leaned on his elbow, looking down at her. "Of course not," he said. "Why would you ask such a thing?"

"Because of this," she said. "I enjoyed what we did. I can't begin to tell you bow much I enjoyed it."

"I enjoyed it too. Does that make me an evil man?"

"But women aren't supposed to enjoy it," Liberty said. "At least, that's what everyone says."

Dan laughed. "Liberty, somehow I have the feeling that you don't give a fig what everyone says."

Liberty laughed with him. "Maybe you're right," she said. She sat up, then leaned over to kiss him, the nipples of her breasts brushing him lightly as she did so. Then she looked at him with a serious expression on her face.

"We mustn't see each other again," she said.

"What? What are you talking about?" Dan asked, puzzled by her remark

"Just what I said. We mustn't see each other again. It can only cause pain."

Dan raised his hand and ran his fingers along her cheek. "No," he said. "Not pain, joy. Liberty . . . this is much too early for me to say it, I know. But I can't help it. I—"

"No," Liberty interrupted quickly, placing her fingers across his lips. "No, don't say it, please."

"But why not?"

"Because ... because it would be too easy for me to fall in love with you."

'What's wrong with that?"

"Everything," Liberty said heavily. "I have no right to fall in love with you, or with anyone. Especially not with you."

"Why especially me?" Dan asked.

"Because I have very strong convictions about what I believe in," Liberty said. "You wont understand those convictions, and you would feel betrayed. It would cause painful misunderstandings."

"Why would that cause misunderstandings?" Dan asked. "Liberty, we're at war now. This is a time that calls for convictions and honor." He laughed, self-deprecatingly. "In fact, it is I who should be apologizing to you, for here I lie with no clear convictions to guide me. But though I have no convictions of my own, Liberty, I have respect for those who do. Who cannot respect honor?"

"Sometimes the line between honor and dishonor may be thinly drawn," Liberty said, her voice and expression reflecting the torment of self-doubt. "Even I have difficulty in drawing the distinction. But I am embarked upon my course, Dan, and I have no choice but to follow it to the end, or admit that I have been wrong. And I can't admit I've been wrong—I fear I couldn't live with the ghosts of the realization."

"Whew," Dan said, frowning, "That's pretty serious stuff."

"Then perhaps you can see what I am burdened with," Liberty said. "Now, I think I'd better get home."

"I'll take you," Dan said, swinging his legs over the edge of the bed and reaching for his clothes.

"You don't have to."

"I know I don't have to," Dan said. "But I very much want to. And, despite what you say, I do want to see you again. Very soon."

"No," Liberty said. "Please, Dan, don't make it harder on me than it already is. Try to understand."

"I'm sorry," Dan said. "But I can't understand."

"Then please forgive me," Liberty said quietly. "For this is the way it must be."

They rode out to Liberty's boarding house in comparative silence. Beneath the lap robe they held hands, not in an intimate, sensual way, but in a way which suggested their hopelessness for a situation which could not be.

When they reached the boarding house, they kissed the long, sad, desperate kiss of lovers who saw their world together ending, before it ever had a chance to start

Chapter 8

DAN COULD STILL feel the heat of Liberty's body and taste the bittersweetness of her kiss as he stepped out of the carriage in front of the Boatman's Hotel. He paid the driver, then stood in front of the hotel and watched the carriage as it slipped off into the darkness. Behind him, and up a set of foot-polished steps, were the glass doors which led into the bright lights of the hotel lobby. In a town dizzy with war fever, such places were golden promises of excitement. Now the golden promise seemed to mock Dan.

What had gone wrong? There had been a mutual attraction between them, he knew. He hadn't forced himself on her; she had responded willingly, even eagerly. And yet, though she had shared her body with him, she had preserved, kept back, the mingling of souls which he yearned for.

Dan thrust his hands in his pockets, and started up the steps. What he needed was a little drink. No, what he needed was a lot of little drinks. Perhaps then he would be able to figure things out.

"Mr. O'Lee, hello to you, sir," a familiar voice called. Dan looked toward the sound of the voice, and saw Captain Todd just rising from one of the many overstuffed chairs which were scattered about on the floral carpet. Todd was carrying a

Hearts Divided

newspaper under his arm, as if he had been waiting for some time and had passed that time by reading. He walked across the lobby toward Dan.

"Well, Captain Todd. I see you're here. This couldn't just be coincidence, could it?"

Todd smiled. "Not exactly," he said. "Miss Welles is a lovely girl, isn't she? I don't blame you for inviting her to your room. I trust your efforts were rewarded?"

Dan's face showed a quick irritation. "Captain Todd, why do you see fit to pry into every aspect of my private fife?"

"Mr. O'Lee, you must appreciate the fact that we are at war," Captain Todd said. "And I have a job to do."

"Assuming I can accept that, captain, why must your job always involve me? What do I have to do with the war?"

Todd pulled a small box of cigars from his breast pocket, offered one to Dan, and when Dan declined, took one for himself and lit it, wreathing his head in smoke before he answered.

"You seem to be right in the center of things, Mr. O'Lee."

"What do you mean, right in the center of things?"

Captain Todd smiled, then pulled the cigar from his mouth.

"Consider my perspective, Mr. O'Lee. You were on the stage when it was jumped by Quantrill's bushwhackers. You spoke with Lieutenant Ward, and delivered what was purported to be his message to General Halleck."

"Purported to be?" Dan asked. "What do you mean by that?"

"I'll tell you what I mean by that, Mr. O'Lee. Suppose you aren't who you represent yourself to be."

"You already know I am Dan O'Lee. Surely your spies have told you that," Dan replied hotly.

"Oh, I don't doubt that you are Dan O'Lee," Captain Todd said easily. "But I may doubt that you are the patriot you claim to be. You see, Mr. O'Lee, what if you wanted to strengthen the Rebel position at Island Number Ten in New Madrid? What better way than to lure our men and material to Sikeston, then fall upon them with massed artillery? We would not only lose several men, we would in all likelihood lose many cannons, much ammunition, powder, food, clothing, and other stocks of war. Stocks badly needed by the Confederacy."

"I see," Dan said. "So what you are saying is that I faked the message, hoping to draw the supplies into Sikeston. Is that it?"

"I'm not overlooking that possibility, Mr. O'Lee"

"Why would you think such a thing?"

"You were on the coach, Mr. O'Lee. You had the opportunity to fake the message, and no one would be any wiser."

"There were others on the stage," Dan said.

"But they're dead, Mr. O'Lee. Except for Quantrill himself. We have only your word that what you say is true, and as there is no one to dispute your version, that puts us in a precarious position."

"Why would you doubt my word?"

"Well, sir, there is the matter of your brother," Captain Todd said. "He is a known Confederate. He was riding with Quantrill, but he was wounded during the stage hold-up. He was treated for his wound by Dr. Coyle, a physician known to have Secesh leanings, in Rolla, Missouri. But Dr. Coyle is also a greedy man, so he attempted to turn Burke in for the reward. By the time he returned to Rolla with a prisoner escort, though, Burke had managed to give the good doctor's wife the slip. Now, we don't know where he is. But we do have an idea."

Dan blinked. Burke with Quantrill? He'd had difficulty assimilating Todd's news; he just hadn't seen or recognized Burke in the band, one or the other.

"You think you know where Burke is?" he said. "Where?"

"We believe he is with Liberty Welles."

"Impossible," Dan said quickly.

"Oh? And why do you think it is impossible? Because you made love to her?"

Dan felt his face burning. "No," he said. "That has nothing

to do with it. It's just that she knows I am looking for my brother. She wouldn't hide it from me . . . she wouldn't deceive me."

"Lieutenant Ward thought that she wouldn't deceive him, either," Captain Todd said dryly, "You see, he was also Miss Liberty Welles' lover. But his trust in her was so misplaced that it got him killed."

"I don't believe that," Dan insisted. "I asked Miss Welles if she knew Lieutenant Ward, and she said she did not."

"She would hardly admit it trader the circumstances, would she?" Captain Todd replied. "Tell me, Mr. O'Lee. Was there any particular reason you asked her? Did the lieutenant mention her name, by any chance?"

"No, of course not," Dan said. He paused for a moment. "At least. . . I don't think he did."

"Aha! You have remembered something," Captain Todd said triumphantly. "Please, tell me what it is."

"I haven't just remembered it," Dan said. "But I was sure that it was of no consequence. Still, I had to be sure, so I checked myself."

"What did he say, Mr. O'Lee?"

"His dying word was liberty," Dan said.

"And you thought *that* insignificant?" Captain Todd said.

"I thought it merely a testimony to the lieutenant's patriotism."

"I see. But now you realize that it was Miss Welles' name the lieutenant spoke ... perhaps as a warning."

"I don't know that," Dan said. "As I said, Miss Welles told me she didn't know the lieutenant."

"I can easily get dozens of witnesses who will swear that they saw them together, including the desk clerk of this very hotel, who often arranged a room for their trysting places. Ironically, they once used room 408. Your room, I believe?"

Suddenly Dan remembered Liberty's strange reaction to room 408, and the memory gave him pause for a moment. Could there be something to Captain Todd's accusation?

But Dan thrust the thought away as being disloyal, and continued to challenge Captain Todd's statements.

"Suppose what you say is true," Dan suggested. "How would Liberty get word to Quantrill?"

"Through your brother."

"Ah, yes," Dan said, sarcastically. "And I suppose you have evidence that my brother is also her lover."

"As a matter of fact, we do, Mr. O'Lee," Todd said firmly.

The cumulative effect of all Todd's information now hit Dan in the face like a slap, and he pressed the knuckles of his fist against his forehead. "Then she did call me Burke," he finally said quietly.

"I beg your pardon?"

"The other evening she called me Burke," Dan muttered. "She covered it up by telling me she had called me Burt, and explained that he was an old beau. I know now, though, that it was Burke's name she said." He laughed a short, bitter laugh. "And to think I was about to tell her ... that I thought I..." He broke it off and looked at Captain Todd with hurt, embarrassed silence.

"Mr. O'Lee, you are not the first man to be taken in by the lady's charms. But if we can put her out of business, you will be the last," Captain Todd said.

"This is what she was talking about," Dan said. "She was trying to warn me."

"What?"

"Nothing," Dan said. "It has nothing to do with the information you are trying to discover. Captain Todd, I assure you that the message is genuine if Lieutenant Ward was genuine. I merely did what I perceived to be my duty in delivering it to General Halleck."

"I would very much like to believe you, Mr. O'Lee. For if the message you handed General Halleck is authentic, it will provide our forces with a great advantage. If, however, it is a false message, planted only to lure us into a trap, then I fear it could have disastrous results should we follow through on it."

"I did not fake that message," Dan said.

"We will proceed on that assumption, Mr. O'Lee, but we shall proceed with caution."

"I'm sure you will," Dan said. "And now, if you will excuse me, I must be going." Dan turned to walk toward the door.

"Mr. O'Lee, are you going out again?"

"Why?" Dan asked. "Have you already let your spies off for the night?"

Todd smiled. "We never sleep, Mr. O'Lee."

"Well, for your information, I feel the need to think about a few things. I would like to be alone."

"Have a pleasant evening, sir," Captain Todd called cheerily as Dan pushed, angrily, through the front door.

A carriage had just deposited a passenger at the hotel, and as the driver started to pull away, Dan hailed him.

"I'm sorry, sir," the driver replied. "I'm goin' home to the wife n kids now. I'm through for the day."

"But I have some place I must get to quickly," Dan said.

"I'm sorry sir."

"I'll double your fare," Dan offered.

The driver hesitated. "I'd like to help you, sir, really I would. But..."

"I'll give you three times your fare."

"Three times?"

"Yes."

"You want to get there awful bad, don'cha'?"

"Yes," Dan agreed. "Will you do it, man?"

"Sure'n for that much I'd carry you on my back," the hack driver said. "Get in."

Dan returned to the block where Liberty lived, paid the driver the agreed-upon price, and stepped out of the carriage. The driver, afraid that Dan would want him for further duty, snapped the reins at the horse, and the horse stepped off at a brisk trot.

The night air was cold, and as Dan walked along the edge

of the street, his breath blew clouds of fog. Finally he reached the boarding house, sneaked up the same stairway he had seen Liberty use, and listened quietly through the door.

"It has to be Corinth," Liberty's voice was saying. "Burke, I heard General Halleck say that within a twenty-mile triangle, he could capture critical railroad junctions which would disrupt one third of the South's railroad system. I was born and raised at Corinth, and I know what he's talking about. He wouldn't say where it was, but it has to be there."

"Then we've got to get word to General Beauregard," a man's voice said. "If he's in time, he can gather enough forces to stop Halleck."

"You must tell him yourself, Burke. Don't trust the message to anyone else."

"I'll leave first thing in the morning."

"Are you going to see Dan before you leave?"

"I think not," the man's voice answered.

"But Burke, he *is* your brother," Liberty's voice said.

"He stopped being my brother twelve years ago."

It *was* Burke! Dan could no longer restrain himself, and he began pounding on the door. "Who is it?" Liberty called.

"Liberty, it's me, Dan. Let me in, please!"

"Dan! It's terribly late, Dan, can't you come back tomorrow?"

"Liberty, I know Burke is in there. Please let me in. I must talk to him."

The door opened then, and Liberty stepped back to allow Dan to enter. He brushed by her quickly, then looked on the bed. There, naked from the waist up, and covered by bedcovers from the waist down, sat his brother. Even though Burke had been only ten the last time Dan had seen him, the features were unmistakable, and he had an urge to rush to him and embrace him. Something in Burke's face stopped him though. Then, with a short gasp of surprise, he recognized what it was. It was hate.

"Well, well, well," Burke said coldly. "If it isn't the long-lost gold hunter."

"Burke, it's good to see you," Dan said.

"I'm sorry I can't say the same of you," Burke replied.

"What are you doing here?" Liberty asked.

Dan looked at Liberty for the first time. She was in a dressing gown, and she pulled it tightly about her, modestly shielding from his gaze that which she had so willingly opened to him only a few hours earlier.

"I see," Dan finally said. "I'm sorry if I arrived at an inopportune time."

"Oh, my, aren't you the wounded brother though?" Burke asked, laughing shortly. "Did you think that by sleeping with her once, you had staked claims to her? Well, how do you think I feel? I've loved her for over a year. At least you can say she's keeping it in the family."

"Burke!" Liberty said, the exclamation coming out almost as a sob. "How could you say such a thing?"

"So this is your little speech of honor," Dan spat.

"I told you, you wouldn't understand," Liberty said. She began crying. "I told you not to try to see me again. I knew this would happen."

"Oh, spare me your tears of remorse, Miss Welles. Lets be honest, shall we? For you, I was merely a means of getting to General Halleck to learn some valuable information. And for me? Well, you were . . . how did you put it? A wartime romance? A woman I could use like a trollop?"

"Dan, it's not like that, believe me," Liberty cried. "I . . . I'm trapped into doing this . . . bound by honor to..."

"Honor?" Dan said. "You don't know the meaning of the word." Dan looked at his brother, and noticed the bandage on his shoulder. "It's true, isn't it?" he said, looking at the wound. "You were one of the gang of bushwhackers who jumped the stagecoach and killed the driver and the lieutenant."

"I didn't kill anyone in that raid," Burke said. "I was flat on my butt in the snow, if you recall. I was lucky to get away alive. I got treated by some sawbones in Rolla, and made it here to Liberty's place."

"Yes," Dan said. "The doctor who treated you is named Coyle. I heard all about it."

"Coyle? Yeah, I think that's his name. How did you know?"

"You aren't safe here, Burke," Dan said. "They know all about you. And you, too, Liberty."

"Me? How do they know about me?"

"I don't know. Perhaps some of the men you've slept with were Union spies." Liberty blinked back the tears.

"Liberty, we've got to get you outta here," Burke said.

"But I can't leave," Liberty said. "My work is too important for the Confederacy."

"Go down to Corinth," Burke advised her. "You carry the message to General Beauregard yourself."

"How will I get there?"

Burke swung his legs over the edge of the bed and started pulling on his pants, wincing as he did so. It was only then that Dan realized that his brother had been holding a gun on him from the moment he stepped into the room. 'I can get you there," Burke replied. He looked at Dan. "The only thing, I don't know what to do with 'brother' here."

"That is a problem, isn't it?"

"Would you give us your word to say nothing to the authorities until we've had time to make good our escape?" Liberty asked.

"My word of 'honor'?" Dan replied, twisting the word so that it became almost obscene.

"Would you rather I just shoot you?" Burke replied, raising his pistol menacingly.

"Burke, you wouldn't really do it?" Liberty sounded shocked.

"I don't see as we have any choice," Burke said quietly. He held the pistol steady, unwaveringly, pointed right at Dan's head. He was so calm, and so cool, that Dan was certain he was about to die. He stood there, rooted in shock, waiting for his brother's bullet to crash into him.

Burke slowly lowered the gun. He looked at Dan with an expression of hurt and anger on his face.

"Why did you leave me?" he finally asked.

"Burke, be reasonable. I wasn't much more than a kid myself. I couldn't have taken care of you."

"You mean you didn't want to."

"I mean I couldn't," Dan said firmly. "I had to do what I felt was best for you. I left you with Aunt Zelda and Uncle Jebediah."

"You would have been better off abandoning me in the street somewhere," Burke said bitterly. "I would have had an easier time of it on my own, than with that sadistic bastard of an uncle."

"Burke . . . Burke, I'm sorry," Dan said, genuinely struck by Burke's revelation. "I had no idea that you wouldn't be well treated."

"What difference did it make to you?" Burke asked. "You had what you wanted. What did you care if a ten-year-old kid had to put up with a beating now and then? After all, it was no skin off your back." Burke laughed bitterly at his metaphor. "That's pretty good, don't you think?"

"Burke, believe me, I'm sorry," Dan said. "I am truly very sorry. If I had only known, I would have come back for you no matter what it took. And I would have gotten you out of there."

"Yeah? Well you never even bothered to check in to see how I was doing all those years. And now you come around telling me how sorry you are. That's supposed to make it all right, is it? You make a confession of guilt, and I, like a priest, am supposed to grant you absolution. Well, it isn't that easy, brother. I can't forgive and forget after what I've been through."

"I don't blame you for being angry," Dan said. "But what can I say now?"

"There is nothing you can say now," Burke said. "And

there's nothing you can do. The damage has been done."

There was a sudden knock at the door, and it startled them all. Burke raised the pistol again, and pointed it toward the door.

"Who is it?" Liberty called.

"It's me, Hiram Dempster," a voice replied.

"He has a letter of introduction for you to General Jeff Thompson," Liberty told Burke swiftly.

"Well, he's just going to have to put one more name in it," Burke replied. "You'll be going with me, Liberty girl. Oh, if that's all right with you, Danny," he added, sarcastically.

"I don't care where she goes, or what happens to her," Dan said, forcing a coolness to his voice. He looked at Liberty, and was surprised to see a hurt reflected deep in her eyes.

"Good," Burke said softly. "Now, Liberty girl, show Mr. Dempster in. He's going to keep an eye on big brother here until after we're gone."

Chapter 9

"SO, WE MEET AGAIN, do we?" Dempster said, after Burke and Liberty had left. He was holding a pistol leveled at Dan, and his thumb played, almost lovingly, with the hammer.

"This is a boarding house, Dempster," Dan said. "If you shoot now, you'll have everyone in here banging on the door, wanting to know what happened."

"Oh, don't you fret about that, dear fellow. I could quite easily explain that my firearm discharged accidentally. But, just to avoid any such embarrassing moments, might I suggest that we go somewhere else?"

"I'm quite comfortable here, thank you," Dan replied.

"You don't understand," Dempster said. The easy smile left his face, and he motioned toward the door with the business end of his pistol. "That wasn't really a suggestion, it was an order. Now move, or I will be forced to shoot you here and try my luck at explaining it later."

Dan reluctantly, but wisely, chose to step through the door into the cold night air. As he descended the steps in front of Dempster, he ran through possible escape plans in his mind. He considered whirling around and trying to grasp the gun away before Dempster could react, or trying to leap over the rail, or even shouting out loud for help. But he discarded each plan as soon as it came to mind, as being unworkable.

There was a carriage sitting at the curb, and a Union officer stepped out as the two men approached.

"Captain!" Dan said happily, calling the officer by rank. "Am I glad to see you! This man is a Rebel spy! You'd better—" Dan stopped abruptly.

The Union officer had shrugged. He opened the holster flap and pulled out his pistol.

Dan turned toward Dempster and was crestfallen to see him laughing.

"Is the fella giving you any trouble, Hiram?" the Union officer asked.

"Not anything I can't handle," Dempster replied. "Mr. O'Lee, may I introduce Colonel Blackie Beauregard?"

"Colonel?'

The man in the Union officer's uniform smiled and preened his mustache and Van Dyke beard. "Don't let this Yankee uniform fool you," he said amicably. "It's merely an expediency. I am, in fact, a colonel in the Confederate Army, in St. Louis on confidential assignment."

"I'm certain you've heard of Blackie's illustrious uncle," Dempster went on. "He's General P.G.T. Beauregard."

"I see," Dan said.

"Yes, unfortunately, you do see," Dempster drawled. "And that brings up a most regrettable point."

"What are we going to do with him, Hiram?" Dempster pondered. "Unfortunately, colonel, we're going to have to find some way to dispose of him."

"Hell, that's not hard." The man who called himself Blackie Beauregard drew back the hammer on his pistol, and once again Dan found himself a breath away from instant death.

"No," Dempster said quickly. "I have a better idea. I have an idea that will make Mr. O'Lee's demise useful to the Confederacy."

"What are you thinking?" Beauregard asked. "We'll take

Hearts Divided

him down to the river and put him on board the *Delta Star*. When the boat blows up, Mr. O'Lee will go with it. And, if they manage to find enough of him to identify, he'll be considered responsible for the blast." Blackie smiled broadly in the moonlight. "Yeah," he said. "Yeah, that sounds like a real good idea. Come on, you, get in the carriage."

It was a private carriage, and the driver, whoever he was, was obviously in the employ of the two who held Dan captive, so Dan realized that he could expect no help from that quarter. And as both Hiram Dempster and Blackie Beauregard held their pistols on him, escape was impossible by his own devices. So there was little Dan could do but ride quietly through the streets of St. Louis, bound for the riverfront.

"There she is," Dempster said grimly, pointing out a side-wheeler paddleboat as the carriage stopped on the levee. "The *Delta Star*. Used to carry cotton from Memphis to St. Louis before the Federals got hold of her and impressed her into, service."

"That pirate, Commodore Foote, stole her," Blackie said darkly.

"Ah, yes," Dempster added. "I forgot to tell you, O'Lee, that the *Delta Star* once belonged to Colonel Beauregard."

"She still belongs to me," Blackie said. "I'll not see her in Yankee hands."

"So we are going to destroy her," Dempster said.

"That doesn't make sense," Dan objected. "You'll get her back after the war. Why would you want to destroy her?"

"I will gladly destroy her to serve the Confederacy," Blackie said narrowly.

"Don't get it," Dan said, fighting for time. "How will destroying her serve the Confederacy?" Dempster laughed. "Oh, dear fellow, didn't we tell you? The *Delta Star* is loaded with ammunition and supplies for General Grant, in Cairo. She leaves tomorrow morning. Grant is desperately in need of those supplies, if he is to have any success in capturing Island Number Ten. I have it on good authority that he has twice petitioned General Halleck for permission to conduct the operation."

"He needs the ammunition almost as badly as he needs the whiskey the *Delta Star* is carrying," Blackie said derisively.

"Unfortunately for General Grant, he's going to get neither," Dempster said to Dan.

"You are going to prevent it, by blowing up the boat."

"We've talked enough," Blackie said impatiently. "Let's do it, and be done."

Still covered by the two guns, Dan had no choice but to walk down the cobblestone levee and step onto the loading gangplank.

"Who's there?" a voice called from the darkened deck of the boat.

"Hello, Carl, is that you?" Blackie said.

Carl came forward into the light.

"Oh, cap'n. What are you doin' down here?"

"I thought I'd take a look at the engine," Blackie said. "The boiler hasn't been holding pressure like it should. It may be being used by the government, but it still belongs to me. Is anyone else aboard?"

"No, sir. They won't be comin' on board 'till six o'clock in the mornin'. I drew the graveyard watch."

"Well, you're a good man for it."

"You can believe it. If any of them Sesesh bastards try anything on this boat, I'll let 'em have what for. If I had my way we'd hang ever' one of the Rebel bastards," Carl said bitterly.

"These two gentlemen are boiler inspectors," Blackie said. "They'll be with me."

Dan wanted to speak out, to deny Blackie's easy lie, but he knew that if he did, it would only put Carl's life in danger as well, so he remained quiet as the four of them went below into the engine room.

The engine room smelled of burning wood, steam and oil. There was also the lingering odor of sweating human bodies, a kind of signature of the toiling firemen who kept the tender stoked. It was warm, and Dan could hear the water bubbling inside the boiler, and see an orange glow from the firebox.

"I see you're keeping some pressure up," Blackie said.

"Right on thirty, just like I'm supposed to," Carl replied. "That way it won't take us long to get underway in the mornin'."

"There," Blackie said, pointing to a maze of pipes behind the boiler. "That's what I'm talking about right there. Isn't that a steam leak?"

"I don't see nothin'," Carl said.

"Get your head down here so you can see," Blackie suggested.

Carl bent down and leaned around behind the boiler, trying to see the leak Blackie had mentioned.

"No, Carl, look out!" Dan shouted, suddenly realizing what Blackie intended to do. But his warning came too late, for by the time Dan perceived Blackie's intent, he had already taken a water-pipe wrench from the worktable and brought it crashing down on Carl's head.

Carl dropped to the deck without uttering a sound, and when Dan looked at the back of his head he could see that the skull was crushed. Blood and brain tissue gushed out of the wound.

"My God, you killed him!" Dan said.

"What difference does it make?" Blackie replied. "He would have died in the explosion anyway. Same as you're going to."

Seeing the lifeless body of Carl lying in his own ooze sharply brought home to Dan his immediate danger, and whereas he had considered and rejected all escape plans earlier, this time he reacted without thought. He shoved Blackie out of the way and started running for the ladderway, which led back to the main deck.

He didn't make it. Before he had gone two steps, he felt a crashing blow to his head and saw brilliant pinpoints of light flashing before him. Then, the lights went out.

When he awakened sometime later, Dan didn't know how long he had been out. For the first few seconds he just lay where he was, feeling a tremendous pain emanating from the back of his head. When he tried to sit up nausea overcame him, and he had to lay back down for a moment.

He suddenly realized where he was and how he got there. He looked around quickly and saw that he was alone, except for Carl's body, which lay in the same place. Dan knew that he had been very fortunate. It had been Dempster who hit him, and Dempster was neither as strong as Blackie, nor did he use as heavy an instrument. Dan had only been stunned. He could have been killed.

And still might be, he suddenly realized! He remembered then that Dempster and Blackie intended to destroy this boat!

Dan stood quickly, and when the wave of dizziness and nausea overwhelmed him, he grabbed onto an overhead beam for support, hanging on until he was sure he wouldn't pass out again. Finally, his reeling senses stabilized, he began to move around on the boat.

He climbed the ladder and walked out on the deck. He was surprised to see that instead of being tied to the levee, the boat was now in the middle of the river, floating downstream. Evidently, the mooring lines had been slipped by Dempster and Blackie as they left the boat, and the current of the river was all that was needed to carry him out here.

The river was chocked with floes of ice, and the current was swift. From this point, Dan was more than a thousand feet from the bank. Even under the most ideal conditions, a swim to shore in the swiftly moving current would be extremely hazardous. Tonight, in his weakened state, and with the temperature of the water at freezing, such a swim would be impossible. So he gave up the idea of diving into the river, deciding instead that his only chance lay in discovering where the explosive bomb was planted. Somehow, he would have to try and defuse it.

Sure that the bomb would be set in the powder locker, in order to take advantage of the remaining powder and thus completely destroy the boat, Dan summoned his courage and ran into the cargo hold to look for it. It was dark inside the hold, and he didn't dare light a lamp for fear of setting off the powder. Still, with no light, it was impossible to see where a bomb might be set.

He stood there, frustrated, freezing, and frightened. There was a bomb set to explode right under him, and he had no idea where it was. His breath was coming in painful rasps now, and he could hear his own heart beating, but though he looked as hard as he could, he could see no tell-tale sign of a sparkling fuse. He held his breath and tried to listen, to see if he could hear a slow burning fuse sputtering, but he heard nothing. Nor did he smell the cordite burning.

Perhaps they were unable to plant the bomb, he thought. But no, that couldn't be. There was nothing to prevent them. Carl had been killed, and he had been unconscious. The very fact that the boat had been slipped from its mooring was proof enough to Dan that the bomb had, indeed, been planted.

But where? he wondered. And how?

He started walking slowly back to the warmth of the boiler room, where he hoped to be able to figure it all out.

Compared to the icy blast of wind on deck, the boiler room was like the hottest summer day. In fact, it seemed to Dan unusually warm even for a boiler room, and almost as he thought that, he realized how Blackie intended to destroy the *Delta Star!*

He ran to the boiler, to check the steam pressure gauge. It had been maintained at a steady 30 PSI when Carl had pointed it out to them as they came aboard. Now the needle was beyond 200, well into the red danger mark, and still moving up.

Dan looked up at the safety valve and saw that it had been wired tightly shut. When he tried to unwire it, he found the wire was much too hot to touch. Besides, it was so intricately wound that it would take him several minutes to release it, even if he could touch it. And a quick glance at the gauge told Dan that he no longer had several minutes. In fact, he might not even have several seconds.

By now the water in the boiler was roaring, and wisps of steam were escaping from any place that would allow it. The needle hit the peg at the top of the gauge, then began clicking as it bounced against it, trying to go still further.

Dan, tasting the bile of panic in his throat, started for the ladder, determined to take his chances in the icy river. Then, just before he reached it, he saw the heavy wrench Blackie had used to kill Carl, and he grabbed it and returned to the safety valve. He began pounding on the valve, praying aloud, and cursing the valve for being stuck. Finally, with one last, desperate swing, he knocked the entire valve off the pipe. A stream of scalding steam shot straight up, roaring as it poured through the hole and filling the entire boiler room with a hot, moist white cloud.

Dan let out a yelp of pain, dropped the wrench, then ran for the ladder to regain the deck.

Steam poured up through the hatch. It rolled across the deck of the boat and drifted across the river in a billowing white puff. All the while, it was giving off a tremendous roar as it issued from the rent he had put in the system.

Dan looked at his hands in the moonlight. Already the pain of the steam burn was subsiding, and he realized how lucky he had been, for he might have prevented the boiler explosion only to be scalded to death. Fortunately, the pressure had been so high that the steam had shot up in a tight jet before dissipating throughout the entire room. Dan had not been directly exposed to it, and was thus spared a severe burn.

"Ahoy, *Delta Star!*" Dan heard someone shouting. He looked back in surprise to see a small, fast, stem-wheeler boat approaching him.

"Here!" Dan yelled, running to the stem of the boat and waving both arms over his head. "Here, I'm adrift!"

The approaching boat closed with Dan, and a sailor on it

tossed a line across. "Make the line fast," he called, and Dan wrapped it several turns around a stanchion.

The sailor on the small steamboat began hauling in on the line, and the boats closed together. Two men stepped from the other boat onto the *Delta Star*.

"It's all right now, Mr. O'Lee," one of them said. "We'll take care of the *Delta Star*. You hop over and they'll take you back to the bank."

Dan was so grateful for the rescue that he didn't inquire as to how they knew who he was. But the mystery was answered for him when he stepped onto the small boat.

"Hello, Mr. O'Lee," Captain Todd said, smiling broadly. "Did you have a nice trip?"

"Well, if it isn't you," Dan said, his gratitude mixed with irritation. "Where the hell were you when I needed you?"

"I was around, Mr. O'Lee," Todd replied.

"You were around? I was nearly killed; do you know that? Why didn't you do something to stop it?"

"I had to know if the message was genuine," Todd said easily.

"You had to what?"

"You were aware that there was some question about the authenticity of the message," Captain Todd said. "I had to be absolutely positive that it was. The best way to validate the message was to validate you."

"Validate me, or kill me?" Dan asked.

"It's the same thing, really. If they had killed you, I would know that you weren't working for them. The fact that they tried is enough."

"Well, thank God for that, at least," Dan said. "I mean I wouldn't want to spoil your plans by living, or anything."

"Why are you so upset? We saved you, didn't we?"

"No, Captain Todd. All you did was give me a ride. I saved myself."

"Well, all's well that ends well, they say. You'll be interested to know that we captured Hiram Dempster. He'll spend the rest of this war languishing in a Federal prison for treason. Unfortunately, we weren't as lucky with Blackie Beauregard. He got away."

"I see," Dan said.

"Aren't you interested in what happened to your brother? Or Miss Welles?"

"I'm sure you'll tell me," Dan said.

"You're right, I will. They both got away too. I'm sure you are equally happy about that."

"Yes, I am glad," Dan said. "I'm glad they are out of my life. Especially Liberty Welles."

"Ah, look at it this way," Captain Todd said. "You met an attractive woman, and you had a fine time. There was no damage done."

"No," Dan agreed. "There was no damage done. Oh, wait a minute! She knows. We've got to tell General Halleck! Liberty knows where Halleck intends to strike!"

Captain Todd laughed. "Corinth, right?"

"Yes. He has to be warned. She's going to tell Beauregard, and he'll have the entire Confederate Army there!"

Captain Todd was still laughing, and he laughed so hard the tears came to his eyes. He wiped them with a handkerchief. "Excuse me," he said, barely able to get the words out. "Oh, you must excuse me, but this is so funny."

"Funny? What's funny about it?" Dan asked.

"I just told you that Liberty knows General Halleck's plans. She's going to have the whole Rebel army there to meet Halleck."

"Mr. O'Lee, that is exactly what General Halleck *wants* them to do," Todd said.

"What? No, he mentioned at the dinner that the very thing he didn't want to do was to meet the Confederates in a major battle."

"He said that for Liberty's ears only," Captain Todd explained. "Don't you see? This is perfect. She thought she was using you, but all along, you were using her. With our help, of course."

"I don't understand," Dan said.

"It's quite simple, really. Lieutenant Ward believed Liberty was a spy, and was working on her case when he was killed. But he passed along enough information for us to have our suspicions. Then, when we learned that she was to be your guest at the general's dinner, we simply set it up. The General gave her just what information we wanted her to have, hoping thereby to lure the entire Rebel army into one major battle. And Miss Welles fell for it, hook, line and sinker."

"I see," Dan said quietly.

Captain Todd began laughing again. "So, Mr. O'Lee. You have achieved your revenge over her, much sooner than you thought. It's really very funny, isn't it?"

"Yeah," Dan said. "So why am I not laughing?"

Chapter 10

THE MISSISSIPPI RIVER starts as a clear stream, no more than eighteen feet wide, in northern Minnesota, and by the time it reaches St. Louis, where it is joined by the Missouri, its chief tributary, it has grown to be nearly a mile across. It was at that point that Dan O'Lee was rescued from the *Delta Star*.

As Dan stood on the deck of the little rescue craft, he looked back across the wide Mississippi, and at the ice floes he would have had to contend with had he elected to jump into the river. He watched one large floe as it floated south at a steady two miles per hour, matching the speed of the river current.

Had Dan been able to follow the ice floe on south, he would have passed such places as Sainte Genevieve and Cape Girardeau, in Missouri, towns whose names still bore the mark of their original French settlers. Then he would have seen Cairo, Illinois, the point at which the Ohio River joins the Mississippi, and the head- quarters for General Grant's field command. By the time the ice floe reached New Madrid, far down in the boot-heel of Missouri, it would have nearly melted, and there, Dan would have gotten a glimpse of Island Number Ten.

Major islands in the river were numbered from north to

south, and Island Number Ten, just north of New Madrid, was one of the larger and more dominating ones. There, the Confederates had built a fort which they called the Confederate 'Rock of Gibraltar.' The fort helped make Island Number Ten a cork in the mouth of a bottle; it kept the Union forces from going any further downriver.

Past that point the ice floes have melted, and their water becomes one with the river, continuing south, passing Kentucky, Tennessee, Arkansas, and forming most of the western border of the state of Mississippi.

The lower course of the Mississippi is between wide, flat shores, mostly mud carried and deposited there by the river itself. This has formed a valley as fertile as that of the Nile River in Egypt, and through this valley the river meanders through bayous, lakes and swamps, depositing rich, black dirt which is the stuff of great plantations.

One such plantation is Calvert Hills, located just north of Natchez, Mississippi. Calvert Hills was founded by Jesse Calvert in 1810, and when Jesse Calvert was buried in his land, he passed control over to his son, Amon. Except that on the afternoon of February 10, 1862, Amon Calvert, a major and the executive officer of the 2nd Mississippi Horse Regiment, fired a ceremonial cannon in salute to the Stars and Bars of the Confederacy. The breech of the gun had been double-charged, in order to make a more fitting salute, and it burst upon firing, killing Major Amon Calvert instantly.

The mythical ice floe had by now reached this point on its steady two-mile-per-hour course toward the Gulf, and was silent witness to the funeral scene unfolding on Calvert Hills.

The rain had fallen steadily all morning long, and the black dirt of the delta land of Calvert Hills had turned to mud. The horses struggled through the mire, pulling their hooves free only with effort.

The preacher who was conducting the funeral had dragged the eulogy on and on while the mourners were in the church, hoping the rain would stop. But the point had been finally reached when the mourners preferred the rain to the sermon, so the great oaken doors were swung open, and the pall bearers bore Amon Calvert's casket to the wagon.

Tamara Calvert sat in that wagon, beside her father's body. She was a striking girl with long, flowing black hair, deep blue eyes, and a flawless complexion. She held an umbrella which did nothing to stop the slashing rain, and her black dress hung heavy with water. She looked at the train of wagons and buggies following them, noting with some pride the many neighbors had turned up for her father s funeral.

The Negroes who had belonged to Amon Calvert struggled through the mud on both sides of the road. They made up a pathetic little army of blacks. They were singing some hymn which, with their own embellishments, was barely recognizable; nevertheless, it was mournful and hauntingly beautiful.

"Miss Tamara," Colonel Putnam said, clearing his throat. Tamara lifted her head and looked at him. It was the first word spoken to her since they had left the church. "I want to express the regrets of the Second Mississippi Horse Regiment about the unfortunate accident which took your father from us. We consider his death to have as much honor and meaning as if he had fallen on the field of battle." The colonel was riding close to Tamara, and he lay his hand on her leg.

"Do you, Colonel Putnam?" Tamara asked indifferently, taking her leg away, not sharply but resolutely.

"Absolutely," Colonel Putnam said, noticing neither the expression in Tamara's voice nor the reaction to his intimate gesture. "In fact, we're leaving soon for an encampment way upriver— I'm not at liberty to tell you just where—and we aim to put your father's name on our flag. It will be carried into combat with honor."

"I am sure I shall take great comfort from that," Tamara said, her voice just short of sarcastic. She was against this war, and had tried to talk her father out of it. But he had insisted, and his insistence had cost him his life. Tamara could not now

Hearts Divided

be bought off with a sham show in his honor.

The grave where Tamara's father was to be laid had been dug by two Negroes while the funeral service had been going on in the church. Now they stood by the hole as the cortege approached, leaning on their shovels and peering at the procession with eyes that looked out from mud-caked faces.

The grave was half-full of water. When the coffin was lowered, it floated, as if Amon Calvert were reluctant to leave the land he and his father before him had built into one of the finest plantations in Mississippi. Colonel Putnam motioned to the two gravediggers, and they began to shovel dirt on top of the casket, which finally forced it down.

"Miz Tamara," one of the blacks said, approaching the wagon respectfully. "I've carved out a headpiece for your papa, 'till you gets a fancy rock one. Do you s'pose it'd be all right if I put it on the grave?"

The man held up a marker inscribed simply; Amon Calvert—Born March 5, 1814—Died February 10,1862.

"Thank you, Troy," Tamara said. "I think it is beautiful, and I'd be proud to have it marking papa's grave."

"What are you aiming to do now, Miss Tamara?" Colonel Putnam asked.

"Do?" Tamara replied. "Why, I'm going to continue on here at the plantation of course."

"Miss Tamara, now that your pa is gone, you don't have anyone to look after things," Colonel Putnam said. "Don't you think it would be best if you come to live with the missus and me, and let us handle the plantation for you?" Putnam put his hand on her again, and looked at her with eyes that were very deep, with red dots far at the bottom. "I'd treat you like one of my own."

"No," Tamara said. She shivered, from the suggestion and from the touch. "Besides, I do have someone to look after things. In less than a month I shall be Mrs. Blackwell Terrence Beauregard. Blackie is coming home soon. Have you forgotten about him, Colonel Putnam?"

"Blackie is away at war," Colonel Putnam said, pulling his hand back. "And operating behind enemy lines like he does, it would be difficult for him to get home frequently enough to take care of you the way he should. The way I could," he added.

"Then I've got Alva and Troy."

"Alva and Troy are both black, Miss Tamara," Putnam said slowly, as if trying to explain something to a child.

"I *know* they are black, Colonel Putnam. But they will watch out for me until Blackie returns."

"Well, don't you fret none about it," Putnam said, as if not hearing a word Tamara was saying. "We'll work something out for you." He reached his hand over to squeeze Tamara's leg a third time, and she pulled it away from him again, this time sharply.

The wagons and buggies were once more filled with people as the procession started back to the big house which dominated Calvert Hills. The house servants had been working all morning, and by the time the mourners reached the house they found food prepared and plates set out on every available table and sideboard.

From the conversation at the table it was hard to realize that the people were gathered for the purpose of mourning. But funerals ranked right behind weddings as social events, and the families who saw each other only occasionally were now able to exchange all the latest gossip. The dinner was gay and noisy, and now and then a trill of laughter rent the air, only to be cut off by a quick, embarrassed shush as someone realized that the mood was supposed to be solemn.

After the dinner, Colonel Putnam stood up and called for the attention of the men.

"Gentlemen, I gave my word to Miss Tamara that the name of Major Amon Calvert would be inscribed on our battle flag and carried in honor. I would now like to propose a toast, to be drunk by all, which binds us to uphold this flag of honor at all times. May it never fall into Yankee hands!"

"Here, here!" one of the other officers shouted, and there was a cheer by all the men, followed by the draining of their glasses.

"Colonel, when are we gonna see some action?" another asked.

"I was waiting for the opportunity to tell you," Colonel Putnam replied. "And I guess now is as good a time as any. We are moving up the Mississippi tomorrow, and my guess is, we will be joining General McCown on Island Number Ten."

"Where is that?"

"It's a large island in the river, just above a place called New Madrid, in Missouri. The river makes a big bend there, and whoever controls that island, controls the river. We aim to make sure that the South controls it. Gentlemen, we'll be standing in the front door of the Confederacy!"

Again there were cheers.

"And now, gentlemen, I think it is time we came to some agreement about Miss Tamara."

"What agreement?" Tamara said quickly.

"There, there, Tamara, honey. Don't you worry about it any. The men folk will think of something," Ellen Putnam said, as she patted Tamara's arm. Ellen was Colonel Putnam's wife. Where Putnam's features were bony and hawkish, Ellen's were full and round.

"I don't want them to think of something," Tamara protested. "I don't need their help."

"Don't worry about it, child," Ellen said. "You won't be a bother to them at all. Come on with us. I had your girl, Alva, fix us up some sassafrass tea. There's nothing like a little sassafrass to keep the chill from settin' in on a body." Tamara was coaxed away by the good-neighbor ladies and given a seat in a rocking chair. A cup of tea was put in her hand and she sipped it absently, straining to hear the conversation of the men who were across the hall in the library.

The ladies pulled out knitting and embroidery and talked among themselves, while their hands moved about their work.

To Tamara, their hands looked like dirt daubers, birds flitting along a fence row.

By ignoring the banal gossip of the women, Tamara was able to overhear snatches of conversation from the men. Colonel Putnam's voice was the loudest, and she could hear him clearly: ". . . and the county clerk told me himself that Miss Tamara approached him on the very day her father was killed and told him of her fool idea for setting all her niggers free. If she sets her niggers free, and with us all gone off to the war, what do you think is going to happen? There won't be a white woman safe on any of the plantations, that's what. I tell you, we've got to do something about it."

Tamara got up from her chair and went into the library. It was full of smoke and the men stood clustered together chewing their cigars and waving their glasses. Tamara stood in the doorway watching them.

"Why, Miss Tamara," Putnam said as he saw her. "You shouldn't come in here. This is just man-talk."

"It's man-talk about me, Mr. Putnam," Tamara said, purposefully disdaining his military title. "I have every right to be in here."

"Let her stay, colonel," one of the others called. "Tamara, I'm going to be honest with you. Your papa would spin in his grave if he knew you were planning on setting all the niggers free."

"I'm doing more than planning," Tamara said resolutely. "I'm going to do it.'

"But think about what you are doing, girl! If you set your niggers free, they'll be wanting to be free on the other plantations too. The next thing you know, they'll start revolting, and then we'll have two wars on our hands. One against the Yankees, and one against our own niggers."

"If you would free your people, we wouldn't have any problem," Tamara said.

There was a rush of protesting voices, some of them raised in anger, until Colonel Putnam raised his hand to silence them.

"It isn't as simple as all that," the colonel said. "There are questions here, far too complex for you to understand."

"I understand the cruelty of keeping another human being in perpetual bondage," Tamara replied evenly. "And I understand the Christian brotherhood that would set them free."

Tamara walked over to the window. It was still raining, and the two little black boys who sat minding the visitor's horses were huddled beneath a piece of canvas, trying unsuccessfully to keep dry. Tamara looked up the long driveway and saw a rig approaching. Whoever it was, she thought, he was too late for the funeral, and if he was going to agree with the others, she'd just as soon he did not come at all.

Tamara started to look away when she noticed something about the driver, a familiar way of his sitting at the reins, which made her heart skip a beat with joy. She let out a little whoop of excitement.

"It's Blackie!" she said, shouting at the others. She turned to look at them with a smile of victory on her face. "What I do now is no one's business. Blackie has come home to marry me!" Tamara ran from the library and out the front door, down the front steps, through the rain, and out into the driveway, arriving just as Blackie pulled his horse to a halt.

"Oh, Blackie, you've come!" she said excitedly. "Oh, darling, I am so happy to see you. Those awful men in there, they—"

"Is Colonel Putnam in there?" Blackie asked, cutting her off.

"Yes," Tamara said. "He's the worst of the lot, Blackie. They keep saying they want to come to some sort of agreement about me." Blackie stepped out of the rig and started toward the house without so much as a perfunctionary kiss for Tamara. Considering that he had been away for over six month, Tamara found his indifference to her perplexing. She was also hurt by it.

Tamara hurried after him, thinking that perhaps he was so

intent upon righting the wrong that had been done her that he had let the greeting slip by for the moment. Such thoughts poured balm on her hurt feelings. But then, with a quick fear, she thought that he might be angry enough to do something unwise.

"Blackie, you won't do anything that might be dangerous?" she asked.

"What do you mean?"

"Like challenge Putnam to a duel or anything like that."

"Don't be foolish, Tamara," Blackie said. "I have no intention whatever of fighting a duel."

"That's good," Tamara said with a relief. "For a moment, I thought—"

"Don't think," Blackie interrupted.

Blackie stepped into the library, and when the others saw him, they greeted him warmly. "How was St. Louis?" one of them asked him.

"Seething with support for our cause," Blackie answered. "I honestly believe that if my uncle were commander of the West instead of Johnston, I could raise an army in St. Louis that would capture the city, then descend down the river to Cairo and crush General Grant."

"Colonel Beauregard." Putnam spoke. "Did you have an opportunity to check on that little matter we spoke of yesterday?"

"Yesterday?" Tamara asked, quickly. She looked at Blackie in confusion. "You were back yesterday, and yet you didn't come to see me? Why not?"

"I had business to attend to," Blackie said. He looked at Putnam with a set expression on his face. "You were right, colonel. You have my undying gratitude, sir, for informing me of the situation before I made a fool of myself."

"It was the honorable thing to do," Putnam said. "That's why I informed you of it, as soon as I discovered it." Putnam looked at Tamara, and Tamara saw the same strange look in his eyes again.

"Blackie, Colonel Putnam, what are you talking about?" Tamara asked, a nervousness rising in her. She looked from one to the other.

Blackie didn't answer. Instead, he looked at the other men gathered there in the library.

"Gentlemen, there will be no niggers freed from Calvert Hills. I can promise you that."

"What?" Tamara asked, stunned. "Blackie, how can you make such a promise? Calvert Hills belongs to me now, and I'll do as I wish with it."

"That's just it," Blackie said easily. "Calvert Hills doesn't belong to you, it belongs to me. So do you, by the way."

"So do *I?* What are you talking about? What do you mean Calvert Hills belongs to you? And how can you say I belong to you? We aren't married yet, Blackie Beauregard, and if this is to be your attitude, we never shall be!"

Blackie smiled. "On that point, my dear, you are one hundred percent correct. I will never marry you."

"What?" Tamara asked in a small voice. She felt her head spinning, and a quick nausea in her stomach. "Blackie, what are you saying?"

"I have no desire to marry you, Tamara, and, according to the laws of this state, I couldn't marry you if I wished."

"But . . . but we are engaged!" Tamara said. "Blackie, don't you remember the night before you left for St. Louis? You asked my father for my hand in marriage, and he said yes. He even made you the executor of his will."

"I remember," Blackie said flatly. "And I am grateful to him for that, for in the same act he made me the ultimate heir, should you be unable to inherit Calvert Hills. By a codicil of the will, Calvert Hills now belongs to me, land and chattel. And, as you are part of the chattel, you too belong to me."

Tamara couldn't believe her ears.

"What do you mean, I'm part of the chattel?" she demanded.

Blackie removed an envelope from the inside pocket of

the gray-and-gold Confederate officer's tunic he was wearing, pulled a paper from the envelope and began reading.

"I, Amon Calvert, do hereby attest and affirm that the following property, herein listed as collateral for a loan . . . and so on and so forth," Blackie said. "Ah, here's the interesting part. Calvert Hills, located north of Natchez where the Mississippi River makes the first large bend to the west, said land to encompass all ground within such bend. In addition to the land there is the main house, stable and outbuildings, a row of ten slaves' shacks, twenty mules, and sixty-five slaves, as of this date, this date being August 10th 1861. The slaves are here below listed by name: Tamara Calvert, my issue by the slave Tricia, now deceased, Alva Morris, housemaid, Troy Parnell, overseer," Blackie looked up at Tamara. "Do I need to go on?"

"I don't understand," Tamara said in a weak voice.

"There's nothing to understand," Blackie said. "Your father was strapped for money, so he borrowed against what he owned. He had to list all his assets, and he listed you among them. Once he made his crop he paid the money back, but the statement he made was still in the bank vault. You are a nigger, Tamara."

There was a stunned silence from the men in the library, and Tamara stood there for a moment, trying to regain her breath. Once, as a child, she had fallen from a tree and lay on the ground for several seconds, unable to breathe. She felt the same way now.

"Isn't that true, Alva?" Blackie called out. Tamara turned to see that Alva had been hiding behind the door. Now she stepped out into plain view, with tears burning her eyes.

"Mr. Amon done give Tricia his word that this girl don't never find out."

"Well, Mr. Amon is dead, and so is Tricia," Blackie said. "And since Tamara is a nigger, and a slave, she can't inherit this plantation. That makes it mine, and I have no obligation to honor any promise made by Amon Calvert. Besides, it serves him right for trying to marry me off to his nigger whelp."

"Alva, is this true?" Tamara asked in a small voice.

Alva hung her head in sorrow. "It's true, girl. I'm sorry," she said. "The Lawd knows I'se tried to pertect your secret."

Alva turned slowly and started to leave.

"No, Alva, wait, please," Tamara said.

Alva stopped. "I know you hates me now, child, for deceivin' you all these years."'

"Hate you? How could I hate you?" Tamara asked. "I love you, Alva, and I always have. Now, more than ever." Tamara ran to Alva and threw her arms around her neck.

"So, gentlemen, we'll leave the two nigger women to themselves, and get down to business. As I said, the niggers here will not be freed, and any future dealings with Calvert Hills will come through its new owner . .. me." "Congratulations," Colonel Putnam said, smiling broadly and offering his hand to Blackie. The others joined in offering congratulations. Tamara and Alva walked back into the kitchen.

"Sit there, child," Alva said, pointing to a chair near the table. "I'll fix you some coffee and tell you a story."

Chapter 11

TAMARA WAS STUNNED by the news that she was herself a slave and not the white mistress of Calvert Hills. In the library, the voices of the men could still be heard, though now their conversation was spiced with ribald laughter. She heard a few shocked comments from the women who sat in the parlor, and though she may have imagined it, she thought she could feel the women slipping quietly in ones and twos down the hall to peek into the kitchen, to stare at her and reassure themselves that her skin hadn't suddenly turned coal black.

Troy came into the kitchen and poured himself a cup of coffee, then settled into a chair quietly, as Alva comforted Tamara.

"Alva, all I remember about mama was that she was so very pretty," Tamara said. "And her skin was as white as mine. I had no idea she was not white."

"Your mama was the smartest and the prettiest woman who ever drawed a breath in her body," Alva said. She picked up a brush and began to stroke Tamara's hair. Tamara had very long hair, which was almost blue-black. It had been the pride of her father, and Alva spent many hours brushing it so that it would shine. "Where did mama come from, Alva?"

"I was with your mama at a fashionable house for ladies

in N'Orleans," Alva said. "Your mama was so beautiful that folks would come from miles around just to see her."

As Alva talked, Tamara closed her eyes to listen. The soothing tone of Alva's voice and the relaxing feeling of the brush allowed her to drift off, and she could almost see the fashionable house for ladies, where Alva and her mother lived. Troy picked up the story in those places where he could add his account:

The river packet *Isabelle Queen* had pulled into the slip at New Orleans amidst the ringing of bells and occasional stomach-shaking blasts froth the deep whistle.

"Captain Reynolds," Amon said as he approached the wheelhouse. "I would like to thank you for the hospitality you have shown me during this voyage. It has been most pleasant."

"Mr. Calvert, I'm mighty proud to offer you any comforts that this old boat has. You are one of my best customers, and many's the time your cotton's been the only paying freight," Captain Reynolds answered.

"Come on, Troy," Amon said to the big man with him. Troy was handsome, tall, and vigorous. A light-skinned, half-caste Negro, he was actually Amon Calvert's half-brother, sired by Amon's father out of a pure Ibo named Harau. Troy had been a childhood companion to Amon, and had grown up to be his personal servant, accompanying him wherever he went.

Although Troy and Amon knew they were related, they never mentioned it. In fact, whereas Amon often spoke of his "father," Troy spoke of the man always as "Masta Jesse."

Troy picked up the baggage and followed Amon down Canal Street until they reached the hotel where they would stay. Amon had a room, to be shared by Troy, though Troy would have to sleep on a pallet on the floor.

"Mr. Amon, where do you know this fella we are goin' to meet from? What's his name? Cap'n Mason?"

"Captain Tom Mason," Amon answered. "He was a classmate of mine at the College of William and Mary. You remember that time that I was gone up to Virginia to go to school?"

"Yes, suh, I 'members," Troy answered. "You was gone a long time."

"Captain Mason was there at the same time, and he is from New Orleans. He wrote me a letter last month, telling me about a plan for shipping cotton direct to England on his own ship. In fact, he wants to sell me half of it."

"Cant you just put your cotton on the boats what stops at Calvert Hills?"

"No," Amon laughed. "Those are just riverboats. They can't go in the ocean. Captain Mason has a large ship that can sail right across the ocean. A big ship like the one your mama come over on."

"For the Lawd's sake, Mr. Amon, you ain't gonna make Troy ride on that thing, are you?" Troy asked, fearfully. Troy's only knowledge of sailing vessels had been garnered from his mother. She had told him of the journey she had made in a slaver's brig.

"Don't worry, Troy. This ship is strictly for cotton. No niggers on it, except maybe some of the crew."

Captain Mason met with Amon and they spent the next few hours discussing the business arrangements and methods of profit-sharing. Finally, after coming to a mutual agreement, they decided to "do the town".

"Amon, there's a place down here that you have got to see. It's the finest sportin' house in N'Orleans, and that makes it about the finest in the world—and I oughta know," Captain Mason said with a wink. "I've been in whorehouses from Frankfurt to Hong Kong, and this one tops them all."

Amon had never been in a whorehouse. He had never even been away from Calvert Hills, except for the time he was away in school. Williamsburg, Virginia didn't have anything in the way of a sporting house, so he was inexperienced. Oh, he had the run of wenches on his and most neighboring plantations. But this was to be a new experience for him.

Hearts Divided

"Welcome, Captain Mason. Welcome to Harmony House," a woman said as she greeted the two men.

"Good evening, Mrs. Drew. This is my friend from Natchez, Mississippi, Mr. Amon Calvert, Esquire."

"*Enchante*, Mr. Calvert. Welcome," Mrs. Drew said, extending her hand.

"*Merci beaucoup, madame,*" Amon answered. He took her hand and kissed it.

"Oh, Captain Mason, your friend is so gallant and charming," Mrs. Drew cooed.

"He wasn't like me, Mrs. Drew. He paid attention to his studies. He was a whiz at college. He never even played hooky with me to go to Norfolk—not even once."

"Will your pleasure be the same tonight, captain?" Mrs. Drew asked.

"Yes, ma'am. I would like to see Fifi, if you please."

"Yes, of course. Go into the Parisian Room. She will be with you shortly. And you, Mr. Calvert. How does your taste run?"

Amon stood there stupidly for a few moments.

He was a little embarrassed and didn't know quite what to say or do.

"You're gonna have to excuse my friend. He's never been to one of these places before. Send him the nicest girl you've got."

"Very well, Mr. Calvert, I understand," Mrs. Drew said with a pleasant smile. "You just wait in the Rose Room. Someone will be in shortly."

Amon walked down the carpeted hallway until he got to the Rose Room. He was alone because Harmony House made provisions for entertainment for the body servants of the gentlemen callers, and Troy was, at this moment, with a girl provided just for that purpose.

"Are you Mr. Amon, suh?" a tall, light-skinned and very pretty Negro girl asked.

"Yes, yes, I am."

"Go right on in, suh. It'll just be another moment."

"Are you the one?"

"Lawd, no, suh! I'se Alva, Miss Tricia's lady-in-waitin'."

Amon eagerly began to look forward to his encounter. If the lady-in-waiting was this pretty, then the lady must be beautiful.

She was. She moved through the door and into the room an effortless glide. Her skin was alabaster, and her eyes were a cool deep, deep green.

"Mister Calvert, my name is Tricia Cote. I've been selected as your companion, and may I say that it is an honor, sir?"

Tricia's voice fell on Amon's ears like the tinkling of wind chimes stirred by the breeze. He was thunderstruck. Never in his life had he seen anyone so beautiful, or heard a voice so soft. He fell instantly in love.

Tricia walked over to the bed and stood quietly beside it, while Alva turned down the covers. She turned her back to Amon, and Alva began undressing her.

Amon watched, spellbound, as the girl's shoulders, then the smooth expanse of skin on her back, and finally the delightfully formed buttocks were exposed. Within moments, Tricia stood nude, though Amon had not yet seen any more than her back.

Amon felt like a field hand; he felt rude, uncouth, clumsy. He knew that the girl he was watching was a prostitute, a common whore. No—not a common whore, an uncommon whore! He should feel superior. He was wealthy, educated, and born of one of the finest families in Mississippi, yet in the presence of this beautiful girl, he felt like the lowest field hand on his plantation.

The girl nodded at Alva, and Alva held the sheet so that she could slip modestly into bed. Never, during the entire episode, had she presented any view to Amon that was immodest or ill-chosen.

Hearts Divided

"Mr. Calvert," Tricia said softly. "If you will pull out the top drawer of that dresser, you will find a robe. Please step into the dressing room and remove your clothes."

Amon wanted to answer, but his tongue grew thick, and his mouth was dry. He took the robe and left without a word.

Amon spent the night with Tricia. Their love-making was not the frenzied wild thrusting that Amon had experienced with the wenches in the quarters. It was tender and sensitive, yet a passionate and complete affair. Amon would have given his life for her by the next morning.

Alva was able to relate the story, because she had spent the night with them in the same room, napping in the chair, always present for her mistress's beck and call. With the coming of dawn's light, Alva began the morning ministrations for her lady.

"Well, Amon," Captain Mason laughed, when they met the next morning. "What did I tell you? Is this a nice place?"

"It's very nice, captain. I enjoyed myself," Amon answered. He kept looking in the back, hoping for another glimpse of Tricia. "I must see Mrs. Drew."

"Not on your life, sir," Captain Mason said. "You were my guest, and I will pay for the services."

"No, you don't understand. I want to inquire about the lady I was with last night."

"You were taken with her, were you? Well, I don't blame you. These women are the highest-class whores in the world. They are all quadroons—only one-fourth nigger. Just enough nigger blood to sex 'em up, but the rest is white, to make 'em ladies."

"You mean she was a Negro girl?"

"The law says one sixteenth is enough to make you a nigger," Mason answered. "I know she is in bondage, and can be bought. The price is awfully high, though. Probably a lot higher'n you'd be willin' to pay."

Amon was struck dumb by the revelation. He had no idea that Tricia was legally a Negro. And he had thought he was in love with her. "I guess you're right, captain. Maybe we'd better go," Amon answered.

But Amon couldn't stay away. Later that same day, he returned to Harmony House, this time without Captain Mason. He was greeted at the door by Mrs. Drew.

"Bonsoir, je suis heureuse de nous voir encore."

"Mon plaisir" Amon answered. "I am happy to see you again too."

"Mr. Calvert, what a gentleman you are!" Mrs. Drew said, beaming. "Now, what can I do for you this evening?"

"I'd like to see Miss Cote, please."

"Oh, dear me. I'm terribly sorry. I'm afraid that Miss Cote is occupied at the moment.

Your French is superb, however. Perhaps Fifi?"

"No. Only Miss Cote."

"I'm terribly sorry, really I am," Mrs. Drew replied.

Amon turned to leave, but as he reached the door he looked back at Mrs. Drew.

"Mrs. Drew, do you own this place?"

"Yes, I do. Is there something I can do for you?"

"I want to buy Miss Cote."

"I beg your pardon?"

"I was led to believe that I could—uh—buy any of your girls if the price were right. I want to buy Miss Cote, and you can name your own price."

"Oh, Mr. Calvert, there is much more than the price. If I were to sell Miss Cote, or any of my girls, I would have to know beyond the shadow of a doubt that they would never, never under any circumstances, be mistreated. And you may have noticed that Tricia has a maidservant, Alva. She would never go anywhere without Alva."

"Your price, Mrs. Drew. I won't haggle."

"Eight thousand dollars for Miss Cote, and two thousand for Alva. Ten thousand dollars total."

Amon opened his jacket pocket and pulled out a bank draft. "Have someone take this draft to the bank. I'll make it out to you for eleven thousand dollars. I want Miss Cote, and Alva, and I want both women to have complete wardrobes. I intend to take Miss Cote with me tonight."

"But the gentlemen who is with her will be offended. He paid one hundred dollars in good faith," Mrs. Drew said.

Amon opened his billfold and took out two hundred dollars in cash. "Give him one hundred dollars in cash, and offer him his choice of any other girl."

"You are most generous," Mrs. Drew answered.

Amon sat on the big overstaffed sofa in the lobby of Harmony House for perhaps fifteen minutes. He picked up a copy of *Harpers Weekly,* and was thumbing through it when he heard his name called.

Again, the tinkling of a breeze through wind chimes.

"Mr. Calvert?"

Amon stood quickly and looked over at her. "You may call me Amon," he said.

"I will be happy to belong to you, Amon," she said, smiling.

"And she was happy," Alva said, as she completed brushing Tamara's hair. "She was happy right up 'till the day she die. Your papa never told a soul that Tricia wasn't a white girl, 'n wasn't his wife."

"You mean papa and mama never were married?" Tamara asked.

"No'm, they wasn't," Alva said. "But they loved each other, same as if they was married. When the big sickness come in 1853, it killed hundreds of folks here 'bouts, both black and white. And your mama, child, was one of the first to go. Now, your papa is buried out there right beside her, and they'll be together in the hereafter, just like they did in this life, with no nevermind that one was white and one was black."

Colonel Putnam stepped into the kitchen at that moment, and Alva and Troy both grew quiet and reserved. Tamara had noticed this subtle but ever present reaction of blacks to the presence of whites before. But now, for the first time, she understood, and realized with sudden insight, that *she had reacted just as Alva and Troy had.*

"Tamara," Putnam said, looking at her with that strange, almost frightening expression she had seen in his eyes earlier. "Under the circumstances, Colonel Beauregard felt it would be best if you didn't stay at Calvert Hills. Therefore, he offered you for sale, and I have bought you. Get some of your things together. I'll be taking you home with me."

Tamara stood woodenly and walked up the stairs to her bedroom. She took a suitcase from the trunk and began packing her clothes, moving mechanically, still too numbed by all that was happening to show any reaction.

The door opened and closed.

"Alva, would you help me..

"It's me," Putnam said.

"Colonel, you've no right to come into a young lady's room without knocking," Tamara said.

Putnam smiled, an evil smile, and now Tamara recognized the expression in his eyes for what it was. It was lust. She realized that he wanted her, and she was frightened by the realization.

"You are no longer a young lady," Putnam said. "You are a slave girl. My slave girl, Tamara, and I can do anything with you I wish."

"What?" Tamara asked, putting her hand up to her mouth. She stepped back, her fear growing to panic.

Colonel Putnam slipped his tunic off, then began unbuckling his belt. "Don't be frightened, Tamara," he said. "This is something all the nigger girls have to go through. Especially the pretty ones."

"What are you doing?" Tamara said angrily. "Get away from me!"

Putnam reached out to grab Tamara, but she jumped back. His hand caught the front of her dress, and he ripped it down the middle, opening it up and revealing her small but perfect breasts. The nipples, reacting to the sudden exposure of air, tightened into tiny rosebuds.

"Look at that," Putnam said. His eyes grew glassy, and he opened his trousers, exposing himself to her. He reached out again and grabbed her, and threw her on the bed. She tried to fight against him, but he was too strong for her, and she was unable to ward him off.

Putnam made no effort to remove her dress. He just tore it from her, ripping it all the way down the front, then laying it open, so that she presented him with her naked body. She tried to hold her legs together, but the effort was futile, and he loomed over her, looking like an apparition from hell.

When she felt his full weight on her, Tamara wanted to scream, but knew to do so would be useless. He entered her brutally, and she felt a searing, shameful pain. It was so acute that she cried out with the agony of it, and wondered how such a thing could happen to her in her own home. That it occurred in her very bed was the final degradation.

Finally Putnam let a grunt escape from his lips, and shuddered once as he finished. He withdrew from her then, and turning his back to her, began dressing quietly.

As Tamara lay on her bed, used, degraded, and injured, she saw a pair of scissors on the bedside table. When she looked up, Putnam was still standing with his back to her, now pulling on his pants. He was talking to her.

"I know you didn't like it much that time," Putnam said. "It's always painful the first time. But you'll get used to it like all the others, I reckon, and then..."

Putnam never finished his sentence, for Tamara brought the scissors down right in the side of his neck. The scissors severed an artery, and a thick, gushing spurt of blood squirted out. Putnam turned to face her with a look of surprise on his face. He made one or two futile efforts to withdraw the scissors. That failed, and he collapsed to the floor. He lay there, jerking convulsively, until he died, never uttering another sound.

Alva stepped into the room a few moments later and saw

at once what happened. She gasped quietly, but she didn't scream.

"Tamara, get dressed and get out of here quick," she said. "You mustn't be here when the white folks find out."

"Alva, I ... I had no choice," Tamara said. "He *raped* me."

"No'm, honey, he didn't rape you. Nigger men rapes white women, but white men pleasures nigger women. Leastwise, that's the way they'll tell it, and you'll hang, girl, sure as Nat Turner. You've got to get out of here."

"But where will I go?" Tamara asked.

"Go north, honey. Go north."

Chapter 12

NORTH OF CALVERT HILLS, but still in the state of Mississippi, was Trailback Plantation, owned and farmed by Mr. A.G. Welles. Mr. Welles' real name was Alexander Grace Welles, but he hated the name Alexander and refused to be called Alex. Grace was his mother's maiden name and, as she was an only child and her father, Charles Grace, had wanted to see the family name carried on, it had been tacked on to Mr. Welles as a middle name. Grace was, of course, too feminine to be used, so Alexander Grace Welles had simply been called A.G. from the time he was old enough to express a preference.

A.G. was sixty years old. His crisp curly hair was silver-white, but his face was unlined, his eyes were sparkling and young, and he wore proudly the uniform of a colonel in the Mississippi militia. He was wearing it now, as he waited at the depot to meet the night train.

Meeting any train was exciting, but night trains were even more so. There was always a carnival atmosphere about the crowd: laughter, good-natured joking, the constant cry of drummers hawking their wares and, since the war had begun, music from a military band. For Colonel A.G. Welles, though, meeting this particular train would be even more exciting, because it would be bringing his daughter, Liberty, back home to

Trailback Plantation.

"Here she comes!" someone yelled, and the band struck up a brisk, military aire.

The train pounded into the station, its great driver wheels flashing by in a blur, while glowing embers tumbled from the firebox and wisps of steam vented from the cylinders. Finally, the train ground to a stop, and through the windows and into the yellowed interiors of the cars, A.G. could see the passengers starting for the doors to disembark at the Corinth station.

"Father, hello!" Liberty called, stepping down onto the platform.

"Daughter!" A.G. replied, running to her with the enthusiasm of a man much younger in years. Liberty had been a late blessing, born when A.G. was already forty and had given up on children. She was an only child, and the absolute apple of her father s eye. And now, she was even more important to him, for she had grown to be a woman who was the exact image of her mother, now dead these many years. To look upon his daughter was a bittersweet experience for A.G., for in her he saw his wife again.

"Father, what is that uniform?" Liberty asked when she saw how her father was attired.

"Do you like it? I am the commanding officer of the Welles' Home Guards. I raised my own regiment, daughter, equipped them, furnished uniforms, horses, everything."

"Good Lord, that must have cost a fortune!" Liberty said.

"I don't mind telling you, daughter, it was no small amount," Welles admitted. "But it is for the Confederacy."

"It is no such thing," Liberty scolded. "It is so you can play soldier and be a colonel."

A.G. Welles looked crestfallen and embarrassed at being subjected to Liberty's perceptive insight. Liberty, not wishing to hurt his feelings, eased the moment by laughing warmly. "Father, if this is something you feel you must do, you'll hear no guff from me. But you must promise me that you won't

Hearts Divided

volunteer your regiment for field duty."

"We are a home guard regiment," Welles said. "If our very homes are threatened, then I shall fight to the last breath in my body."

"I hope such an occasion never presents itself," Liberty said.

There had been a young man hovering near Liberty for the duration of their conversation, and A.G. finally noticed him. "Why is that man staring at us?" he asked.

"Father, I'd like to introduce Burke O'Lee. He saw me safely out of St. Louis, and will be returning to Missouri tomorrow to join with General Jeff Thompson's army."

"Have you been fighting with Thompson?" A.G. asked.

"No, sir," Burke said, now stepping up to join them, having been invited to. "I have been with Quantrill."

"With Quantrill, you say? Well, now, I guess you've seen some action then, haven't you?" A.G. said, obviously impressed.

"Not the type I wanted to see," Burke replied. "Colonel Welles, Quantrill is nothing but a common criminal, using the Confederacy as a cover. I have no pride in my association with him."

"Acts of war can sometimes be cruel, son. Perhaps you shouldn't be so quick to judge."

"I make the judgment against myself," Burke said. "For I have been as guilty as the rest. But I hope with Jeff Thompson to participate in a way which will have more relevancy to the southern cause."

"Father, is General Beauregard still in Corinth?"

"Yes," A.G. said.

"I must speak to him."

"I'll invite him over tonight," A.G. said. "He has been a frequent house guest. I'm sure he will come."

"Good."

"And you, Burke. Will you stay with us tonight? I'm sure we can offer much more comfortable arrangements than would the hotel."

"I'd be happy to," Burke said. "If it won't be any trouble."

"It won't be any trouble at all," A.G. said. "Liberty, take the carriage. I shall invite Beauregard and ride out with him when he comes."

"Impress upon him that it is important," Liberty said.

"I shall, daughter, I shall," A.G. promised. "You take your young man on home now." Liberty kissed her father again, then, as a porter appeared with her bags, she pointed to the carriage. After the bags were loaded, she climbed onto the seat, handed the reins to Burke, and showed him which way to go.

Burke was quiet for several moments, concentrating more than necessary on driving, speaking only when they were well on the road to Trailback.

"Am I?" he asked.

"Are you what?" Liberty asked, puzzled by the odd statement.

"Your father said take your young man on home now. Am I your young man?"

"Well, you are here with me, aren't you?"

"But you aren't with me."

"Of course I'm with you. What are you talking about?"

"You aren't really with me, Liberty. You're thinking about something else. You're thinking about *somebody* else."

"Suppose I am?" she said. "It's just that I can't get over how badly Dan must be hurt."

"What about me? Have you no sympathy for my feelings?"

"Burke, I haven't hurt you. Besides, I haven't forgotten that comment you made about sharing me with everyone. How could you say such a thing? That made it sound as if I'd been an easy mark for anyone to sleep with . . . and I've never slept with anyone but you."

"And Dan," Burke said.

Liberty was silent for a long time.

"You did sleep with Dan," Burke said again. "Didn't

you?"

"Yes," Liberty said quietly.

"And you say you've never hurt me."

"You've been chaste, I suppose?" Liberty replied hotly.

"No, of course I haven't. But it's different with a man."

"How well I know," Liberty said. "Though I hope the time will one day come when men and women are equal."

Burke laughed. "That day will never come." They were quiet for several minutes more, then Liberty spoke again. "I'm sorry I hurt you, Burke," she said quietly. "I didn't want to hurt anyone . . . and it seems I've hurt everyone."

General Pierre Gustave Toutant Beauregard, known as the Great Creole, was a dashing and argumentative figure who already, in the short war, had clashed with Jefferson Davis. But he was the hero of Bull Run, and had been in charge of the southern troops which had fired on Fort Sumner, so he was highly regarded throughout the South, despite his difficulty with the President of the Confederacy.

Beauregard arrived with A.G. Welles and listened attentively as Liberty related the conversation which had taken place at General Halleck's dinner.

"I believe you are correct," Beauregard said. "He intends to strike at Humboldt, or Corinth. At any rate, it will be somewhere in this area."

"General, I can have the home guards out in a moment's notice," A.G. offered hopefully.

Liberty looked at her father sharply, but was relieved to hear that Beauregard had other plans.

"I thank you for your offer, colonel," Beauregard said. "But I fear your home guards won't be up to the task. In fact, my entire army is insufficient to defend the junctions, without reinforcement." He smiled. "But we have been anticipating just such a move somewhere. We just had no idea where the major push would come. Miss Welles, I thank you very much for your information. I shall contact General Johnston immediately. This is just the break we've been looking for.

And you, young man, I appreciate your contribution as well. Will you be joining us here?" he asked Burke.

"No, general," Burke replied. "I'm going over to join General Thompson tomorrow."

"Ah, yes, the Swamp Fox. Give him my regards, and inform him of my appreciation for his job in holding New Madrid. I have overall command of the Mississippi River, you know, and right now, Island Number Ten is one of the most important points in the entire Confederacy. As long as we hold it, we are keeping the front door shut and locked, so to speak."

"Then we shall hold it forever," Burke said.

"Let us pray that we do. And now, Miss Welles, colonel, Mr. O'Lee, if you will excuse me, I must return to camp. Due to the information you have brought us, I have much work to do."

Colonel Welles escorted the general to his horse, then returned to spend the rest of the evening in conversation with Liberty and Burke. They talked long into the night, and only when Burke began yawning openly did A.G. realize how late it was.

"You must forgive me," he said. "You have to leave early to catch the return train tomorrow, and here I've kept you up. Liberty, show the young man his room." A.G. yawned, then smiled. "I guess I'm sleepy too," he said.

A.G. kissed Liberty goodnight, then went off to his own room. Liberty led Burke up the stairs, then down the hall to the room which would be his.

"I can get you a few extra pillows if you'd like," she said, after turning down the covers to his bed.

"It's not pillows I want," Burke said. 'It's you." He reached for her, but Liberty turned, ostensibly to fluff the bed, but in reality to avoid his embrace.

"I thought you were sleepy," she said.

"I just let on that I was sleepy, in order to get an excuse to come to bed." He reached again, and this time Liberty didn't try to avoid him. But she didn't help him either. After a brief kiss, Burke let her go, then stepped back and looked at her. "What's wrong?" he asked.

"Nothing," Liberty said. "I suppose I'm just tired. It's been a long trip."

"Yes, it has," Burke admitted. "I'm sorry. Of course you're tired. I'm tired myself." He leaned forward and kissed her lightly. "You go on to bed. I'll see you in the morning."

"Goodnight," Liberty said, returning his kiss.

Too many things were on Liberty's mind. Though she was very tired, she was unable to sleep. She tossed and turned, fluffed up her pillows, smoothed her covers, and nothing helped. Finally, after laying in bed for nearly an hour, she got up and walked over to the window and pulled the curtain to look outside.

Under the full moon, the well-kept lawn was very bright, and a large magnolia tree, its leaves shining like silver ingots, kept the same patient vigil over the house that it had since long before Liberty was born.

Liberty slipped into a robe and decided to take a walk, thinking that perhaps the fresh night air would help her to sleep.

The stars were incredibly bright. Some of them seemed to be hung so low that she could reach up and grab them. Even the black of the night sky itself was dusted with so many tiny stars that it looked as if a star-blue powder had been spread through the heavens.

"I saw you from my window," Burke's voice suddenly said, and Liberty turned with a start. Burke laughed softly. "I'm sorry, I didn't mean to frighten you."

"It's all right," Liberty said. "I was just lost in my own thoughts and didn't hear you." Burke looked up at the sky, then out across the gently rolling fields. "It's so quiet out here," he said. "It's hard to even imagine there is a war on somewhere."

"The war is coming here," Liberty said.

"Yes, I know."

They were silent for a moment longer, then Burke started

to ask a question. But even as he drew the breath for his comment, Liberty interrupted him.

"Don't ask, Burke. Please don't ask."

"Don't ask what?"

Liberty looked at him, and her eyes were brimming with tears. "You *know* what you were going to ask. If I was in love with Dan."

"I have to ask," Burke said. "Can't you see that?"

"Oh, I am, Burke. What am I going to do?" Liberty asked. She began crying and Burke took her in his arms. He held her close to him and she cried against his chest, letting the tears of despair flow freely, undammed at last.

"There, now," Burke said, stroking her hair gently. "There, you go ahead and cry. Let it all out. It'll do you good."

Liberty cried until she could cry no more. Then, when the tears would no longer come, she just leaned her head against Burke's chest and let him hold her. After a moment, Burke put his finger under her chin and gently turned her face up toward him. He kissed her, and she put her arms around his neck and pressed her body tightly against him. Burke began to fumble with the tie of her robe.

"No," Liberty suddenly said. She pulled back away from him and looked into his face, her eyes pleading with him.

"Liberty," Burke said. "I just..."

The tears were flowing freely down Liberty's face again. "No, Burke, please don't."

"All right," Burke said quietly.

Liberty took his hands in hers. "I'm sorry."

"I understand," Burke said.

"Do you? Do you really understand? Because, God help me, Burke, I don't understand at all."

Burke smiled, the same, boyish smile which had so endeared him to her. "Liberty, believe me, I know what it's like to love someone with your heart, and not with your head. My head has always told me that the day would come when you would tell me you were in love with someone else, but my heart wouldn't listen." He laughed. "I just never thought it would be my brother, that's all."

"Forgive me, Burke."

"Oh, I forgive you, Liberty girl," Burke said easily. "And, whether you believe me or not, I hope it works out for you."

Liberty smiled at him through her tears. "It can't possibly work out," she said. "But you're sweet for wishing so."

Chapter 13

ARTICLE APPEARING in a St. Louis newspaper:

The streets of this city are full of passing troops. Until the last two or three weeks, the impression has prevailed that the forces of this department were all in the field, but day by day one column arrives and another departs, until the reserve seems to be inexhaustible. And still they come. Of the numbers and direction, we may not speak. Stalwart thousands march through our streets; and one thinks each regiment must be the last, but tomorrow brings another. The physique of the men in the newly arrived regiments is remarkable.

One new member of these regiments is Second Lieutenant Dan O'Lee, most recently noted for his bravery in thwarting an attempt by Rebel spies to destroy the *Delta Star*, and the valuable arms and powder she was carrying. Lieutenant O'Lee has been assigned to General Halleck's staff.

Dan folded the newspaper and lay it aside, then looked up at the others in the lobby of the Boatman Hotel. As usual, the lobby was exceptionally busy, and as usual, the majority of the men wore uniforms. Now Dan had become one of them, wearing the dark blue and gold uniform of an Army lieutenant. Because of his mining background, he had been commissioned in the Engineers, and he wore the Engineers' castle emblem on his collar. As second lieutenants did not wear any insignia of rank, there was only the cut of the uniform and the castle to identify him as an officer.

All around Dan, conversations were going on about the war. They spoke of the war in the east, the war in the west, and the war in Missouri. It seemed clear to everyone that a battle was shaping up further south, for control of the river. Ideas and plans curled and seeped through the group as very senior officers advanced their pet theories as how best to accomplish the upcoming mission. Dan smiled to himself. There be little risk involved, he decided, for a Rebel spy to just sit in the lobby and listen to the conversation.

But then, there was such confusion as one plan seemed to supersede another that Dan decided that confusion was itself the best security against unwanted information leaks to the Confederacy.

A carriage pulled to a stop at the curb in front of the hotel. Dan, sitting next to the window, looked out and saw a woman sitting in the shadows of the back seat. He watched as she passed money across to the driver. When she stepped out of the carriage, Dan recognized her as Verity Eternal.

Dan watched as she approached the entrance. He guessed her age as around twenty-five. She had high cheekbones, not prominent but well accented. Even at this distance, Dan could see that her eyes sparkled like set jewels, and were framed by eyebrows as beautiful as the most delicate lace. Her movements, as she walked toward the hotel entrance, were as graceful as a willow in a breeze, and Dan was struck again by her beauty, moved by it as greatly as he had been the first time he had seen her.

Dan found himself standing up and moving toward the front door to meet her as she entered.

"Miss Eternal, it is a pleasure to see you again," he said, offering his hand.

Verity looked at him, puzzled for just a moment, then smiled broadly. "You are Mr. O'Lee, aren't you? Liberty's friend. Only I see you are a lieutenant now."

"Yes," Dan said, flattered that she remembered him. "But I'm not exactly a friend of Liberty Welles."

A shadow came across Verity's eyes. "Yes, I heard what happened with her. I'm terribly sorry. I'm sorry for Liberty, but I'm especially sorry for the cause of abolition. She was a powerful force for good here."

"A force for good?" Dan asked, as if unable to believe what he had heard. "Miss Eternal, didn't you hear that Liberty Welles is a spy? She is a southern sympathizer."

"Well, she is, after all, from Mississippi," Verity said, being charitable in her appraisal of Liberty.

"Then how can you say she was doing good?"

"Oh, but she was, Mr. O'Lee," Verity insisted. "The fact that she was a southerner . .. even the fact that she has now, evidently, gone back south to help the confederacy, doesn't mean that she meant the movement any harm. Liberty Welles was, and is, an abolitionist, as dedicated to the cause of freedom for all slaves as I am."

Dan laughed, a short, disbelieving laugh. "I must say, I admire your loyalty," he said. "I am unable to remain so loyal to people who fail me.

"That's just it, Mr. O'Lee," Verity said. "Liberty hasn't failed me. But, what are you doing here, in this hotel?" she asked, changing the subject.

"I live here," Dan said.

"Oh? I would have thought you would have to live in a barracks somewhere."

"Not yet. Quarters have grown scarce in the city. Besides, as a member of General Halleck's staff, I can pretty much live where I please. Do you live here as well?"

Verity laughed, and the laughter fell from her lips like the musical trill of a bubbling brook. "No, Mr. O'Lee, I don't live here," she said. "I am here to make arrangements for a talk I shall be giving later. I can come to such places as this to give a speech, but I must choose another place to live."

"Oh," Dan said, awkwardly. "I'm sorry." He laughed self-consciously. "I guess that eliminates my next question as well."

"And what would have that next question have been?"

Dan cleared his throat. "I was going to invite you to dinner," he said. "Again."

Verity laughed again. "You seem determined to take me to dinner, Mr. O'Lee," she said.

"I can't help it. I find you a fascinating woman, and I would like to get to know you better."

"Then I have a proposal. Since it is not possible for me to go to dinner with you . . . how would you like to come to dinner with me?"

"What? Are you serious?" Dan asked. "Yes ... I'd love it. But . . . how, I mean, where could we go?"

Verity opened her purse and removed a card. "Be at this address tonight at eight," she invited. "You won't disappoint me now?"

"Disappoint you? No, what are you talking about? Of course, I'll be there. I'll be there at eight.. . sharp."

"Good," Verity said. "Now, I must see the gentleman at the desk, and explain my presence to him. Already, he is beginning to wonder why a Negro woman has come into the lobby."

"Well, you just let me . . ." Dan started.

"No, Dan, please," Verity said, using Dan's first name for the first time. She put her hand on his arm, and though her fingers felt amazingly cool, they seemed to generate a heat within him. "I'm used to this sort of thing," she said. "I'll handle it."

"Very well, if you insist," Dan said, wondering how she could generate such heat with such cool fingers. "I'll see you at eight tonight, then."

"You've got three blocks to go yet, before you reach that address," the hack driver said, stopping his carriage.

"Then why are you stopping here?" Dan asked.

"Look down that street, lieutenant. What do you see?"

"I don't see anything. What are you talking about?"

"I see niggers," the driver said. "Nothin' but freed niggers, and freed niggers is the worst kind. Like as not, most of them ain't free anyhow, they's just runaways."

"What difference does that make?"

The driver spit a chew of tobacco over the rim of the wheel, and pushed the hat back on his head.

"I don't like niggers," he said. "And I ain't gonna drive my hack down a street where that's all there is. Now you pay me what you owe me, and walk the rest of the way. Unless, now that you've seen where you was goin', you've changed your mind, and'll be headin' back."

"I've done no such thing," Dan said. He stepped out of the hack, and handed the driver some money.

"Hey, this isn't the right amount," the driver said, looking at the fare.

"This isn't the right place, either," Dan replied easily. "Take me the rest of the way, and I'll give you the rest of the fare."

The driver looked at the money for a second, then put it in his pocket. "I'll settle for this," he said, flicking the light whip against the horse's hide.

Dan started down the street, and a small, black child started following him.

"Is you Marse Link?" the boy asked.

"I'm Lieutenant O'Lee," Dan replied.

"Marse Link," the boy said again.

The young black boy was joined by another, and then another, and still another, until by the time Dan reached the address given him by Verity, there were dozens of kids, laughing and shouting at him, all calling him "Marse Link."

Hearts Divided

"Here, you children," Verity said, stepping out to meet Dan and escort him the rest of the way. "Scat. Go home now, you hear me?"

"Marse Link," they called as one. "Marse Link, Marse Link, Marse Link."

"What are they saying?" Dan finally asked. Verity laughed. "They think you are Abraham Lincoln," she said.

"Oh, Lord, no, I'm not that ugly, am I?" Dan replied, laughing.

"No, but you are a white man in the uniform of Lincoln's army. They don't fully understand, but they know that a war is being fought which may mean the end of slavery. They know that Lincoln is the President, and they just make the natural connection, that's all. Please, come in, Mr. O'Lee."

"You called me Dan earlier," Dan said. "I think I liked that better."

"Then I shall call you Dan," Verity said. She touched him, and again he was amazed by the coolness of her fingers, and the heat her fingers spread.

Inside the small house, Dan saw that Verity had taken great pains to prepare a fine dinner for him.-A table was laid with china and silver, and she led him to it.

"It looks beautiful," Dan said.

"Thank you. It isn't exactly the dining room at Antoine's, I'm afraid."

"No, it isn't," Dan replied. "It is much better than that." He held the chair for Verity, then sat across from her. They were served by another black woman, darker and older than Verity.

"Thank you, Mandy," Verity said, as the older woman withdrew. "Mandy came to St. Louis six months ago," she said. "She ran away from her owner in Arkansas. I'm actually violating the law by sheltering her, you know. She is a fugitive slave, and Missouri is a slave-holding state. You won't turn me in, I hope?"

"No, of course not," Dan said.

Verity laughed. "I was teasing. I knew you wouldn't, or I would have never mentioned it to you in the first place."

"Are you a runaway?" Dan asked.

"No. I was free-born, in Memphis, Tennessee. But even though I was free-born, I could not enjoy my freedom. Just seeing so many of my people in bondage . . . that was in itself a sort of bondage. I began agitating for freedom for my people as soon as I could speak, and I've never stopped."

"You are an amazing woman, Verity Eternal," Dan said. "And a beautiful one as well."

Verity looked down in modesty as Dan complimented her, then looked up once, raising her eyelids as though they were exquisite fans. Her eyes shone gold in the candlelight.

"Have I embarrassed you?" Dan asked.

"No," Verity replied. "But..."

"But what?"

"I am a Negro," she said.

"What difference does that make?"

"It makes a tremendous difference," Verity said.

Dan reached across the table and took her hand. He held it for a moment, then raised it to his lips and kissed it lightly. At first, she tried to pull her hand away, but Dan held it more firmly and kissed it again. Finally he released her.

"Are you turned away by the fact that I am white?" Dan asked. "Is that the tremendous difference you speak of?"

"No," Verity said. "That's not it at all."

"Then you will not be offended if I call on you again?"

"I would be honored," Verity said. "If you really want to."

"I really want to."

Mandy interrupted their conversation with the second course of the meal, and though they spoke of many things that night, exchanging anecdotes of their past, discussing their philosophies of life, they never reopened the subject of their own relationship with each other. But though the words were unspoken, a deeper and more meaningful communication took place between them that night. They exchanged intimate glances, looking at each other with eyes which were windows to their souls. They touched, lightly, lingeringly, over wine and dessert. When Dan left later that evening, he offered a kiss which she accepted. Before either of them could control it, the kiss began to deepen, until finally Verity pulled away with a gasp of breath.

"You'd ....you'd better go now," she said.

"Goodbye," Dan said, making no effort to leave.

"You must go," Verity replied.

"I'm going," Dan said. He kissed her again.

"No," Verity said, but she found that she was speaking into his mouth as his lips closed over her own, and this time as they kissed, she knew that it was too late. There would be no turning back.

Now time and circumstances hung suspended as Dan and Verity came together. They were not principals in one of the world's major conflicts—they were not black and white—they were not representatives of opposing cultures. They were a man and woman, complete within themselves.

Verity took Dan's hand and led him into her bedroom. There she lit a candle, and began removing her clothes for him. Behind her was a window, opening onto the Mississippi River, and in the dark the black water twinkled with reflected light as it flowed, ever, ever southward.

Dan removed his clothes as Verity did, and when both were nude, they went to bed, not in a hot-blooded rush of desperate lovers taking sex from each other, giving nothing in return, but in the tender and passionate way of people who care for each other and are capable of sharing.

When they made love it was rich and fulfilling. It was strongly physical and immensely satisfying, as if their passions were perfectly orchestrated to move in harmony, so that there was a tremendous sense of mutual need and attainment.

Afterward, they both slept.

Dan awoke once in the middle of the night. The moon was

shining brightly, sailing high in the velvet sky. It spilled a pool of iridescence through the window and onto the bed. It bathed Verity in a soft, shimmering light.

Verity was asleep, breathing softly. Dan reached over gently and put his hand on her naked hip. He could feel the sharpness of her hip bone and the soft yielding of her flesh. The contrasting textures were delightful to his sense of touch. He let his hand rest there, enjoying a feeling of possession, until finally sleep claimed him once again.

Dan awoke the next morning to the smell of bacon sizzling in the pan. A moment later Verity came in to tell him that breakfast was ready.

"When I accepted your dinner invitation, I had no idea that breakfast would be part of the deal," Dan said, smiling.

"No, but you hoped it would, didn't you?" Verity asked, laughing at her own ribald jest.

"Touché, madame," Dan said, buttering a steaming hot biscuit.

"Dan, there's something that needs to be said," Verity ventured a moment later.

Dan held his hand out, as if to stop her. "Verity, if you're going to bring up the fact that you are a black woman and I am a white man, it is obvious, and doesn't need to be discussed. We will be who we are, and the color line will not come between us."

"It isn't the color line that's between us, Dan O'Lee," Verity said plainly.

"I don't understand. What are you talking about?"

"Liberty Welles," Verity said.

"Liberty Welles?" Dan gave a weak laugh. "Why would you mention that Rebel spy?"

"Why indeed?" Verity said.

"I told you what she did ... or rather, what she tried to do. As it turned out, she was hoist by her own petard, and I say fair enough."

"Say what you really think," Verity said.

"I don't understand," Dan said.

"Yes, you do," Verity insisted. "You understand perfectly. Dan, do you think a woman can let a man make love to her, and not know that his heart is with another?"

"No, that's not true," Dan said. "I don't love Liberty Welles. I don't."

Verity smiled, a slow, understanding smile. "Keep talking, brother, maybe you'll convince yourself. You certainly won't convince me."

Dan sighed. He lay his biscuit down, then looked at Verity, his face displaying the hopelessness of it all.

"It's true," he finally said. He gave a short, unconvincing laugh. "I don't think I had even admitted it to myself, until this moment. I don't know how it can be true, Verity, but it is. I do love her, even though a love between her and me is as impossible as a love between you and me."

"No," Verity said. "Love between you and me is not impossible. It is just forbidden. But forbidden fruit is always sweetest, so we'll take what we can, Dan O'Lee, while we can. And when the time comes for us to part, we shall do so without looking back, and with no regrets."

"You're willing to do that?" Dan asked.

"I *want* to do that," Verity said.

"You are an amazing woman."

"And Liberty Welles is a lucky one," Verity said.

Chapter 14

THE SNOWS OF February were blown away by brisk March winds. During the last two weeks of February and the first two weeks of March, Dan spent all his spare time with Verity Eternal. He knew that their love affair was star-crossed and destined to be short-lived, but he determined to make the most of it, for in the words of an old Chinese philosopher he had met in San Francisco: "It is not the time granted a love, but the love granted a time which is important. The flower that buds, blooms and dies in a single day does not differ at heart from a tree that lives a thousand years."

Thus it was, that when General Halleck told Dan that he would be sending him south to Sikeston the next day, Dan was prepared for it. After all, he had already enjoyed more time than he expected.

"What do we know of Sikeston, general?" Dan asked.

"Very little, I'm afraid," General Halleck answered. "It doesn't even show up on most maps, the town was only begun two years ago. It's important to us though, because it sits at the western terminus of the railroad which starts at the river, and there is a good road through the swamp south from Sikeston to New Madrid."

"I see," Dan said, looking at the map General Halleck

spread before him.

"I have a man here who does know the town," Halleck said. "I've asked him to brief you."

"How well does he know it?"

Halleck smiled. "About as well as anyone, I reckon. His name is John Sikes, and he started it.

Dan looked up a moment later as a tall, thin man stepped into the room. He had piercing brown eyes, and rather prominent cheekbones, and he extended his hand in a perfunctory, businesslike way when Dan offered his.

"Major Lathrop will be in command of the detachment at Sikeston," General Halleck continued. "It will be his job to supervise the offloading and assembly of the artillery. Your job will be to secure the road south from Sikeston, protect it against Confederate raiders, and effect such construction as is necessary to allow cannon caissons and wagons to pass across it."

"Would you tell me something about that road, Mr. Sikes?" Dan asked.

"It's part of the old El Camino Real," Sikes said. "King's Highway, we call it now. It's a road that stretches from St. Louis to New Madrid, and though much of it has fallen into disrepair, the stretch from Sikeston to New Madrid is quite good."

"Is it surfaced?"

"Yes, sir," Sikes said. "It is a plank road, made of crossed logs."

"The trouble is, we don't know whether or not the Rebels have torn it up," Dan mused.

"The road was in good repair as of two days ago," Sikes commented. "I rode it myself then."

"As you can see, Lieutenant O'Lee, speed is important," General Halleck said. "You must get down to Sikeston immediately, lest the Rebels decide to cut the road."

"I'll arrange for transportation," Dan said.

"That's already taken care of," General Halleck said.

"You'll leave, at once aboard the ironclad, *Cairo.* Mr. Sikes will be returning to Sikeston with you."

"General, will I have time to tell someone goodbye?" Dan asked. "

General Halleck pulled his watch from his pocket and looked at it. "I'm afraid not, lieutenant," he said. "If you wish, you may write a note and I'll have it delivered."

Dan thought about it for a moment, then decided that it would be better not to send a message to Verity by someone else. It might lead to embarrassing questions being asked of her and he had no wish to complicate her life. They had both realized that the time would come when he would have to leave St. Louis, and he knew that Verity would understand that they had said their goodbyes.

"No, sir, thank you," Dan said. "That won't be necessary." Dan looked at John Sikes. "Are you ready, Mr. Sikes?"

"Quite ready, thank you," Sikes answered. "I am looking forward to returning home."

One hour later, Dan was leaning over the railing looking at one of the huge paddle wheels, now lifeless in the water. He studied a twig as it floated along the waterline of the boat, then got caught in the wheel. John Sikes was standing beside him.

"Has there been much action around Sikeston?" Dan asked, wondering if he was about to see any.

"Well, the actual fighting has been going on down around Island Number Ten," Sikes said. "But we've suffered terribly from the bushwhackers. Raiders ride through the town, terrorizing our citizens, robbing and burning. In truth, lieutenant, more than two thirds of the townspeople have abandoned Sikeston."

"And yet you're staying on?"

"I will as long as I can," Sikes said. "But if this war continues much longer, I fear there will be little to stay for."

The boat sounded its whistle and started reversing the paddle wheel on the left while going forward with the one on the right. The boat turned, then, both paddles slapping at the water together, bubbled up a frothy white wake as it moved majestically into the center of the river before turning downstream.

Though the *Cairo* would ultimately be going into battle as a gunboat—and indeed cannon protruded from both sloping, iron-clad sides—it was now being used as a troop boat. In addition to Dan, there were nearly one hundred other soldiers on board the vessel. They sat, or lay around where they could find space, playing cards, writing letters, talking, or just staring off into space, lost in their own private thoughts.

Facing them was a twenty-four hour trip downriver. Dan sought out a small corner where he could stretch out during the long, cool night. Though he had figured on getting in only a few hours' sleep, when he was awakened by the heavy blast of the ship's whistle, he saw the red smear of an early morning sky through one of the gun-ports. He stood up, stretched, and walked out on a small afterdeck which was unprotected by the iron plate.

He'd no sooner reached the deck when he heard a pinging sound against the plate behind him. He turned, curiously, to see what had made the noise.

"Get down, lieutenant!" a voice called, and someone ran quickly across the deck, crashing into him and knocking him down, just as a large splinter of wood was torn from the rail near where he had been standing.

This time Dan heard the unmistakable sound of a rifle shot, a flat sound that echoed across the water.

"Raise up ag'in, Yank, 'n give me another potshot at ye," a voice called from the shore. The voice rolled, amazingly clear, across the river, aided by the sound-carrying property of the water.

Dan looked over to see who had saved his life by knocking him down. It was a young, handsome, rather small soldier. He smiled broadly at Dan.

"Sorry I had to bowl you over like that, lieutenant, but there are Rebel sharpshooters all along the river, just waiting for an opportunity like you gave them." The soldier s voice was soft, with an unmistakable southern drawl.

"Don't apologize to me, soldier," Dan said quickly. "I should apologize to you for being such a damn fool as to make you expose yourself to danger in order to save me. And I thank you for it."

"No thanks needed, lieutenant. I was only doing my job. I'm Private Cote. Cal Cote, now of the 24th Missouri, though a Mississippian by birth." Cote stuck out his hand, and Dan shook it, knowing that wasn't protocol for an officer meeting an enlisted man but not caring. This man had saved his life; he couldn't help but be thankful, as well as drawn to his friendly ways. "Dan O'Lee," Dan said.

"I know who you are," Cote smiled broadly. "Fact is, when I saved you just then, I was saving my own commanding officer. I'm in the company that's been assigned to work on the road leading down to New Madrid."

Dan laughed. "I guess news gets around fast," he said. "I wouldn't be surprised if everyone on the boat knows about me."

"Everyone does know," Cote said. "And you can bet the Rebels know too."

"Then I expect we'll get a welcome from them."

By mid-afternoon of the second day, the boat reached its destination, and most of the soldiers, weary now, were ready for anything, even immediate action, if it meant relief from the cramped voyage. They were mustered into squads by the N.C.O.'s, and now stood around anxiously, as the boat's captain and crew members shouted landing instructions to each other.

The boat was putting ashore at Bird's Point, Missouri, just opposite Cairo, Illinois. The paddle wheels stopped as it glided up to a mooring. There was a small scrape as the boat rubbed against the bottom, then a rush of steam and a frantic beating of paddle wheels as the captain "pegged her to the bank" by running the bow slightly aground.

"Well, hello, John," a Union major greeted Sikes as he and Dan stepped off the boat. "And you must be Lieutenant O'Lee."

"Yes," Dan said. "You are Major Lathrop?"

"Right you are, lieutenant. The artillery pieces are already loaded on the train. I need only you and your men, and we're ready to go."

"They are loading now, sir," Dan replied. He looked over toward the standing box cars and saw the soldiers, Cal Cote among them, climbing on, handing up their long rifles, jostling and joking with each other to take the edge off their nervousness.

"Mr. Sikes, I honestly didn't think you would return after that hanging," Major Lathrop commented.

"Hanging? What hanging?" Dan asked.

John Sikes put his hand to his throat in an unconscious move as Lathrop told the story.

"It happened about two months ago," Lathrop said. "John, and in fact, most of the good citizens of Sikeston, were asleep, when a group of bushwhackers rode into town. They burned a couple of houses, then threatened to burn John's if he didn't come out. When he did, they strung him up to a tree and left him hanging there. They meant to kill him, but a young black girl who knew where John hid his money offered to tell the bushwhackers where it was it they would cut him down. So they did, just in time."

"You mean you would let them hang you, without telling them?" Dan asked.

"I didn't have any choice," Sikes replied grimly. "You can't talk with a rope around your neck."

The whistle on the train sounded a warning.

"Come on, we'd better get," Lathrop said, starting toward the train.

The cattle cars were loaded with soldiers, and the flatcars with equipment. Dan, Major Lathrop and John Sikes climbed into the engine cab as the train got underway, puffing loudly and throwing great pillars of smoke into the sky.

Riding in the cab, Dan kept his face in the wind, trying to overcome the excitement that was brewing inside of him. When he looked back along the string of cars, he could see that the men were all as excited as he. They were cheering and shouting at each other, trying to be heard over the sound of the train.

The train approached a long trestle, which stretched out over swampland, and it roared and clacked out onto it. Suddenly Dan's heart leaped to his mouth, because the opposite end of the trestle exploded and erupted in a sheet of flame!

"Engineer! Back this thing down!" Dan yelled. "The Rebels have the other end . . . it's on fire!"

The engineer threw the lever into reverse and opened the steam valve full. The wheels began reversing, throwing up a shower of sparks that bathed the inside of the cab in a glow of orange.

The sudden stopping of the train threw many of the soldiers against each other, cursing and shouting. Some of those riding in the open doors fell out, and Dan saw one unfortunate soldier get crushed by the car wheels.

A mounted band broke out of the woods and raced toward the train, firing and yelling as they approached. Bullets began crashing against the engine cab, and Dan and the others ducked down. One bullet hit the steam gauge, and a hissing rush of white steam spurted out. Dan pulled his pistol and began returning fire.

The Rebels only made one pass, then broke away and rode off into the woods, still shooting and yelling. Dan raised up and looked in the direction they had gone for a moment, then realized that the troops were still firing into the woods, now just wasting ammunition.

"Cease firing!" he yelled, finally leaving the engine cab and waving his arms at them until they heard his order. Their guns fell silent.

Hearts Divided

Major Lathrop and Dan walked down the track to inspect the damage. They were surprised to see that there was practically no damage at all.

"Whoever laid the charge didn't know what the hell he was doing," Lathrop commented, kicking at a singed but still intact railroad tie.

"Luckily for us," Dan replied.

Lathrop waved the engine on, and with he and Dan walking the track in front of the train, it proceeded slowly across the trestle. Sikeston was now less than a mile ahead, and with Dan and Lathrop back aboard, that last mile was turned quickly.

Major Lathrop wasted no time in assembling the artillery, and Dan formed up his company to inspect the road from New Madrid. They began moving down it, and were approximately one mile south when one of Dan's outriders came galloping back, his horse's hooves drumming on the plank road like the beating of a drum.

"Lieutenant, it's Thompson's raiders!" the rider warned. "They're comin' up fast."

Dan yelled at the men who were working with pick and shovel, and the tools were quickly cast aside in favor of rifles. The men spread out along both sides of the road and waited for the Rebels.

Dan took a position behind their line, watching down the road. His heart was in his stomach, for here would be his first actual battle.

They could feel the vibrations of the approaching cavalry in the road planks before they could hear them, and they could hear them before they could see them. Then, finally, they saw them, moving up the road in mass, a tiny dot of red waving above the column.

Dan felt a slight thrill as he realized that he was seeing an enemy flag in battle for the first time. He stared at it until it was close enough to make out... a circle of white stars in a field of blue, and three broad, horizontal bars of red, white and red.

The approaching riders halted approximately five hundred yards away. Dan heard the tinny blast of a distant bugle and saw the column spread out into a wide front.

"Get ready, men," he said, forcing a calmness to his voice which he did not feel.

There was another faint, tinny sound from the bugle, and then the riders started toward them.

At first Dan could hear only the beat of the hooves, then the jangle of the gear and the rattle of sabers. Finally he heard the Rebels themselves, shouting and screaming at the top of their lungs as they approached his line of soldiers.

Dan knew that his men had the more favored position. They had cover behind trees, logs, and mounds of earth. But he also knew that his men were raw recruits, seeing combat for the first time. The riders advancing toward them had many battles under their belt.

"Hold your fire, men, until I give the word," Dan called. He pulled his pistol out of his holster, and leveled it at the approaching army.

Closer and closer they came, until the great, gray mass became distinguishable as horses and riders, then closer yet until even the Rebels' faces were visible.

"Now, men, fire!" Dan yelled, shooting even as he spoke.

There was a deafening rattle of musketry as Union and Confederate soldiers opened fire. A soldier standing less than two feet from Dan suddenly spun around with blood spurting from his forehead, and Dan saw one of the Rebels he had shot pitch forward from his saddle.

The Rebels came close enough to cut down a few of Dan s men with saber slashes, then, just as Dan was afraid some of his men might turn and run, the Confederates suddenly, and inexplicably, wheeled and started back down the road.

Dan's men began cheering.

"Lieutenant," one of his sergeants shouted. "Lieutenant, let's mount up and chase the bastards down! We'll give them a thrashing they won't soon forget!"

"Right you are, sergeant!" Dan yelled, new caught up in the same infectious excitement that swept over his men.

With a shout Dan's men leaped into their saddles. Seconds later, they were pounding down the road in hot pursuit.

Dan kept up the pursuit for nearly an hour, until he suddenly realized what he was doing. He wasn't chasing the enemy! He was being led by them! They were taking him right into New Madrid, where all the Confederate forces were concentrated!

He held his arm up, signaling for his men to stop.

"Don't stop now, lieutenant, we've nearly caught them!" his sergeant yelled.

"Sergeant, we've got to get out of here," Dan said. "Do you know how many of us there are?"

"About eighty," the sergeant said. "And I didn't count more'n fifty of them."

"But in New Madrid, and around Island Ten, there are nearly ten thousand Rebels," Dan said.

"My God, lieutenant, you mean we're ridin' into a trap?" The sergeant's eyes grew wide with fear.

"Not if I can help it," Dan said. "Let's get out of here."

Dan turned his company around and led them back up the road toward Sikeston, feeling very exposed and very foolish.

But he had accomplished one thing. He had reconnoitered the road almost all the way to New Madrid, and he could report to Major Lathrop that the cannons could be brought down and put into position immediately.

And, small though it had been, he had fought his first battle. And he had survived.

Chapter 15

BURKE O'LEE rode across the water to Island Ten in a small skiff. Large cannon protruded from earthen works on the island, pointed upstream to turn back the gunboat flotilla of Union Commodore Foote. Thus far they had been successful.

The guns were heavy and mounted in fixed positions, commanding the river approach only. That had made Burke feel uneasy, but when he commented on it, his apprehension was laughed off.

"We control the Tennessee side of the river," General McCown said. "There is absolutely no way heavy artillery can be brought through the swamps to threaten us at New Madrid. And as for the river . . . now we can hardly expect an attack from the southern approach, can we? Your fears, captain, are unfounded, though I appreciate your interest. You just do your duty in harassing the enemy with your cavalry raids. And leave the fortifications up to us."

Burke, who had been appointed a captain by General Jeff Thompson in recognition of his experience with Quantrill's raiders, had accepted General McCown's assurance when he first arrived at Island Number Ten. But having seen with his own eyes Union artillery being assembled in Sikeston, he knew that heavy guns could indeed be brought to New Madrid.

The only thing that would prevent it would be to destroy the road. Though he had petitioned to do this several times, General McCown had refused to grant permission. Now, with the guns in Sikeston, General McCown had no choice. The road, Bruke thought, would have to be destroyed.

The Confederate soldiers on Island Number Ten were composed of troops from General Polk's regular army, which included the Second Mississippi Horse Regiment, now commanded by Colonel Blackwell Beauregard. Blackie had succeeded Colonel Putnam in command after Putnam's murder by the runaway slave, Tamara Calvert. Blackie, from having spent some time in St. Louis disguised as a captain in the Union army, knew Burke and welcomed him warmly when he stepped off the skiff onto the island.

"Blackie, we've got to cut the road," Burke said.

"Impossible," Blackie replied. "It would not be politically expedient to do so."

"Politically expedient? What the hell are you talking about?" Burke asked.

"Governor Jackson has announced his intention to convene the Missouri state legislature in New Madrid in one week," Blackie said. "There are only two roads coming into New Madrid now, one from Charleston and one from Sikeston. The Charleston road is controlled by Yankee troops. If you cut the Sikeston road, New Madrid will be cut off from the rest of the state, and none of the legislators will be able to get here."

Burke ran his hand through his hair in exasperation. "Governor Jackson is a damned idiot! He's been run out of Jefferson City, and the state government has been taken over by the military. Who the hell does he think he is kidding?"

"Nevertheless, it is Governor Jackson's government which is recognized by the Confederacy, and it is important that he hold a meeting of the general assembly."

"If I don't cut that road, colonel, the only people who will come to his meeting will be Yankees," Burke stormed angrily.

"Now, please step aside and let me speak with General McCown."

"I'll do better than that," Blackie said easily. "I'll take you to see the general."

Burke followed Blackie through the breastworks of the Island, then down an excavated stairway until they reached General McCown's bunker. The General was sitting behind a small field desk, looking at a map. He glanced up when Burke and Blackie entered.

"Hello, Blackie," General McCown said. "And, O'Lee, isn't it? You're with Thompson?"

"Yes, sir," Burke said.

"General, Captain O'Lee wants permission to cut the Sikeston road," Blackie said. "I told him it was quite impossible."

"Quite right," General McCown replied. "I'm afraid that we can't cut that road."

"But, general, I just returned from a raid at Sikeston," Burke said. "The Yankees have brought in a whole trainload of supplies and equipment, including heavy guns. If you don't let me cut that road, were going to be dodging cannon balls around here in less than twenty- four hours."

General McCown laughed. "Oh, I hardly think so. At any rate, I'm leaving the Island shortly, and it will be the responsibility of General Gantt. You'll have to get permission from him."

"Where is General Gantt now?"

"He won't be here until midnight," General McCown said. He rolled the map up and handed it to Blackie. "Colonel, I've marked all the known positions of Union forces on the map. Please see that General Gantt gets the information immediately when he arrives."

"Yes, general," Blackie said.

General McCown looked around the bunker. "I'd like to stay here," he said absently. "I think this is truly the Gibraltar of the South."

Burke swore under his breath. After receiving permission to withdraw, he returned by skiff to Fort Thompson, as the Confederate works on the Missouri side had been named.

"What about it, cap'n? Have we got permission to cut the road?" Sergeant Chism, his first sergeant, asked.

"Yeah," Burke said, in a sudden decision to disobey specific orders. "Yeah, let's get out there and get it done."

There was a sudden rushing noise, then a loud explosion, followed immediately by another rushing noise, and another explosion.

One of the men who had been posted as a picket came running back into the encampment. "Cap'n O'Lee!" he yelled. "My God, cap'n, there's Yankees out there, and they've got the biggest goddamn cannons I've ever seen!"

By now the night was raining shot and shell. Flashes lit up the sky and explosions shook the ground. Burke ran for shelter in the earthworks of the fort.

So, he thought. Events had proved him right after all. But the distinction of being right left a bitter taste in his mouth.

By the time Dan and his troops had returned to Sikeston, Major Lathrop had already assembled the cannon. Dan reported to him that the road was intact as far as he had gone—which was within a mile of New Madrid—so Major Lathrop moved his entire command out in force. Though they expected to be jumped by Confederate raiders at every turn of the road, they proceeded unmolested all the way to the Rebel's advance picket lines, from which point they were well in range of Fort Thompson, though not within range of Island Number Ten itself.

The fire from Major Lathrop's guns was the first notice General Gantt, who was in Fort Thompson preparing to assume command of the island, had of the proximity of Union batteries. He ordered that Fort Thompson return fire with all its guns, and Commodore Hollins of the Confederate navy brought his gunboats in close enough to shore to aid.

General McCown visited Commodore Hollins on his flagship, and, after a brief conference, decided to order Fort Thompson abandoned. Under cover of the commodore's gunboats, the Confederate troops fled from Fort Thompson, crossing the river to the Tennessee shore.

The Union troops, unaware that the fort had been abandoned, continued to pour artillery fire into it through the rest of the night. They were receiving return fire from the gunboats, and mistakenly assumed that some of it was coming from the fort. To make matters even more difficult for them, it began to rain, a cold, drenching rain, which filled the shelters with water and turned the ground into near quicksand.

Dan had his troops in position to repel any Rebel advance against their batteries. He shivered in the cold, and pressed himself down into the mud to avoid the flying shrapnel of the incoming fire. It was one of the longest and most miserable nights of his life.

The rain stopped just before dawn, but daybreak itself was masked with a very thick fog, which rolled in off the river and lay its oppressive wet blanket about everything. The fog was so thick that Dan could see no more than fifty feet in front of him. This would be a perfect time, he thought, for the Rebels to counterattack.

"Cote," he called quietly. The soldier who had saved his life on board the riverboat a few days earlier now seemed always to be nearby.

"Yes, sir?"

"Pass the word to all the men to be especially watchful of a counterattack. I couldn't think of any better time to do it than right now."

"Yes, sir," Cote replied, and Dan heard the young soldier pass the word down to the next man in line, and so forth, until his entire company had been alerted.

Strange, muffled sounds floated up to Dan's ears distorted by the fog, until even his own breathing sounded like the approaching footsteps of an army. Finally the fog began to roll away, and he could see trees and bushes and, finally, after nearly two hours, the river itself.

And the fort.

All was quiet in the fort. There were no flags flying. From his vantage point, Dan could see no sign of life.

"Cote," he yelled.

"Yes sir?"

"Tell Major Lathrop I believe the Rebels have abandoned the fort."

"I'll find out, sir," Cote said, raising up quickly and starting toward the fort in a low, crouching run.

"No, Cote, come back here!" Dan called, but it was too late. Cote had gone. "Sergeant, have the men cover Private Cote!" he shouted, when he realized he wasn't going to return.

An anxious moment later, Cote was standing on the parapet of the fort, signaling for Dan to come down.

"All right," Dan shouted happily. "Sergeant, send word to the major that the fort has been abandoned. Men, to the fort, on the double!"

Dan ran down to the fort with the others from his company, and Cote met him, smiling broadly.

"What are you trying to do, get your fool self killed?" Dan scolded.

An expression of hurt passed across Cote's handsome features, and Dan upbraided himself silently for speaking so sharply. After all, it had been a brave and important act, and Cote deserved praise, not reprimand. It was just that he had grown attached to the little soldier and was solicitous for his welfare.

"Ah, don't mind me," Dan said, smiling. "I guess I'm just angry because you've made more work for me."

"I've made more work for you? How?" Cote asked, confused.

"Now I'll have to mention you in the dispatches," Dan said.

Cote rewarded him with an even broader smile.

Major Lathrop's artillery and Dan O'Lee's engineer and recon company were both part of General Pope's army. On word that the fort was abandoned, General Pope moved his Union forces quickly to take up positions inside it and bring their guns to bear on the river. Five Confederate gunboats steamed upriver, and moved into position to try and destroy the Union batteries. They started steaming in a big circle, each boat, as it arrived in position for firing, delivering a broadside that rent the air with its thunder. The fort returned the fire, and the battle continued for an hour and a half, resulting in the sinking of one of the gunboats and severe damage to the others.

But Fort Thompson also received damage, and casualties, as one shell exploded not ten feet from Dan, killing two of his men.

And wounding Calvin Cote.

"Cote!" Dan shouted, when he saw the brave little soldier trying to crawl away from the carnage the shell had caused.

He ran out of his shelter toward Cote to help him. A quick glance at the other two told him that they were beyond help.

"How badly are you hit?" he asked Cote.

"Not too bad," Cote said. "I'll be all right, I just . . ." Cote passed out. Another shell burst nearby, and Dan had no recourse but to pick up the small soldier and carry him out of the field of fire. He scooped Cote up in his arms, then ran back across the open ground until he returned to his own position. There, he lay Cote gently on the ground and looked at the blood-stained tunic.

Much of the blood looked like it might have been splashed onto Cote from his two dead comrades. The tunic wasn't heavily soaked, and there didn't seem to be any fresh blood pumping out of his chest, but Dan knew that he had better check more carefully, so he opened Cote's tunic to examine the extent of the wound.

Then he was staring disbelievingly.

Cote was a woman!

For a moment, Dan stood stock-still in a surprise bordering on shock. Then, confusedly, he checked the severity of the wound and saw, thankfully, that it wasn't critical, though it was serious enough to require immediate attention.

Dan began administering to the wound. Cote, whoever she was, had been struck just below her right breast by a shell fragment. The fragment was still imbedded in her flesh, and, after first checking to ensure that its removal wouldn't cause immediate hemorrhaging, Dan pulled it out. The wound, he saw, wasn't too deep, though it was of the type which could easily fester if not properly attended to.

Cote's eyes fluttered open as Dan was working. At first she lay there dazedly, then realizing what was happening, tried to sit up.

"No," Dan said sharply, holding her down gently, but firmly. "You've been wounded."

"But I . . ." the girl said, trying to pull her tunic closed.

"Shh," Dan said. "So far your secret is safe with me." He looked at her face more closely, and saw that the features which he had thought were the young, handsome lines of a boy were in fact, the beautiful lines of a clear-skinned woman of about twenty-one or so. She winced once as he began applying the bandage, and he made an effort to be more gentle.

"Who are you?" Dan asked quietly.

"My name is Tamara Calvert," the girl replied. "I'm a ... a runaway slave."

"A what?" Dan asked in surprise. "But you re. . ."

"White?" Tamara said bitterly, finishing Dan's statement. "Yes."

"Ah, but that's only my skin. Look at my blood, for there is the true test. My blood is black. Or at least, one-eighth black, and that's enough to make it all black."

"From what I can see of it.. . and at the moment I see a great deal of it, your blood is red, like everyone else's," Dan said. "How could anyone say..." he started, but when he looked into Tamara's face, he saw that she had passed out again.

Dan stood up and looked around the fort. The bombardment was still going on, and everyone had taken cover, so that he was, for the moment, unobserved.

He wondered what to do about Tamara. As a woman, she would be turned out of the service, and once turned out, she would technically be a fugitive from justice, and thus enjoy no special protection from the government.

Dan knew he would have to sneak her off the battlefield. And that presented a problem of what to do with "Cal Cote." Suddenly, he saw the body of a Rebel soldier about thirty yards away. The dead Rebel was about the same size as Tamara, and, as he had been the victim of an exploding shell, was not easily identifiable. Looking around to make certain he wasn't being observed, Dan removed Tamara's tunic entirely, then ran to put it on the dead man. Then he put the Rebel's body alongside the two men who had been with Tamara when the shell exploded, so that it looked as if the shell had killed all three. Now, Cal Cote was dead. And Dan had only Tamara Calvert to contend with.

Chapter 16

SHORTLY AFTER TWO in the morning, while the Confederates were abandoning Fort Thompson, General Jeff Thompson, after whom the fort was named, sent for Burke O'Lee. When Burke reported to him, General Thompson was just getting around to having his supper.

"They tell me you warned General McCown of this," Thompson said. He was sitting on a log, eating a piece of cornbread, shielding it from the rain which had already started by holding it under the apron of his poncho.

"Yes, sir, I warned him," Burke replied. "I warned him at least two times."

"Well, he's a hard man to figure out sometimes," Thompson said. "Like, you take now, for instance. He's determined to make a fight for Island Number Ten, when any fool can see the writing on the wall." Thompson pointed to the island. "He's sendin' half of his troops over there, and the other half over to the Tennessee side. He's wanting to send my men as well."

"Are we going?"

"I don't know," Thompson said. He finished his cornbread, wiped his hands on his pants, then went on with his explanation. "I'm trying to talk him into freeing my men and let them slip away to act as raiders. Like I said, though, McCown is a hard man to figure out. He may let us go, he may not. Truth is, I get the impression that he's just about written Missouri off. If he knew about the money I had, I think he would take it for his own troops."

"Money?"

"Yeah." Thompson grinned. "I got nearly one hundred thousand dollars from Governor Jackson, to be used for equipping my men. All in gold," he added. "It's not going to do me much good now, so I want you to take the money to General Sterling Price. Tell him where ole' Jeff Thompson and the boys are. Tell him we need more guns and ammunition, maybe a few horses and some staples too. There's a lot depending on you now, Burke. You've got to get out of here on your own. Get through, for the Confederacy in Missouri."

"When you reckon would be the best time to go?" Burke asked.

"I don't know. I've got the two best horses ready for you, one to ride and one to pack with. I'd say go ahead and get ready to make a getaway whenever you think you can."

"And leave you fellas to do all the fighting?" Burke asked.

Thompson smiled. "My friend, I have a feeling you'll be seeing all the fighting you want when you get out of here. Grant has an entire army moving this way. They'll have patrols out on both sides of the river, and you're more'n likely gonna be running into them."

"I'll get through, general."

"I figured I could count on you," Thompson said.

"General Thompson, sir, his respects, and General Gantt would like a word with you," an approaching officer said. The new officer was dressed in the gray and gold-trimmed uniform of Gantt's regular troops and he looked with ill-concealed contempt at Thompson and Burke in their homespun denim clothes.

Thompson stood up and pointed to a pair of saddlebags. "Take care of that for me, will you?" he asked, pitching his voice in a careless inflection which told the visiting officer nothing of the contents of the bags.

"Yes, sir, right away," Burke replied.

After General Thompson and the staff officer left, Burke hefted the saddlebags, surprised at their weight, then went to the remuda and took the two horses General Thompson had ready.

"Wait," another voice called.

Burke turned to see Sergeant Chism, his first sergeant.

"Cap'n, let me go with you," Chism said. "I know what you're doin' 'n bein' as I was born down here, I think you'd have a better chance with me along."

"You'd be safer staying here," Burke said.

"And I'd be safer yet back home plowin' the field for spring plantin'," Sergeant Chism answered, smiling wryly.

Burke had learned to trust Chism since joining with Thompson's irregulars, and he returned Chism's easy smile with one of his own. "All right," he said. "Let's go."

They mounted their horses and rode through the abatis construction out into the dark, rainy night. They rode north along the Missouri side of the river. Mingled with the sounds of the night were the occasional sounds of Federal troops. On the opposite side, they could make out a few campfires, although they didn't know whether they were northern or southern fires. Occasionally they would hear a shout, or a guttural laugh. Once a skiff moved down the river quickly, a dark shadow slipping through the night rain.

"You're crazy. Grant ain't half the gen'rl Fremont is," a strange voice said loudly.

Burke held up his hand and the two riders stopped. "There's a Yankee patrol comin' in," he hissed at Chism.

The two men moved into the shadows of the trees and waited while the patrol moved through. Burke and Chism were veterans of a hundred raiding campaigns. They knew how to use the night to mask their moves, how to strike and then melt back into the trees before the advancing Federal troops. The Yankee patrol they had just encountered had spent their entire period of service in a garrison. They marched as if on parade, talking in loud voices.

There was no way out of the woods, for the entire Union attacking force had landed on the Missouri side by then, so Burke and Chism had to slow their horses to a walk through the thick, tangled undergrowth, picking their way around swollen sloughs and patches of quicksand.

Always as they moved, they heard the constant sound of artillery fire as the duel between the Union and Confederate cannoneers continued. Then they heard an explosion so close that they were sure a cannon ball had landed right between them. To their surprise they discovered that they had blundered into a Union battery. The gun had just been fired, and one of the soldiers was swabbing the barrel with water to prevent premature detonation of the next charge. The soldier looked up just as Burke and Chism burst onto them. The two men weren't in uniform, and the soldier didn't realize who they were.

"Hey, you two civilians get the hell out of here! There's a battle going on!"

"We're sorry," Chism answered, exaggerating the flat southeast Missouri twang. "We'uns is a lookin' for some stray hawgs."

The battery commander came toward them. "We haven't seen any pigs around here," he said. "You'd best get on out of harm's way."

"Thank'ee. We'll be goin' then," Chism said. "Who the hell ever heard of goin' out at night in a rainstorm, in the middle of a battle, just to look for some damn pigs?" one of the soldiers commented suspiciously.

"Hey!" the battery commander said. "Wait a minute. That's right. Maybe you two fellas better climb down off those horses."

Hearts Divided

Burke and Chism slapped the reins of their horses and darted away. The Union soldiers yelled at them to stop, but as they were working the cannon, none were armed with sidearms, so they had no way of stopping them.

Burke and Chism managed to get away from the Federal battery, then rode north along the riverbank. The riverbank was badly overgrown, and the established roads were full of Union soldiers, so the progress was very slow. Finally they halted for a break.

"There's only one way we're going to make it out of here," Burke said. "We're going to have to bury the money somewhere. Lugging it around is going to get us caught."

"But that's the only reason we left Fort Thompson," Chism protested. "We've got to get that money through to Price."

"And we will," Burke promised. "But right now it's pulling us down. Which would you rather have, the money hidden safe so we could come back for it, or have it captured by the Yankees?"

"I guess you're right," Chism said.

"We'll bury it right here."

"No," Chism said. "This section is being farmed—it might get dug up before we can get back to it. I have a place in mind not far from here. It's right near the river and can't be farmed. It'll never be discovered."

Burke followed Chism to a place on the river that Chism indicated would be the best spot, then stood guard while Chism buried the money. Once or twice Burke glanced down by the riverbank and saw Chism by the light of a lightning flash, busily shoveling the wet sand. After a while Chism came back, brushing his hands together.

"If a person didn't know exactly where to look, he couldn't find that money in a hundred years," Chism said. "Let's go."

The two men continued north trying to avoid the roving bands of soldiers as they headed for their rendezvous with Price.

Just at dawn, their luck ran out. They blundered into another Union column and were challenged by the pickets. The two men spurred their horses in an attempt to run away, but the terrain was so badly undergrown that the horses couldn't run much faster than a man on foot. The pickets fired, and Chism fell from his horse, mortally wounded. Burke's horse was shot out from under him, and he pitched over the animal's head onto the ground. When he came to a moment later, there were four bayoneted rifles pointed at him.

"Easy, boys," Burke said. "I know when it's foolish to keep on running. You got me."

"He's alive, sarge," one of the Union soldiers yelled. "What should we do with him?"

"Take him to New Madrid," the sergeant answered. "General Pope will know what to do with him."

Burke was jerked roughly to his feet and prodded in the rear with one of the bayonets, just enough to make him wince and elicit a bit of laughter from the soldiers who were guarding him.

"You just keep it movin right along there, Reb, and I'll try'n keep my bayonet outta your ass." The others laughed, and the soldier, enjoying being the center of attention, added a bit to hold the limelight as long as possible.

"Mind you now, I'll just try. But my arms is itchy, and ever' now'n then I'm liable to lose control, 'n the next thing you know, somethin' like this will happen."

The soldier jabbed Burke again, this time more painfully than before. But Burke refused to give them the pleasure of watching him wince a second time.

Back in New Madrid, Dan had commandeered an empty cabin for his personal quarters. He attended to Tamara himself, intending to explain her presence away by saying she was a wounded civilian, should her presence be discovered. In the meantime, the casualty report he turned in included Private Calvin Cote among the killed.

Tamara responded to treatment well. Within a short time,

she had told Dan her entire story: how she had been raised as a southern belle, only to discover that she was not who she thought she was, but the illegitimate child of a black slave. And she told of being raped, and then murdering her rapist.

"No, Tamara, that wasn't murder," Dan said softly, brushing her hair away from her face tenderly.

"I killed him, Dan," Tamara said. "I stabbed him in the neck with a pair of scissors. If that wasn't murder, what was it?"

"It was self-defense if nothing else," Dan said. "Whatever it was, it was certainly justifiable. Any court in the land would defend your right to do what you did."

"Any court?" Tamara asked. "Even a Mississipi court, if the murdered man was the owner of the slave who did the killing?"

Dan looked at Tamara, and his heart suddenly went out to her. So this was what Verity had been telling him about? Here, right before him, was a helpless victim of the evils of slavery. He felt a quick, burning rage, and knew now, more than at any time before, the fundamental right of the cause of abolition.

"That's what we're fighting for," he said.

"That's what I'm fighting for," Tamara replied. "Or was . . . until this happened. Dan, please, you must let me get back into the fight."

"There, now, Tamara, your fighting days are over. Besides, it shouldn't have to be your fight."

"But I want it to be my fight," Tamara insisted. "You don't understand. I can know no peace until I know I have done everything I can do to change the way things are. I must fight."

"You must also see that I can't allow it," Dan said quietly. "Please, Tamara, let's not speak of it again."

Tamara looked up from the pillow and smiled, a small, conspiratorial smile. "Dan, I know what we could do," she said. "You could make me your aide. I would always be by your side. That way you could keep an eye on me, and satisfy yourself as to my safety."

"I don't know," Dan said.

Tamara's smile broadened. She reached up and took Dan's hand in hers, kissed the end of his fingers, then brought it down to her breast. "There would be other advantages too," she said.

"Tamara, I ... I couldn't take advantage like this," Dan said. But even as he spoke, he felt the heat of her breast burning his hand even through the thin nightgown he had found for her to wear.

"It is an advantage I would gladly give," Tamara said.

Dan felt his breath quicken, then, before he could stop himself, found himself kissing her. His arms went around her, and he pressed her down into the mattress.

Tamara felt his weight upon her. For an instant she wished she could call back what she had started. She meant only to play the game with him, entice him with a promise of things to come, not offer him herself. But his hand on her body roused unexpected passions, and soon she was so caught up in the rising tide of pleasure that she was scarcely aware of Dan removing her nightgown, exposing her naked skin to the cool air. When he began removing his own clothes, she lay on the bed silent and unprotesting, still riding the cresting wave of pleasure which had begun to sweep over her. Then she felt him return to her, and she opened to him, welcoming him into her with a small groan of pleasure.

Dan took her with amazing tenderness, as different from the brutal pounding she had been subjected to under Putnam as a gentle shower is from a ripping thunderstorm. And yet, though he was as tender as a gentle shower, the passions he released in her flashed through her like charges of lightning.

Tamara had never before felt such jolts of pleasure, and she cried out in ecstasy as they occurred, once, twice, three times in rapid succession, then a fourth time which was as great as the first three combined and lasted for several seconds, causing her to arch her body up to him, holding him in her for as long as possible, then feeling him join her as he spent himself in her.

Finally a last shudder of ecstasy convulsed both of them, and they collapsed back to the bed, lying in each other s arms for a long moment before Dan rolled away from her. Tamara lay with her eyes closed for a long while, listening to the sounds from outside ... the occasional crump of distant artillery, a sergeant shouting impatient orders to his squad, a group of men laughing over some shared joke.

Finally she opened her eyes and looked into Dan's face. He was on one elbow, looking down at her. Somewhat hesitantly, he spoke to her.

"Forgive me," he said. "I had no right to do that."

"You had the right of my consent, sir," Tamara replied. She smiled. "Dan, other than the rape I spoke of, this has been my only experience." Dan returned her smile. "And tell me, madam," he teased. "Was it a pleasurable one?"

"Uhmmm," Tamara replied, rolling her eyes impishly. "You have no idea. Let's do it again."

"What? You mean now?" Dan asked in surprise.

"I mean right now," Tamara replied, reaching her arms up for him.

Suddenly the door to Dan's cabin burst open and slammed shut. Tamara let out a small scream, and Dan whirled in anger.

"So, brother, we meet again."

Burke O'Lee, wild-eyed and wounded, stood just inside the door, holding a pistol.

"Burke, what the hell are you doing here?" Dan asked.

Burke coughed, and when he did, blood came from his mouth. The gun he was holding lowered, and he grabbed his chest with his free hand. Blood spilled between his fingers.

Dan started toward him, but Burke recovered. He brought the pistol up again. "No," he said. "Stay where you are."

"I... Burke, may the lady and I get dressed?" Burke looked toward the bed, seeing Tamara for the first time. He smiled a small, strained, smile. "Excuse me, ma'am," he said to her. Then to Dan: "I didn't know you were engaged. I would have knocked."

As they hastily pulled their clothes on, Dan questioned Burke again.

"I asked you what you are doing here?"

"I was a prisoner," Burke said. "And I escaped." He coughed again, and more blood came up. "But not before your brave boys in blue tried to get me to answer a few questions."

"Burke, are you saying we did that to you, just to get military information?" Dan asked in surprise.

Burke gave a short, bitter laugh. "No, brother, military information didn't have anything to do with it. It seems some of your soldiers discovered that I rode away from here last night with one hundred thousand dollars in gold. They wanted to know what I did with it, and they tried to prod the answer from me with their bayonets. I managed to grab a pistol from one of them, and I killed the son-of-a-bitch who was asking all the questions. I got away, and intended to steal a boat to make it to the other side, but the bayonet jabs started bleeding and I had to take a rest. While I was hiding, I heard someone mention your name, and saw them point out this cabin, so here I am."

"Burke, I've got to get a doctor for you."

"A Yankee doctor?" Burke asked.

"That's the only kind around," Dan said.

"No, thanks."

"But you'll die!"

"I'm going to die anyway," Burke said. He laughed. "It's funny, isn't it?"

"What?"

"You left me twelve years ago to look for gold. Now I'm about to leave you and I know where gold is. All the gold you could ever use." Burke laughed again. "And I'm not going to tell you, any more than I would those sons-of-bitches who were torturing me."

"I wouldn't ask you, Burke," Dan said quietly.

"I know you wouldn't," Burke said. He coughed again, and this time he dropped his pistol. Dan rushed to him quickly and caught his brother just as he collapsed. He held him and lay him gently on the floor.

"Dan, I want you to know why I won't tell you about the gold," Burke said weakly.

"It doesn't matter," Dan replied. "I understand."

Burke waved his hand. "No. No, you don't understand," he said "You think it's because I want to get even with you, but that's not the reason. S'funny, but I don't have any hate left in me. But if I tell you, it'll wind up in Yankee hands, I know it will. I can never get it to General Price now . . . but at least I can keep the Yankees from usin' it. I've not done a lot of things to be proud of in my life, Dan." He smiled, weakly. "But I'm going to die a noble death. I'm not sure I'm fightin' for the right side, or the right reason. But I aim to be loyal to the side and the reason I've chosen. I hope you can understand that."

"I think maybe I do," Dan said.

"Dan, I hope you do. There's somebody else who is true to a cause too, and you know who I'm talkin' about. I'm talkin' about Liberty. You've got her all wrong, brother. She's a good woman. And what's more, she's in love with you.

"What makes you say a thing like that?" Dan asked.

"Believe me, brother, I don't want to say it. But she told me herself, and I know it's true." Burke paused for a moment to get his breath. He looked up at Tamara, who was now standing over them, looking down. "Excuse me, ma'am, I know it's indelicate to be talkin' about another woman in front of you, but it needs sayin', n I don't have that much time left."

"You're talking about Liberty Welles?" Tamara asked.

Dan looked up in amazement. "You know her?" he asked.

"Yes," Tamara said. "She's a good woman."

"There," Burke said. "You see? Even your lady friend agrees with me. She is a good woman. She's torn between two loyalties, Dan. She's a true abolitionist. .. but she's a southerner. It's not easy for her. If you see her again, and I hope that you will, remember that. And tell her I died with her name on my lips." Burke smiled, one last time. "It's a pretty name, isn't it? Liberty." Burke broke into another convulsion of coughing and this time when he finished, he made a last, rattling gasp for breath, then died.

"Burke! Burke!" Dan shouted, pulling his younger brother to him and cradling him in his arms. "Burke, no, don't die!"

Dan had an eerie feeling as he realized that, for the second time, someone had died in his arms with Liberty's name on his lips.

His door burst open again, and this time there were four armed soldiers standing there.

"Lieutenant, did you see . .." one of them, a sergeant, started to ask, then stopped as he saw Burke lying on the floor.

"That's him," one of the other soldiers said, pointing at Burke. " I told you I seen him run in here."

Dan looked up at the sergeant. "Are you the one who did this to him?" he asked coldly.

"No, sir. We just knew that there was an escaped Rebel prisoner somewhere here'bouts, and Marty here seen this fella come runnin' into your cabin. We thought you might be in danger, that's all."

"I'm in no danger," Dan said, looking sadly into Burke's face. He took his fingers and gently closed Burke's eyes.

"Is he dead, lieutenant?" one of the others asked.

"Yes," Dan said. "He's dead."

"I wonder who he was?"

"His name was Burke Patrick O'Lee," Dan said.

"O'Lee? But see here, ain't that your name too?"

"Yes. Burke was my brother."

The sergeant paused awkwardly, "I know how you feel, lieutenant," he said then. "I got me a brother who is a Secesh hisself." He turned to the other men. "Let's go, men."

The detail left. Dan stood there, looking down at the lifeless body of his brother for a long moment. He had forgotten all about Tamara, who finally spoke.

"I'm sorry, Dan," she said. "I'm truly very sorry."

Dan sighed, then turned to walk back and sit on the bed with her. He looked back at Burke again.

"Was he in love with Liberty too?"

"Yes," Dan said.

"Then he did die a noble death, telling you how she felt. I hope you won't let his death be in vain."

"What are you talking about?"

"I'm talking about Liberty Wells," Tamara said. "I know her, and I know she is a fine woman. You are a lucky man to have her love."

"Tamara, you needn't be self-sacrificing," Dan said. "I'm not about to go to her."

Tamara smiled. "I'm not being self-sacrificing in the least," she said. "What we have just had, Dan O'Lee, is all I can ever give you. There will never be room for love in my heart again. There is too much hate. Too much pain."

"You don't have a patent on pain, Tamara," Dan said resolutely. "You'll learn that pain is a universal human experience."

Chapter 17

ISLAND NUMBER TEN fell under constant bombardment for the next week, but despite the terrible rain of shells upon the defenders, the island held fast, accomplishing its avowed purpose of keeping the Union fleet bottled upriver, above the New Madrid bend.

Commodore Foote made several sorties against the island with his gunboats, but each attack was driven back by deadly accurate cannon fire. Finally, in frustration, Foote withdrew his gunboats and asked for a conference with General Pope, commanding general of all New Madrid forces.

"I can't knock that island out with gunboats," the commodore said. He had just come to Pope's headquarters from one of the boats, and had gratefully accepted a cup of coffee.

"We have to capture that island," Pope replied. "It is beginning to stick in my craw. Grant wants it, Halleck wants it, McClellan wants it. . . even the Secretary of War has sent a telegram asking when we can expect it to fall."

"General, if I could sink that damn island for you, I would readily do so," Foote said. "It won't sink, but my boats will. I've already lost eleven, and a goodly number of men. I'm telling you, I can't take that island with a frontal attack."

Hearts Divided

"We've captured Fort Thompson," General Pope replied. "We've at least relieved the pressure from you on the Missouri side of the river."

"The guns at Fort Thompson won't reach the island," Foote said. "What I need is a few batteries on the Missouri shore, just opposite the island. Perhaps the combined effect of your shore batteries and my gunboats would reduce it"

General Pope unrolled a map on the table in his tent, and held the corners down with a pistol, his coffee cup, field glasses and a book. "Then you are asking the army for help, is that it?" he asked with a superior air in his voice.

"If it is within your power to do so, then please help," Foote said.

"What about this?" Pope asked, pointing to the map. "I propose to build a road from the Sikeston-New Madrid road, stretching over to the riverbank at this point. If we erected batteries here, we could aid in the bombardment."

Foote put the cup down and looked at the map where indicated. "I agree, it would be a great help," he said. He rubbed his chin. "The question is, how are you going to build a road across the swamp?"

"Simple, my dear fellow," Pope replied, smiling. "I am going to order it done. That is the way we do things in the Army."

"Ordering it and doing it are two different things," Dan said a bit later, after he heard of General Pope's comment. Dan was assigned to Colonel Bissel of Pope's engineers, and to the two men fell the task of examining the area where Pope wanted his road built.

"Perhaps we could fell enough trees to lay a foundation," Bissel suggested. "We could build a corduroy road like the one from Sikeston."

"That road follows a ridge line of high ground," Dan said. "Look at this swamp, colonel. It is absolutely impassable. A man on foot would do well to make it to the river. There is no way we can build a road good enough to haul in cannons and ammunition. The only thing we can do is disassemble the artillery, and pack it in by hand."

"I suppose you're right," Bissel said. "But that limits us to the smaller guns, and I don't know how effective that will be against the island."

Dan stood alongside a winding slough of water, looking at it, lost in thought. "Colonel," he said, "let me look at that map for a moment."

"Sure," Bissel answered easily. "Do you think you've found a route for the road?"

"Not a road," Dan replied. "A canal."

"A canal?" Bissel mused. "You may have something, Dan." Bissel looked at the map with him. "Of course. Why didn't I think of it? We could just follow the St. John's here . . . damn, that would take a lot of digging though, wouldn't it?" Dan laughed. "Colonel, you're looking at the most experienced digger of all diggers. I've moved enough dirt looking for gold to change the course of this damned river."

"So, you were a gold digger, huh?"

"Mostly I was a dirt digger," Dan answered, and both men laughed.

"Let's get this idea to General Pope," Bissel suggested.

When the two returned to Pope's headquarters, they found him posing for Mr. Simplot, a staff artist from *Harpers Weekly*. He was sitting stiffly in a chair, gazing off into space, holding one hand thrust inside his tunic jacket, in a pose that was considered very appropriate for military pictures.

"Well," Pope said, not looking at the two men as he spoke. "My two road-builders. What have you come up with?"

"General, there's no way a road can be built through that swamp," Bissel said.

"What?" Pope said, jerking his head toward them.

"General, please, just a moment longer," Mr. Simplot pleaded.

General Pope returned to the original pose. "What do you mean, a road can't be built?" he barked.

"General, what we are dealing with is swampland, pure and simple. We'd have to lay a roadbed fifteen feet thick just to keep it from sinking," Bissel explained.

"Then build the road fifteen feet thick," Pope said, taking a sidelong glance at the artist's sketch to see if Simplot was capturing the look of authority he wanted to portray.

"General, I think Lieutenant O'Lee has a better idea," Bissel suggested.

"How can a lieutenant have a better idea than a general?" Pope wanted to knew.

"It is merely a recommendation, for your action, general," Bissel corrected. "Lieutenant O'Lee wants to build a canal."

"Why would you want to build a canal?" Pope asked.

"General, a canal would allow the boats to pass through the swamp and approach the island from the rear. As the island's guns are all pointed upriver, that would put Commodore Foote's gunboats in an excellent position to rout the enemy."

"And give credit for the victory to Foote and the navy?" Pope replied. "Absolutely out of the question. Foote has already admitted defeat, and I'll be damned if I'll hand him victory on a silver platter."

"But General, it could shorten this campaign by . . ." Dan started.

"Lieutenant, I have made my decision, and until such time as I am overruled, that decision will stand, You will proceed to Cairo at once, secure the tools you need, then return here and build that road."

"Yes, sir," Bissel replied. "Let's go, Dan."

"Oh, colonel, before you leave, check my likeness, will you? This picture is going to appear in *Harper's Weekly.* People all over the country will read of this battle, and about me. Does the picture do me justice, do you think?"

Bissel looked at the drawing, a highly romanticized rendering of General Pope. "It is one you will appreciate, general, I'm sure," he said dryly.

"Ah, excellent, excellent. This war is going to create some powerful political personages you know, colonel. People like McClellen, Halleck, Grant and, if I may say so in all modesty, even myself, are going to be touted by many as possible presidential material. It doesn't hurt to start getting a little advance publicity . . . and it's wise to make sure that you don't miss out on every opportunity that presents itself by foolishly squandering it away. That's what I would be doing if I allowed Commodore Foote to reap the rewards of my victory."

Dan and Colonel Bissel left Pope's headquarters frustrated that their idea hadn't fallen on favorable ears.

"At least we'll get a chance to spend one night in Cairo," Bissel said. "One good meal, and a clean, dry bed before we come back to this Godforsaken swamp."

"Colonel, there is someone I would like to take to Cairo with me," Dan said. "A civilian."

"A civilian?"

"Yes, sir. It's a girl. She was wounded in the fighting when we took Fort Thompson. I've been tending to her in my cabin, but as she's getting along nicely now, I feel that it wouldn't be proper to keep her any longer."

Bissel laughed. "Why you sly old dog, you. You can find a girl even on the field of battle."

"Well, she was wounded, sir, and . . ."

"And you never thought to report her to the division surgeon," Colonel Bissel interrupted. "Ah, never mind. Perhaps I would have done the same thing, had I the opportunity. Don't worry. I'll talk to General Pope and get him to issue her a pass through the lines. But you must promise to tell her that I came to her rescue."

"I promise, colonel," Dan said, laughing easily. Tamara, as Dan knew she would, protested when she discovered that he intended to take her to Cairo. But her protests went unheeded. When Dan and Colonel Bissel stepped on board Commodore Foote's flag vessel later that day, Tamara Calvert was with them.

Dan couldn't help but notice the several sidelong admiring glances the soldiers gave her. Colonel Bissell was as obvious in his attentions as the others, and Dan chuckled to himself, thinking of how many of these man had served with Tamara when they thought she was a soldier like them. It was amazing that she hadn't been discovered by virtue of her beauty alone, but as women never affected men's clothing, they could often pass just by their sheer audacity in dressing as one.

The steamer on which they took passage was also carrying the dead and wounded back to Cairo, and the bodies of the soldiers who had been killed during the Fort Thompson fighting were wrapped in canvas bags and laid on the deck. There were some Confederate dead among them, one of whom was Dan's brother. It had been Dan's unpleasant duty to verify the identity of Burke in the casualty letter which was exchanged with the Confederates, and, as he was Burke's next-of-kin, he had authorized the return of the body to St. Louis, to be buried in the same cemetery as their parents.

When the steamer reached Cairo, Dan placed Tamara in the only available boarding house, then joined Colonel Bissel in securing the equipment they would need to build the road.

"It's a shame," Dan said as they acquired the floating steamshovels, saws, axes, etc. "These same tools could be used much more effectively in building a canal."

"I agree," Bissel said. "But Pope is in command." Bissel rubbed his hands together. "Now, my boy, we've done all that we can do tonight. The Little Egypt Hotel has been converted into an officers' dining hall, and the food is delicious. Suppose we try it out?"

Dan smiled. "The biscuits and salt pork are getting a little tiresome," he said. "I would be most happy to join you."

They went to the officers' dining hall, anticipating their first good meal in weeks. They were still studying the menu, when Bissel suddenly pulled Dan's menu down and looked at him with a conspiratorial expression on his face.

"Dan, how serious are you about that canal?"

"What do you mean?" Dan replied, puzzled that the subject had been introduced anew.

"Are you positive that you can do it?"

"Of course I can. Why do you ask?"

"Because if you are really serious, I think I know how to get permission to build it."

"What? How?"

Colonel Bissel pointed to a table on the far side of the room. "That man over there is General Grant," he said. "Do you know him?"

"No, sir."

"Well, I do," Bissel said. He smiled dryly. "The fact is, when he was a captain, I was a major in the same regiment, and so was his superior. Come over with me. I'll introduce you."

"Should we disturb him? I mean after all, he is the top commander of all forces in the field.

He has more important things to do than talk to us.

"Trust me, Dan," Colonel Bissel said. "Sam is as approachable as they come. And if he likes your idea, he'll authorize it."

"Are you going to tell him about it?"

"No. You are," Bissel replied.

"I think you should. You're senior in rank, and you know him."

"But it's your idea, and it'll be better coming from you," Bissel said. "We'll wait until he's finished his meal, then we'll talk to him."

Dan studied General Grant as they were eating. Until a few months ago, Dan had never heard of Grant. In fact, there were few in the country who had. He had been a captain, and he was a veteran of the Mexican War, but his military career had been undistinguished. He'd resigned his commission in 1854, but when the war started, he'd managed to be appointed to the rank of colonel in an Illinois regiment. He was advanced to the rank of brigadier general during the general mobilization, was posted to Cairo, Illinois, then was catapulted to national prominence with his twin victories at Ford Henry and Fort Donnelson, opening up the Cumberland and Tennessee Rivers. Now he needed only a victory at Island Number Ten to open up the Mississippi as well, and thus own every waterway leading into the south.

General Grant was a very short man, with a full beard and mustache. His beard was a little long, unkempt and irregular, of a sandy, tawny shade. His hair matched his beard. At first glance he seemed to be a very ordinary sort of man. Indeed, he was a little below average attractiveness in appearance. But as Dan sat watching him, the general's face grew on him. Grant's eyes were gentle, with a kind, thoughtful expression. He was listening to his table guest with quiet attention, and was smoking a pipe which he often had to relight. Finally he signaled the waiter to remove his plate.

"Now," Bissel said. "If we don't see him now, I feel we will lose our opportunity."

Bissel stood up and walked toward the general's table. Dan had no recourse but to follow him.

"Hello, Sam," Bissel said. "It's good to see you again."

Dan was surprised by Bissel's familiarity, but Grant showed no displeasure at the lack of respect. On the contrary, his face lit up in genuine appreciation of seeing an old friend again.

"Harry, well, you are looking very well Won't you join me?"

"Thank you, general, I will. This is Lieutenant Dan O'Lee.. He has an idea that I think is worth listening to."

"I'm always open to ideas," Grant said. "What is it?"

Dan looked at Bissel nervously, then cleared his throat. "General, I would like to build a canal at Island Number Ten."

"A canal, you say?"

"Yes, sir," Dan said. "As you know, the New Madrid bend forms a large letter 'U.' Island Number Ten sits in the bottom of the U, with all its guns pointing north, keeping our gunboats away. But if we cut a canal across the top of the U, we could run gunboats through that way and attack the island from the rear."

"Good heavens, what a good idea," Grant said quickly. "But tell me, is such a canal possible?"

"Yes, sir," Dan said. "There is no doubt that I could build it."

"Then do so, lieutenant. Do so at once."

"There's a catch, Sam," Bissel said.

"What's that?"

"General Pope wants a road."

"A road?"

"Yes, sir," Dan said. "He wants a road built down to the river, so he can put artillery on the Missouri side."

"That sounds feasible," Grant said. "If you can build a road, perhaps you should do it."

"We can built it, general, but it would take at least two months to get a solid enough foundation to move cannons through that swamp."

"I see," Grant said. "How long would the canal take?"

"Less than thirty days, I'm certain," Dan put in.

"Then why in blazes would Pope want a road?"

"Because Foote can't run his gunboats down a road," Bissel said dryly.

Grant chuckled. "I see. He wants the credit, is that it?"

"Yes, sir," Bissel answered.

Grant drummed his fingers on the table in silence for a long while, puffing on a curved-stemmeers cham pipe which wreathed his head in blue smoke. Finally he spoke. "Build your canal, Captain O'Lee."

"I'm a lieutenant, sir," Dan corrected him.

"You were a lieutenant when you were in Pope's command. Now you are on my staff and you are a captain. Build the canal, then return to Cairo." Grant chuckled again. "I'm about to go into the railroad business down south, and I want you to come along."

"Are you talking about the railroad junctions in and around Corinth, general?"

"Yes," Grant replied.

"I would be glad to join you. I have a personal interest in that campaign."

"Oh?"

"Dan is the man who set up the Rebel spy to draw the Confederate forces into Corinth," Bissel said. Bissel had heard the story, first from General Halleck himself, and then had it confirmed by Dan during the long night duty-hours he and Dan had spent together.

"That's not entirely true, sir," Dan said quickly. "I was involved, but I didn't set Miss Welles up. In truth, she set me up."

"You sound as if there was some personal betrayal involved," Grant said.

"There was," Dan said. "She was a person who thought nothing of trifling with a man's affections, if in so doing she gained her objective. She was a woman totally without honor."

"Don't be so harsh on her," General Grant said. "After all, didn't you do the same thing to her?"

"Not knowingly, general. Not knowingly," Dan insisted.

"But you used her, none the less. I fear that the line between honor and dishonor is thinly drawn here, and you should not be so quick to cast stones."

Dan felt a sudden chill pass over him. It was a touch of *deja vu,* for those were the same words he had heard Liberty speak.

"I'm sure you're right, general," he said. "I must confess to my own confused emotions when dealing with this. Liberty Welles was a woman who made a lasting impression in my heart. And now that heart is divided as to loyalty and love."

"There are many hearts divided by this terrible war," Grant said "But if fortune smiles upon us, we may be on the verge of an engagement which could hasten the end of it."

"Do you think the fighting to come will be significant?'

Dan asked.

"Yes," Grant answered. "We have information that General Johnston is joining forces with General Beauregard. That should bring a sizeable portion of the Confederate army together, and it will give us the opportunity to deal them a terrible blow."

'But what if they defeat us in battle?" Dan asked.

"They cannot win," Grant said simply. "If we are better armed, which we are, if we have more men, which we do, and if we can sustain the greater losses, which we can, then it is a question of mathematics, pure and simple. Masses of men and materiel against masses of men and materiel, and the side with the most surviving men and materiel will be victorious. We shall be the survivors, Mr. O'Lee."

"And what of the losers?" Dan asked. "What is to become of them?"

"That I shall leave in the hands of the politicians who shall come after this war," Grant said. "Our duty, as soldiers, is merely to fight the war. I have resolved myself to the conduct of that duty."

"As have I, general," Dan said resolutely. "As have I."

Chapter 18

"GENTLEMEN ARE NOT allowed beyond the lobby, sir," a rather plump, frumpy looking woman said. She was the registration clerk at the Ladies' Temperance Boarding House, the hotel where Dan had left Tamara.

"Yes, I know," Dan said. "I would like to call on Miss Calvert. She checked in earlier today. Would you notify her that Captain O'Lee is here to see her?"

"Have a seat," the unsmiling woman said. "I'll send for her."

"Thank you," Dan replied. He walked over to one of the hard, uninviting chairs and sat down. The room was very spartan. Dan didn't know whether it was to maintain the image of tempeance or to discourage men visitors. This would not have been his choice as a hotel for Tamara, but the population of Cairo was swollen by the war, and rooms were at a premium—even rooms in such uninviting establishments as this.

Tamara came to the door a moment later, looked toward Dan and smiled. "Well, is it visiting day already?" she asked, walking toward him.

"Visiting day?"

"As you have placed me in a jail, sir, I thought perhaps

you were now coming to visit me."

"Tamara, be fair," Dan said. "You know this was the only place we could find. What other choice did I have?"

"You had the choice of leaving me as you found me," Tamara said. "I managed to carry off my deception until you discovered my identity. Were you to say nothing, I could no doubt continue the charade indefinitely."

"No," Dan said. "That is absolutely out of the question. I won't allow you to return to the battlefield. I want you to stay here in Cairo, where it is safe for you."

"You forget, sir, I am a runaway slave," Tamara said. "I'm not safe anywhere until this war is won."

"You are safe here, and you know it," Dan said. "Besides, I've been assigned to General Grant's staff, Tamara. After I complete the project I'm working on, I'll be able to return to Cairo. When I do, I shall request a furlough to see you safely to St. Louis."

"I don't want to go to St. Louis," Tamara said. "I want to return to the battlefield."

"There are other ways of fighting which are just as effective as risking your life on the battlefield," Dan said.

"Those ways do not suit me," Tamara said. "I am a simple girl who has been wronged. I know only the simple solution to right that wrong."

"Tamara, believe me, I am only doing what is best for you. You've let your emotions blind your reason."

"And you have not, sir?" Tamara challenged.

"What do you mean by that?"

"You were hurt by Liberty Welles, and now everything you do is colored by your reaction to that hurt. If that is good enough for you, why shouldn't it be good enough for me?"

"I ... I don't have an answer for that," Dan said. "And I shan't try. But you must promise me that you'll be here when I get back."

"Ill see you again," Tamara said. "I promise you that."

"Good," Dan said. "In the meantime, you get plenty of

rest. Your room and board is paid for two months. That should give you plenty of time to recuperate."

Dan left, smiling and waving at Tamara, who was smiling and waving back at him. She laughed at her little joke. He had asked her if she would be here when he got back, and she had answered only that she would see him again. That she could do on the field of battle.

Tamara remained in the lobby until she saw Dan hail a carriage and drive away. Then she hurried back up to her room and closed the door, locking it behind her. Then she reached under the bed and pulled out a box, removing the contents and laying them on the bed.

The box contained the uniform of a captain in the Union Army. It was among the stores carried by the steamer, and Tamara had managed to move it into the pile of her personal luggage. Dan himself had seen to the transfer of her luggage to her room, and once, when he dropped some of the boxes, part of the uniform had come out. Tamara had held her breath for a moment, but Dan had stuffed it back into the box without paying attention to what it was, and she'd breathed easier as they continued toward her hotel.

Getting the uniform on the steamer had been easy. But when she'd looked into the box during an unguarded moment and saw that she had acquired the uniform of a captain, she'd feared that identity papers might be difficult to obtain. Then she'd remembered the bodies being returned to Cairo. It was a gruesome task, but Tamara had managed to search them until she found the body of a captain with identity papers. Distasteful though it was, she'd removed the papers. Now, armed with them, and the uniform, she was ready to rejoin the army.

Tamara modified the uniform to fit. A short time later, she climbed through the window and down the back of the hotel. When she saw a transport being loaded with soldiers, she stepped easily into the group and boarded with them.

"You, captain," a colonel said, noticing Tamara a moment

later. "What is your name?"

"Savage, sir," Tamara replied, taking the name from the identity papers. "Captain Bill Savage."

"What is your assignment?"

"Replacement pool, unassigned."

"Good. You will take command of G Company. I've just sent the previous commander to St. Louis under arrest for being drunk on duty." Tamara felt a quick beat of fear. Passing herself off as a private was one thing, since she could lose herself in the crowd. But to become a commanding officer of a company was something entirely different. She would be highly visible, and the least mistake might compromise her identity.

Well, she decided resolutely, she just wouldn't make any mistakes.

"Colonel, I've just arrived in Cairo. Where is this boat going?"

"Up the Ohio until we reach Paducah, then down the Tennessee to Savannah."

"Then there is a chance that we are going to see some fighting?" Tamara asked, enthusiastic at the prospect.

"Not much chance, I'm afraid," the colonel said. "It'll probably just be guard duty. There aren't any Confederates there. They're all down at Island Number Ten. That's where the fighting is."

On the night of the day that Tamara started toward Pittsburgh Landing, General McCown and General Gantt left the Confederate works on the Tennesee side of Island Number Ten, taking ten regiments with them. They proceeded downriver to Fort Pillow, then overland to Corinth, Mississippi, there to join the growing army of General P.G.T. Beauregard. The Confederate force left on the island was greatly reduced. Numbered among its units was the Second Mississippi Horse Regiment.

"Colonel, it isn't fair," Major Owens, one of Blackie's staff officers argued. "We're havin' to stay here to fight in

Missouri, when there is likely to be a big battle fought in Mississippi. We are Mississippians, by God, 'n by rights that's where we ought to be."

"Major Owens is right," another put in. "General Beauregard is your uncle, sir. Don't you think he'd rather have the Second Mississippi Horse Regiment at Corinth than here in New Madrid?"

"We've received no orders to that effect," Blackie said.

"Well, hell's bells, colonel, you give the orders. The men want to fight for you and Mississippi, not MacKall and Missouri. Besides, what right did McCown and Gantt have in making MacKall a general over you anyway? You were senior to him," Owen said.

Upon that point, Owen had struck a telling blow, for Blackie had been offended that MacKall, not he, had been selected to assume command of the island.

"All right," Blackie said. "Alert the men. We'll leave tonight."

"Yes, sir!"

Less than thirty minutes later, newly appointed General MacKall came to see Blackie, who was now gathering the personal belongings he intended to carry with him.

"Sir, I have been informed that you intend to quit the island. Is that true?" MacKall asked.

"Yes," Blackie said.

"Colonel, I consider that desertion under fire, and I will personally carry the report to General Beauregard."

Blackie smiled. "I'm sure my uncle will see things my way. Besides, we will be of some use to the South in Mississippi. We are of no use to them here."

'That is not true, sir," MacKall replied. "We are keeping the Yankees bottled up. It is my intention to erect batteries facing south, and thus render the island impregnable from all sides. But I can't do that without your men and equipment."

"You're going to build batteries facing south?" Blackie asked, laughing. "And whom do you expect to drive off?

Admiral Semmes?"

"No," MacKall said. "Yankees. They now own New Madrid and Fort Thompson and may devise some means of putting floating batteries below us. We would be highly vulnerable to such an attack."

"General MacKall," Blackie said, twisting the word general as he spoke, so that his face looked like an image in a distorted mirror. "I feel that you are trying to keep my men here merely to swell the numbers of your command and thus inflate your importance. Well, sir, I have no intention of remaining on this island while my home state is being threatened. I am taking my men out of here tonight."

"And I will personally carry my report of your disgrace to General Johnston when he arrives to take command of the combined armies." General MacKall refused to authorize the transports which were under his command to carry Blackie and his regiment to the Tennessee shore, so they made the trip across in skiffs, carrying four and five men at a time. It took almost three hours before the entire regiment had abandoned the island. Blackie then led them straight toward Reelfoot Lake, where he hoped to catch a ferry the rest of the way.

Blackie was unfamiliar with the country, and, unknowingly, led his men right into the middle of the swamp. All pretense of command and order failed. His regiment disintegrated from a military unit to a band of nearly one thousand fugitives, each man on his own, fighting the forces of nature inherent in the swamp. A journey which on the map appeared to be a distance of no more than an hour's duration stretched through the whole night, until finally, cold, drenched with water and caked in mud, the men began to straggle in the next day. It was after noon before the forlorn band had completely traversed the swamp. Without knapsacks or blankets, many of them without arms, they began their weary march toward Corinth.

Chapter 19

ARMED WITH INFORMATION supplied them by Liberty Wells, Generals Albert Sidney Johnston and P.G.T. Beauregard brought their two armies together under the command of the former and prepared to defend the critical railroad junctions in and around Corinth, Mississippi. Thus far, there were thirty thousand Confederate troops in position, and the numbers continued to grow as new regiments came in daily.

General Beauregard, who had command responsibility for the defense of the Mississippi River, was less than enthusiastic when he learned that his nephew had quit Island Number Ten at a time when its defense was most critical. But short of a general court martial, an action he was loath to take against his only brother's son, there was nothing he could do but accept the Second Mississippi Horse Regiment into his command.

The soldiers of the Second Mississippi Horse Regiment, having been exposed to battle at Island Number Ten, swaggered around the camp grounds, lording it over those troops who were as yet untested. There were few now who had seen no action. Most of the soldiers gathered by Johnston and Beauregard were veterans of a string of campaigns, from

Bull Run to Fort Donnelson and Island Ten, and they bore the bragging of the Second Mississippi stoically, knowing that a few more campaigns would make the Second Mississippi as jaded as the rest of them. They were young men who were aged long before their time, who had seen and smelled death far too often to find any degree of glory in war.

Colonel Blackie Beauregard was invited to dine at Trailback Plantation by Colonel A.G. Welles. Generals Johnston and Beauregard would also be guests, the invitation noted, as would Colonel Welles's daughter, Liberty.

Blackie found his freshest tunic. When he appeared at the Welles home, he was greeted by Liberty.

"Liberty, you are as beautiful as you were the last time I saw you in St. Louis," Blackie said, removing his hat and bending low in a sweeping bow.

"And you as gallant, sir," Liberty replied.

Blackie looked around. "Has General Johnston or my uncle arrived?"

"They sent word they would be detained on some military business," Liberty said. "But they will be here shortly."

Blackie smiled. "Good. That means that I, as a result of my punctuality, will be able to enjoy the full measure of your company all alone for a brief time."

"Why, colonel," Liberty said, smiling coyly. "Is that any way for an engaged man to talk?"

"Engaged? But I'm not engaged," Blackie said.

"Oh, forgive me," Liberty apologized. "I thought you were engaged to Miss Tamara Calvert, of Calvert Hills."

The smile left Blackie's face, and a dark mask descended over his eyes. "No," he said. "But I shall live with the shame of having been engaged to her for the rest of my life."

"The shame?"

"You mean you haven't heard?"

"No."

"I wish I could keep my silence, and thus spare myself the embarrassment," Blackie said. "But as the matter has been raised, I feel I owe you an explanation." Blackie drew a deep breath. "I discovered, just in time, I might add, that Tamara Calvert is a nigger."

"What?" Liberty asked.

"Yes, I can see you are surprised, as I'm sure you can appreciate I was."

"Surprised? I'm more than surprised," Liberty said. "I know Tamara very well, have known her for years. She is not a Negro. Where did you get such an idea?"

"Her mother was one-fourth nigger, bought and paid for by Tamara's father as his slave girl," Blackie said. "That makes Tamara one- eighth nigger."

"It also makes her seven-eighths white, and eight-eighths a person, so what difference does it make? Did she tell you this?"

"Did she tell me? No, she didn't tell me. She didn't even know. It came out after her father was killed. Tamara was due to inherit Calvert Hill, and she tried to free all the slaves. I'm sure you can well imagine what a dangerous thing that would be ... it could start a general uprising. Then Colonel Putnam discovered that while negotiating a loan last year Amon Calvert had to list all his holdings, and he listed Tamara as one of his slaves."

"Oh, how awful," Liberty said.

"Yes, that's what I thought. Here I was engaged to a girl, and all the time she was a nigger slave. Fortunately, Calvert had placed a codicil in the will leaving the place to me, should Tamara be unable to inherit. She, being a slave, cannot hold property by Mississippi law, so the property became mine, and I put a quick end to the idea that the niggers would be freed."

"I meant how awful for Tamara," Liberty said. "To discover that she was no more than property."

"Well, I thought of that too," Blackie said. "And I figured that it would be best if she left the place. So, for her own good, I sold her to Colonel Putnam. And now, here's the really terrible part, Liberty. She *murdered* Colonel Putnam. She stabbed him in the neck with a pair of scissors."

"Why?" Liberty asked. "Did he abuse her?"

"Abuse her? He owned her. He could do as he liked with her."

"What happened to her?" Liberty asked.

"I don't know. I do know that the girl, Alva, had something to do with helping her get away. But even though I tore the hide off her back with a whipping, she never told me where Tamara went. She's a fugitive, all right, and right now there's a warrant out for her arrest on the charge of murder."

"Oh, the poor thing," Liberty said. "What she must be going through."

"She's not going through half what I'll put her through if I ever find her," Blackie said. His eyes narrowed menacingly. "If I find her, I'll kill her."

"Then I pray that you never find her," Liberty said quietly.

"I will find her, Miss Welles. You may count on that."

There was a noise in the entry foyer as Generals Johnston and Beauregard arrived. They came into the parlor, escorted by Colonel Welles.

"Miss Welles," General Johnston said, bowing before her. "May I say that it is an honor to see you again? Allow me once more to give you my thanks, and the thanks of the entire South for your services."

"It is a privilege to serve, general," Liberty said. Her eyes got a troubled look about them. "Though it is not always an easy thing to do. I am as dedicated to the cause of abolition as I am to the cause of the Confederacy. It is only because I hope eventually to serve the abolitionist cause in the new South that I am able to abandon my work in St. Louis."

"You mean you were *serious* about freeing the niggers?" Blackie asked. "I thought you were just using that as a cover."

At that moment a black servant walked in, carrying a tray of drinks. Blackie took one, then smiled. "But, I see, you have niggers of your own here."

"I have no slaves," Colonel Welles put in quickly. "Those

who work for me work for wages."

"Well, if you'll excuse me, sir, that's a very dangerous precedent to be establishing," Blackie said. "I don't approve of it at all."

"I would hope that there will be room in our new nation for diversity of thought," General Johnston put in. "I feel no threat from such beliefs. General Lee himself has freed his slaves."

"Nevertheless, it doesn't set well with me, and I feel it won't set well with many others," Blackie said.

"Then they shall have to accommodate themselves to it," Liberty said resolutely. "For I shall continue the fight for abolition with all my energies."

General Johnston laughed. "And colonel, as you have seen, she is a person of immense energies. Her service to us in the past is witness to that."

"General, will the Yankees attack anyway, now that we have brought in more troops?" Colonel Welles asked.

"They will attack all right. In fact, I think the biggest battle of the war is about to take place here within a matter of a few weeks."

"How big?" Blackie asked.

'Very big," General Johnston answered. "General Halleck is putting as many divisions together as he can to make his demonstration here, and we have nearly as many men assembled to meet him."

"Will we win the battle?" Colonel Welles asked.

Johnston got a faraway look in his eyes. "Yes," he finally said. "I think we will. Our chances improve each day we continue to hold Island Number Ten. You see, that not only ties up General Pope's army but it keeps the river open to us, and as long as the river is open we can move men over here. But I'll tell you this. The creeks and streams are going to run red with the blood that will be shed in this battle. There will be a carnage such as this continent has never before witnessed. And all of us must accommodate ourselves to our own mortality. The angel of death may be waiting for me, as well as for any of my command, and I must be prepared to accept this."

"General, I pray that isn't true," Liberty said. "The South needs you badly. Not only as a great general, but as a statesman who will help in establishing our new society."

"I shall give my all for the South, my dear, but I fear I shall not live to see our new society established," Johnston said.

There was a moment of awkward silence. Then Johnston smiled, dispelling the mood. "However, we must not dwell on such things," he said. "The purpose of this dinner is to honor one of our genuine heroines. If we are successful, it will be due to Liberty Welles." Johnston held his drink out in a toast. "May we drive the Yankees out of Mississippi."

"General, I look forward to the small part I shall play in serving Mississippi," Blackie said, holding up his own glass.

General Johnston looked at Blackie with narrowed eyes. "You would have served Mississippi better by helping in the defense of Island Number Ten. By leaving it, you may have cost us thirty-five thousand men."

General Beauregard cleared his throat in embarrassment, and Blackie looked at the floor, his cheeks burning in shame. Liberty smiled a small smile of satisfaction. Blackie had gotten his comeuppance.

Chapter 20

TO GENERAL POPE'S credit, he responded to General Grant's directive that a canal be built by offering immediate cooperation in all ways. He authorized Colonel Bissel, his chief engineer, to set his entire command to work and even got assurances from Commodore Foote that he would provide manpower too, if need be.

It was a formidable task to build the canal. Dan had to cut through the forest a channel fifty feet wide, four-and-a-half feet deep and twelve miles long. In order to accomplish this, he and his men waded through mud and stood waist deep in icy water to saw through the trunks of trees. The trees, once felled, had to be cut up and disposed of. The overhanging boughs of other trees, which were standing outside the channel, had to be lopped off, and their limbs cleared away. Shallow places were excavated, and men worked around the clock in three shifts. Dan drove himself and his men relentlessly, often working two full shifts himself, then showing up to oversee a portion of the third.

On the seventeenth of March, General Grant moved his headquarters from Cairo to Savannah, Tennessee. He checked on the progress of the canal before he left Missouri. Dan was standing chest deep in water, straining with nineteen of his men to dislodge a fallen tree from the mud and thus clear away a portion of the channel.

"Cap'n, we're gettin a current from the river now," one of his sergeants said, after they had tried unsuccessfully to dislodge the large trunk. "That's fightin' us."

Dan scratched his cheek, leaving a smear of mud there as he did so, and examined the problem. "All right," he said finally. "Let's clear a little path out that way, and we'll use the current to help us carry it out."

The sergeant looked in the direction Dan had indicated, then spit a chew of his tobacco and smiled. "Well, now, I reckon that's why you're a cap'n 'n I'm a sergeant," he said.

"He's a captain because I made him a captain," General Grant grunted, and the men, who had not heard Grant approach, looked around in surprise.

"General Grant, sir," Dan said. "I didn't know you were coming, or I would have come to meet you." He climbed out of the water and reported to the general.

"That's precisely why I didn't let you know I was coming," Grant said. "You would have come to meet me, and we would have lost your services here for a few hours. The canal is much more important than protocol, Dan, believe me. How is it coming along?"

"It's coming along fine, sir," Dan said. "We'll meet our deadline, with time to spare."

"The sooner the better," Grant replied. "If we can control this river, we'll have a waterway that leads right into the heart of the South. But we'll have something else, which right now is even more important."

"What's that, general?"

Grant put both hands behind his back and looked southeast. "There's a big battle brewing down there, Dan. The biggest of this war. Johnston and Beauregard have been fortifying Pittsburgh Landing and the railroad junctions around Corinth, thanks to the information Miss Welles carried to them. They're pulling in troops from all over. But if we can control this river, we'll have some thirty-five thousand Confederates trapped west of the Mississippi. That would be thirty-five thousand people that Johnston won't be able to use. You can see, then, the importance of taking out Island Number Ten and establishing control of the river."

"Yes, sir," Dan said.

"Fire in the hole!" someone yelled. The yell was repeated down the line until one of the men in Dan's party picked it up and passed it on.

"Watch yourself, general," Dan said. "We're about to blast away some trees." He put his hand on General Grant's arm and led him back a little way. Seconds later there was a deep, stomach-jarring explosion, and water, mud, smoke, and small pieces of tree flew into the air where the blast had occurred.

General Grant chuckled. "It's too bad we can't get the Confederates to fire a few explosive shells this way. They might do some of our work for us."

"They might at that," Dan agreed.

"Captain, I'm most impressed with your work here. Keep it until the canal is opened, then report to me at Pittsburgh Landing."

"Yes, sir," Dan replied.

Grant waved goodbye, then began walking slowly, picking his way back through the swamp. Within a few moments he was swallowed up by the twisted tangle of trees and vines. Dan thought how easy it would be for a lone Rebel soldier to sneak into the swamp, hide and kill General Grant, then escape without ever being caught. It would be a small act, but one with a tremendous consequence. He shuddered at the thought.

"Hey, cap'n, was that feller really Gen'rul Grant?" one of Dan's men asked.

"He sure was, Charlie," Dan said.

"I'm gonna write my pa' that I seen him," Charlie replied. He looked at his rope-burned hands. "That is, if I got anything left to write with after diggin' this here damn canal." Charlie's eyes suddenly brightened, and he smiled broadly. "Hey, fellers, did you hear what the gen'rul said? What we're 'a doin' here is important! Come on, let's get with it. We can't stand around here 'n lollygag all day long!"

Dan laughed, but appreciated the fact that General Grant's visit had instilled in his men an understanding of the degree of importance of the canal. It would make the task of motivating them a little easier.

If motivation was easier, the actual work was not. There were twelve tortuous miles to be completed. The canal was dug, chopped and blasted through for twenty-four hours a day, in every condition of weather, without letup. Finally, on the twenty-eighth of March, thirteen days after Dan had turned the first spade of dirt, the way was free and clear. He reported to General Pope and Commodore Foote that the canal was open.

"We have your guarantee that safe passage can be effected through your canal now, is that it, captain?" Commodore Foote asked, pulling on his chin whiskers.

"No, sir," Dan replied.

"What? You don't feel your canal is safe?"

"The canal is passable, sir," Dan answered easily. "And it will allow your boats to be put into position behind the enemy. But I don't guarantee that it has not been mined with floating torpedoes, or that some enterprising Confederate officer hasn't found a way to move cannons into position to bear on its mouth."

Colonel Bissel, who had gone with Dan to make the report, threw his head back and laughed richly. "Dan," he said. "Let's hope that the Confederates don't have an officer as enterprising as you are."

"I would not wish to underestimate them, colonel," Dan replied.

"Nor I," Pope agreed. "But decisions have to be made, and risks must be taken. Based on Captain O'Lee's report, it is my decision that the canal be declared open. Commodore Foote, I suggest that you try and effect a passage as soon as possible."

"Of course, general," Foote replied. "Though I can't help but notice that it is your decision, and my risk. Or, rather, the risk of Commander Walke, who has already volunteered to take the first boat through."

"Balls of fire, commodore!" Pope exploded. "What do you want? We've done all the work for you now, and you stand to reap the glory. Were it my risk to take, I would gladly take it!"

"I'm thinking of Commander Walke and his men," Foote said. "They must face this alone." "Commodore, I have already spoken with Commander Walke," Dan said. "I intend to be on the boat with him."

"We don't need an army officer to give us courage," Foote replied rather stiffly.

"Courage has nothing to do with it, sir," Dan said. "Who better knows the canal than I?"

"The captain has a point, commodore," Pope said.

Foote stroked his chin whiskers again, striking a thoughtful pose for a moment He was cleanshaven around his mouth, and he pursed his lips. Finally he spoke. "Very well, I have no objections. But I want it clearly understood that Commander Walke is in command. From here on out, it is a naval operation."

"I appreciate that fact, commodore," Dan said. "And now, if I may be excused, I promised to help Commander Walke prepare the *Carondelet*."

The *Carondelet* was a beehive of activity by the time Dan returned to the boat. Its crew, along with Dan's men, were covering the decks with heavy planks. Chains were coiled over the most vulnerable parts of the boat, and an eleven- inch hawser was wound around the pilot-house, as high as the windows. Barriers of cordwood were built around the boilers. Finally, protected in every way possible, the boat was ready to make the passage.

-"Dan," Walke said. "Are you absolutely positive you want to go with us? It will be dangerous, and you did your part when you cut the canal."

"I'm ready to go," Dan said.

"All right. It's your funeral."

"Thanks," Dan said, grinning dryly. "But couldn't you have chosen another metaphor?"

Walke returned the grin, then added, with another touch of grim humor, "I'll make you an honorary member of the United States Navy," he said. "If you get killed, we'll bury you at sea ... in the swamp."

"That'll make me the first sailor in history to have dug my own grave at sea," Dan replied, laughing.

"Commander Walke, Commodore Foote says you may proceed at your discretion," a sailor reported, coming aboard the *Carondelet* with the message.

"Very well, tell the commodore we will get underway just after sunset," Walke replied.

Clouds had been building all day. By the time the sun set, the sky was hazy and overcast. Walke called for the guns to be run back, and he closed the ports. The sailors were all armed with handguns and put in strategic positions to be used in resisting any attempted boarding. Men were also put in position to open the petcocks and sink the boat if she appeared likely to fall into enemy hands. Walke signaled the pilot, and the boat was cast loose to steam slowly down river, heading toward the mouth of the canal.

By now a storm was gathering, and the boat was little more than a dark shadow against the night, practically invisible as it moved downriver.

"Damn," Dan said, shortly after they got underway. "Listen to the noise this son-of-a-bitch is making. I never paid any attention to how loud these things were before. We might as well have a brass band on board."

"You're right," Walke said. "But I know how to take care of it. Phillips," he called to the pilot, a man who had plied the river as a civilian pilot for many years and was now offering his services to the Union. "Pull the flue-caps shut. That'll keep

Hearts Divided

the steam from puffing up through the stacks."

"Cap'n, that could be dangerous," the pilot replied.

"I hope you're not doing anything that might make the boiler explode," Dan put in quickly. He remembered his experience on the *Delta Star,* and the prospect was more frightening to him than the possibility of coming under Rebel cannons.

"No, nothing like that," Walke said. "The steam'll just vent through the cylinder ports; it won't build up an explosive pressure. But Phillips is right about being concerned, because the steam is the only way we have of keeping the soot wet. If the soot dries out, there could be a stack fire."

"There will be a stack fire, cap'n. I've seen it happen too many times," Phillips said.

"We've got to take that chance," Walke said. "Pull the caps shut."

The valves were pulled shut, and the puffing noise ceased almost immediately, so that the boat, in addition to being practically invisible, was now nearly noiseless as well.

"Here we are," Walke said quietly, as if even his voice could give them away. "The first Rebel position is right over that point. The gun they have there can throw a ball four miles."

Suddenly a sheet of flame, five feet high, shot up from the stack.

"Open the flue caps!" Walke shouted.

A rocket darted skyward from the riverbank.

"It's too late! They've seen us!" Walke shouted. His shout was followed by the explosions of heavy cannonading.

As if on cue, the storm which had been threatening broke. Streaks of lightning flashed through the sky, commingling the flashes and thunder of the heavens with the flashes and thunder of men.

Shrapnel from exploding shells crashed through the window of the pilothouse. One of the armed sailors let out a scream, then crumpled to the floor.

"What is that?" Phillips shouted during one of the lightning flashes. "Cap'n, there's an obstruction ahead!"

Dan strained to look through the broken window. Then he could see it too, a long, low-lying mass stretched across the river in front of them.

"It's a chain!" he shouted. "They've stretched a chain across the water!"

"Phillips, back down!" Walke shouted.

A cannon ball passed through the wheelhouse at that moment, not exploding but crashing through with a ripping, smashing sound. The ball cut right through Phillips. When Dan looked, he saw the macabre sight of the top half of a man hanging from the wheel, still holding on tightly, while the bottom half was torn away and flattened against the bulkheads on the other side of the wheelhouse.

"My God!" Dan said, fighting instant nausea. Walke moved quickly to take the wheel. "There's no time to reverse the engine," he shouted. "We're going to hit the chain!"

"Commander, try and hit one of the supporting floats," Dan yelled. "Maybe it'll give way there!"

Walke grabbed the wheel and spun it, heading them toward the nearest float. Seconds later the boat hit it with a jar which was great enough to pitch Dan against the front of the wheelhouse. He put his hand out to brace himself and was painfully cut by the jagged pieces of the remaining glass. The boat shuddered, then continued forward.

"We made it through!" Walke shouted happily.

The storm continued to vent its fury upon the river and combatants, but the fire from the shore batteries was no longer effective as the *Carondelet* passed into the mouth of the canal.

Once the *Carondelet* was through the canal, Walke fired a signal rocket, and the other gunboats of the fleet started through. From the deck of the *Carondelet,* Dan and the others watched anxiously, as the flashes of the batteries competed with the lightning to illuminate the night sky. Finally the first boat appeared, then the second, then another, until the entire fleet had made the passage.

By the break of dawn, in a still pouring rain, the defenders of Island Number Ten saw a ghost fleet materializing out of the swamp, steaming toward their island with all guns firing.

Chapter 21

AT THE HEIGHT of the cannonading, one of the guns burst on the island, killing three men and wounding four others. That left the commander of the artillery, Captain Jeremy Humes, with only seven working guns. He went to General MacKall to make a desperate plea to move some of the guns from the Tennessee side of the river onto the island.

"No," MacKall said. "I don't think that would be practical."

"But, general, with just a few more guns, I feel like we could hold the Yankees off indefinitely," Humes said. "Look what we're doing now with only eight. Seven, now that the *Belmont* is out of action."

MacKall put his hand affectionately on Captain Humes's shoulder. "Captain, you have done an admirable job here. You've stemmed the tide against impossible odds. But the truth is, this island is going to fall, despite all we can do to hold it. And when it does, we'll lose all materiel on it. It would be folly of me to bring more guns into a position where they are likely to fall into enemy hands."

"But, general, with a spirited defense the island need not fall at all," Humes protested.

"It is going to fall," MacKall said flatly. "But we have

accomplished our mission thus far. We have kept the Yankees bottled up here while Johnston and Beauregard have gathered their forces at Corinth. Now I'm off to join them with what remains here."

"You mean we are abandoning the island?" Humes asked.

"I'm leaving you in command, Captain Humes. You, and one battalion of artillery. I'll take every remaining unit, slip across to the Tennessee shore under cover of darkness, and try and make it to Johnston's position."

"I wish you luck, sir," Humes said.

"Jerry," General MacKall said, looking at the junior officer with deep, sad eyes. "I wish there was a way we could all get out of here. But I must ask you to stay and hold the enemy off for as long as possible, in order to give us the chance to get away. I'm asking a great deal of you, I know."

"We'll do the best we can, sir."

"I'm not asking for a stand till you die in defense of the island," MacKall said. "After we've slipped away, your conduct will be up to your own discretion. You may slip away if you feel you can ... or surrender, if need be."

"General, the boats are ready to take us ashore," a colonel called.

"Start the evacuation," MacKall ordered. He looked at Humes for a long moment, then shook his hand warmly. "Good luck, captain."

"Give my best to Pelham, will you?" Humes replied, smiling cheerfully. "He's with General Johnston."

"I'll do that," MacKall promised.

When Captain Humes returned to his batteries, his men started plying him with questions.

"Are we gettin' ready to skedaddle?" one of them asked.

"No, gentlemen, we are going to stay right here and make a fight of it," Humes said. Even as Humes spoke, another volley of shells arched in from the gunboats, which now invested the island from both sides.

"We're gonna stay here 'n fight? What the hell are we

gonna fight with?" another said. "Damn it, cap'n, there ain't but seven guns still firin'.' "Then double the rate of fire," Humes said. "That will make seven guns do the work of fourteen."

"We'll burst another breech," one of the men protested.

"Which gun is most likely to go?" Humes asked.

"The MacIntyre, in number three."

"Then I'll thumb the touchhole on the *MacIntyre* by myself," Humes said. "If the breech bursts, I'll be the only one hurt. Let's go, men, we've got some fighting to do."

Captain Humes's talk managed to instill a little spirit into his men, and they let out a cheer of defiance and returned to their guns. Though the rate of fire wasn't doubled, it was increased, and moments later they let out a lusty cheer as one of Foote's gunboats left the line, burning badly.

The increased rate of fire was enough to provide the cover General MacKall needed. He and his men slipped across the water to the Tennessee side, then started south and east to link up with Johnston.

Dan was still on board the *Carondelet* with Commander Walke and determined to stay with him until the island was completely silenced. Commodore Foote had assigned Walke the task of taking out the remaining Confederate batteries on the Tennessee shore. Dan stood behind the iron-plated shields as the guns boomed away, throwing shot and shell at the shore batteries. The shore batteries consisted of three sixty-four pound guns, standing half a mile apart, and they maintained a spirited contest for a couple of hours until they were finally silenced by the gunners on board the *Carondelet.*

"You want to go ashore and have a look around?" Walke asked, after the Confederate guns quit answering the fire.

"Sure," Dan replied, effecting a calm which he didn't feel. "We might as well."

Walke headed the boat into a sandbar and grounded the bow, so that a reconnaissance patrol could disembark. Dan, going ashore with the patrol, found the Rebel guns, two of which had been knocked out by fire from the *Carondelet* and one of which had been spiked by the retreating Confederates. The works were abandoned, though a few bodies had been left behind. One, a boy who couldn't have been over seventeen, sat in an upright position against the gun carriage, his arms by his side, his hands lying on the ground palms up, his mouth hanging slightly open and his eyes wide, as if staring accusing at the men who killed him. The sailors spoke in hushed tones around the body, as if the boy could hear them and would be disturbed by their conversation.

One cannon ball had chopped through a tree, and the tree was akimbo, leading to a great height at an angle that was easy to climb. Dan, on impulse, climbed it. From his position near the top, he could look far up and down the broad, amber-colored river. He could see the gunboats sailing in circles to either side of the island, firing as they came into position, and he could see the island returning the fire. The sounds of the cannons rolled across the flat space like thunder, and though he knew they were sending missiles of death, he was nevertheless thrilled by the sight.

Dan had turned to come back down the tree when he saw something that made him gasp. A large body of troops, the largest he had ever seen assembled in one place, were moving south and east. He looked closer and saw that they were Confederates!

Dan scrambled down the tree quickly. "Come on!" he shouted to the others. "We've got to get word to General Pope! The Rebels are getting away!"

The men ran back to the *Carondelet,* and Walke made a quick run across the river to New Madrid to communicate the news to General Pope.

"We've got 'em!" Pope said, hitting his fist into his hand. "Walke, General Paine's division is on board boats, ready to assault the island. Tell them to land on the other side of the river and go after the Rebs!"

"I'd like to go with General Paine, sir," Dan requested.

"Go ahead," Pope said. "You found them, you earned the right." Pope laughed. "I shall be anxious to see the headlines in the eastern papers after this engagement is concluded."

Dan left General Pope and returned quickly to the *Carondelet* with Walke. The *Carondelet* pushed back into the river and joined with the three transport boats which had on board General Paine's troops. There Dan transferred to the flag vessel, where he told Paine what he had seen and delivered General Pope's instructions.

Paine landed his division in two brigades, one commanded by Colonel Morgan, the other by Colonel Cummings. They passed by abandoned camps and artillery. Straggling prisoners were gathered up. Finally they came in sight of a detachment of enemy cavalry, but the cavalry fled without giving a fight. About nine miles from the landing, the two brigades, in a pincer movement, flanked the fleeing Confederate army, trapping them against the swamp. Now the Confederates had no way out, except through the Union army.

Confederate pickets brought news of the Federal position to General MacKall, just before midnight. MacKall was sitting on a log, wrapped in a blanket, fighting the effects of chills and fever. His troops had lit no fires, for fear of exposing their position, and had eaten no food since before leaving the island.

"What are we gonna do, general? Fight 'em?" his adjutant asked.

"What is their strength?" MacKall asked, shivering in the cold night air.

"I'd estimate two full divisions, maybe more," the adjutant replied. "They're fresh troops too, prob'ly just brought down from St. Louis in the last week or so. They look awful healthy."

"Look at our men," MacKall said. "Less than half of them are armed. Most have dysentery or some other ailment. We have no food, no ammunition, and the man who owns a pair of shoes is considered lucky," MacKall sighed. "We've but one recourse."

"I know, sir," the adjutant said.

"Tell the officers I have decided to sue for surrender."

"You tried your damnedest, general," the adjutant said.

But MacKall couldn't answer. He had hung his head, in shame and sorrow, to hide the tears which were now streaming down his face.

During that same night, thinking that by now General MacKall would have effected his evacuation, Captain Humes sent two men across the river in a boat, flying a white flag, offering to surrender the island and all that was on it.

General Pope was elated, and sent the following telegram to General Halleck:

"General, yours to report that on the night of the 2nd, instant, I have succeeded in opening the Mississippi River all the way to Memphis and Fort Pillow. The spoils of my campaign include one general, two hundred and seventy- three field and company officers, six thousand seven hundred privates, one hundred and twenty-three pieces of heavy artillery, thirty-five pieces of field artillery, all of the very best character and of the latest patterns, seven thousand stand of small arms, tents for twelve thousand men, several wharf-boatloads of provisions, an immense quantity of ammunition of all kinds, many hundred horses and mules with wagons and harness, six steamboats, including officers, crew, laborers and employees."

General Pope was most generous in his appraisal of the spoils, as most of the materiel and many of the prisoners he mentioned had actually been in possession of the Union army for as much as six months previous, and some of it had been captured by General Grant in earlier campaigns. In fact, General Paine had taken eleven hundred prisoners when he captured General MacKall, many of them unarmed. On the island with Captain Humes there were sixteen officers and non-commissioned officers, and three hundred and sixty-eight privates. These nineteen hundred men had kept General Pope's army of fifteen thousand tied up for three months, while much of the Confederate army in the area had slipped away, like quicksilver, to join General Johnston and Beauregard along the Tennessee- Mississippi border. The two nations then turned their eyes toward a small log-house church known as Shiloh,

Chapter 22

GENERAL BRAXTON BRAGG, with ten thousand battle-proven veterans, reported to General Johnston at Corinth. Bragg's men, joining those who had managed escape from Island Number Ten before the escape route was cut off, thus swelled the Confederate forces at Corinth. The governors of the Confederate states were called upon to recruit new men, and they added still more to the numbers. Then General Beauregard made a personal appeal for volunteers, and as a result of his efforts the army at Corinth grew larger still.

General Johnston inspected this growing army and discovered that if all the soldiers detailed as cooks and teamsters were relieved of these duties, he could muster yet another brigade of effective men, so he sent messengers through the surrounding country urging citizens to provide their Negroes as cooks and teamsters for sixty days. Unfortunately, the messengers returned with the answer that though the planters would freely give their last son, they wouldn't part with a Negro or a mule.

Despite General Johnston's failure to recruit blacks, he still had an effective army of more than forty thousand men. They were poised, ready to strike at the Union army at the moment he gave the word.

Twenty-three miles away, General Grant was also assembling an army. Grant had nearly as many effectives as General Johnston. In addition, only ninety miles away and coming to join him, was General Buell with his army of the Ohio . . . another forty thousand men. News of Buell's advance was provided to Johnston on the night of April third, and he called an emergency war council of his Generals Beauregard, Bragg, Polk, Hardee and Breckenridge.

"Gentlemen," Johnston said when he had them assembled. "While I have guarded against an uncertain offensive, I am now of the opinion that we should entice the enemy into an engagement as soon as possible, before he can further increase his numbers."

"General, I think we should strike at Pittsburgh Landing right now, while the Yankees are landing. They haven't built any fortifications. My scouts tell me they've set up tents like they were on parade," General Bragg said.

"I'm opposed to that," Beauregard put in. "I would prefer the defensive-offensive; that is, we should take up a position that would compel the enemy to develop his intentions, to attack us. Then, when he is within striking distance of us, we should take the offensive and crush him, cutting him off, if possible, from his base of operations at the river."

The others made their comments as well, and finally Johnston held up his hand to quiet them.

"Well, then, we've all had our say, but as I am in command here, gentlemen, the ultimate responsibility rests with me. I feel that it is imperative to strike now, before the enemy's rear gets up from Nashville. We have him divided. We should keep him so if we can."

Johnston's word was final, so there was no further discussion on that subject. The discussion then turned to the plan of battle, and in this, Johnston decided to form the army into three parallel lines, the distance between the lines to be one thousand yards. Hardee's corps was to form the first line,

Bragg's the second. The third would be composed of Polk on the left and Breckenridge on the right.

"Gentlemen, I propose that you have your elements in position by seven o'clock Saturday morning, and we shall begin the attack at eight. Now, as I know you will have staff meetings to conduct, I shall let you return to your units." The corps commanders saluted, then climbed on their horses to return to their positions. Only Beauregard, who was second in command and had no specific corps, remained with Johnston.

Johnston remained seated for a long time, with his head hung, as if praying. Beauregard didn't speak during that time, and the only sound was the popping and snapping of the wood burning in the room's small pot-bellied stove. A pot of coffee sat on the stove, and after a few minutes General Beauregard poured two cups, setting one of them in front of Johnston and taking the other himself.

"Thank you," Johnston said. He sucked the coffee noisily through extended lips. "Gus, I've drunk coffee around hundreds of fires in dozens of campaigns, but I tell you now, this will be my last."

"What do you mean?"

"I fear I will not survive the battle which is coming."

General Beauregard tried to dismiss Johnston's statement with a light laugh. "Sid, every man, be he general or private, feels fear before a battle."

"You don't understand," Johnston said. "I am not afraid. I am certain that I shall be killed, and with that certainty has come a sort of peace. I can't explain it to you, Gus. It's something you must feel, though you can't feel it until you are facing the same situation."

"But you can't know with a certainty," Beauregard argued. "The hour of death is known to no man."

"Until it is upon you, Gus, then you know. Then you know," he said again, quietly, as if talking to himself. He took another drink of his coffee. As Beauregard could perceive that Johnston wanted to be alone with his thoughts, he made an excuse to check on the disposition of the pickets and left the Confederates' commanding general in the small log cabin which was his headquarters.

As he stepped outside, Beauregard saw his nephew Blackie approaching. Blackie swung down off his horse and hailed his uncle.

"General Bragg has just informed us that we will be going on the attack Saturday morning. Is that true, uncle?"

"Yes."

"Uncle, give me a division to command," Blackie said.

"I can't just give you a division," Beauregard said. "To do so would mean that another commander would be deprived. It would be unthinkable."

"You could create a new division," Blackie implored. "I have my own Second Mississippi Horse. Detach two more regiments from two other divisions and you can create one new division. Uncle, it is only right. I was passed over at Island Number Ten. MacKall was made general over me."

"Is that why you abandoned Island Ten?" Beauregard asked sharply.

"I abandoned it because I felt I would be of more value here. And it is well I did, for General MacKall and his entire force is now in an enemy prison camp. I, on the other hand, am here."

General Beauregard looked at Blackie for a moment, then sighed. "Very well," he said. "Inform General Bragg that you're to be attached to his corps. You will have your division, Blackie, but God have mercy on you if you dishonor the family name a second time."

"I am to be a general?" Blackie asked, hopefully.

"No. That I will not do. You'll have your division, but you'll lead it as a colonel. If you are successful, then, perhaps, you'll be made a general."

"I shall be successful," Blackie said. He returned to his horse, then looked back toward his uncle just before mounting. "You won't regret this, uncle."

"I regret it already," Beauregard muttered under his breath.

Blackie let out a whoop of excitement and slapped his legs against his horse, riding off through the woods. General Beauregard let out a sigh of resignation, then walked over to his tent to write out the necessary orders, transferring two new regiments to Blackie's 'division.'

"What are you doing, father?" Liberty asked, as she saw him packing a haversack.

"My regiment is taking to the field," Colonel Welles replied.

"What? No, General Beauregard himself told me that your regiment would be held in reserve."

"I know, and I was resigned to that," Colonel Welles said. His eyes were sparkling in excitement. "But now I'm to get a field command. I'll be part of a new division, assigned to General Bragg's corps."

"I'm going to talk to General Beauregard," Liberty said, starting for her coat. "I'll get this changed."

"No, daughter, you are not," Colonel Welles said quickly.

"Father, you are much too old for this. Please, send your executive officer."

"Liberty, what sort of man would I be if I did that?" Colonel Welles asked.

"You'd be alive," Liberty replied.

"Life without honor is no life at all."

"Honor," Liberty said bitterly. "I wish I had never heard the word. Doing the honorable thing has brought me nothing but pain. I would do many things differently if I could do them over, father, and the very first thing I would do would be to redefine the word honor. Now, please, I beg of you, let your executive officer go in your stead, and you remain behind."

"Liberty, I'm going to the field, and that is all there is to it," Colonel Welles said. He looked at his haversack. "I believe that is about all. . . . Oh, the gloves your mother knitted for me that last year before she died. Where are they?" "They're in your overcoat pocket, father," Liberty said. Tears started welling to her eyes. "Is there no way I can talk you out of this?"

"Absolutely no way at all," Colonel Welles said. He smiled. "But cheer up, Liberty. I shall be with one of your old friends."

"Who?"

"Colonel Blackie Beauregard. He is to be the commander of the new division."

Liberty said coldly, "I do not number Blackie Beauregard among my friends."

Colonel Welles looked at her and frowned. "Well, no matter," he said then, shrugging, "This is something which must be done, and I shall do it, daughter, with or without your blessing." He walked over to Liberty and kissed her lightly on the lips. "We begin our march tonight. Take care."

Liberty stood quietly after her father left, fighting back her stinging tears. Her father was sixty years old. Thus far his age had kept him out of the war except for the most perfunctory of duties. He had wanted to participate, and to that end he had raised and equipped a regiment from his own resources.

But the regiment was a home guard regiment, composed in the main of old men and young boys, part-time soldiers whose dreams of glory had been satisfied by the weekly drill meetings. It had never dawned on Liberty that the regiment might really be called to battle.

Blackie, she thought. Surely he doesn't know about her father's regiment. If he knew it was composed of old men and young boys, he would want to leave it behind.

Liberty hurried to get her coat. If they were marching out tonight, she would have to see Blackie quickly, before it was too late.

When she reached the road that passed in front of her house, she was overwhelmed by the sight that greeted her. It was as if the road itself had come alive, rising into one great gray mass, flowing inexorably north. Company after company of men marched by, like giant centipedes. Sometimes there would be a subdued flash of silver, as their bayonets, sticking up like picket-fence posts, caught an errant moonbeam. Their equipment made small, jangling sounds, and their feet rustled against the dirt road like a heavy brushing on cloth.

Occasionally Liberty would hear the sound of rapid hooves coming up the road, and the moving columns of men would give way as an artillery battery rushed by—the caisson wheels spinning rapidly and rooster-tails of dust all but obscuring the cannon, which pointed back down the road, silent now but wicked-looking nonetheless.

Liberty stepped on the road just as one such cannon rushed by. She heard it barely in time to leap back and thus avoid being struck by it.

A soldier from the ranks called to her. "Miss, them cannoneers don't stop for nothin' or nobody. I done seen 'em run down folks. You'd best mind your way there."

"Who are you with?" Liberty called.

"We're with Whitman's brigade."

"Is this General Bragg's corps?"

"No'm. We'uns is with Hardee. Bragg's corps, hit'll be back down the road a mite." "Thank you," Liberty replied, and she started back against the mainstream of soldiers.

She'd walked, less than half a mile when she saw several men sitting and standing on both sides of the road. There were a few low-voiced comments about a lady being here, at night, but she closed her ears to them. Then, seeing an officer, she inquired if this was Bragg's corps.

"Yes'm," the young lieutenant answered. He tipped his hat. "Can I help you, ma'am?"

"I'm looking for Beauregard's division." "Beauregard? Ma'am, he ain't got no division. He's second only to Johnston for the whole danged army."

"I think she means Colonel Beauregard," a captain said, walking over to join them. "I just heard that we had a new division join us, and it is to be commanded by Colonel Blackie

Beauregard. Would that be it, ma'am?"

"Yes," Liberty said. "Could you tell me where to find Colonel Beauregard?"

The captain pointed into the woods. "I figure he'll be no more'n five hundred yards that way," he said.

Liberty thanked him, then started into the woods.

"Ma'am, there's likely to be Yankee patrols operatin' in these parts," the captain said. "You'd best stay out of the woods."

"I was raised in these woods, captain," Liberty called back over her shoulder. "I'll be all right."

Though she had indeed been raised in the neighborhood, Liberty had not often been in the woods at night, and she found passage exceedingly difficult. The briars formed barriers and the tree limbs reached out to hold her back. The sounds of the moving army grew muffled and distorted. Though she was less than two hundred yards from the main road and no more than a mile from her house, she felt as if she could have been a thousand miles away.

The briars tore at her clothes, pulled at her hair, and slapped her in the face. Her breath started coming in ragged gasps. Then the ground fell off into steep ravines and wide creeks, throwing still more obstacles in her way. But still she went on.

"Well, Angus, what do we have here?" a voice suddenly asked.

Liberty stopped short, feeling a quick chill rim through her. "Who's there?" she asked.

"Naw, lady, you tell us who's there?" the voice replied from the dark.

Liberty looked toward the sound of the voice, but she could see nothing. "I'm looking for Beauregard's division," she said.

"So are we, lady," the voice answered dryly. There was the sound of branches and twigs breaking as whoever owned the voice started walking toward her. A second later, three men stepped out of the woods, all holding pistols. One of them smiled broadly. "Fact is, we're lookin' for the whole damned Rebel army, so's we can carry a report back to Gen'rul Prentiss."

"You're . . . you're *Yankees!*" Liberty said, gasping in recognition.

"Yep, we are," the smiling soldier said. "And you must be what they call a 'southern belle.' "

"What. . . what are you doing here?" Liberty asked. She felt a quick fear growing inside, not merely because they were Union soldiers, but because she sensed in them an even greater danger.

"Angus, you've been down south. Is them southern belles as good in bed as they say they are?"

"I don t know," the soldier named Angus answered. "I never had me no chance ter try one of 'em out."

"Well, grab aholt of this one," the smiling soldier said, unbuckling his belt. "We'll all try it."

Liberty opened her mouth to scream, but no sooner had she done so than it was stuffed with a foul-smelling, awful-tasting rag. "This'll just keep you from screamin' out when you starts enjoyin' it," Angus said.

Liberty felt her dress being pulled off her, and a moment later, she was thrown down onto a bed of wet leaves. They felt cold and clammy on her skin, but concern over the leaves quickly faded away when the grinning soldier descended over her.

His brutal entry into her brought excruciating pain. Somewhere in the recesses of Liberty's mind, she wondered how this same activity could be so pleasurable under the right circumstances, and so painful under the wrong. She cried out under his assault, but the rag muffled her scream so that it came out as a small, squeaking noise.

"Listen to her squeal," Angus said. "Hell, she's likin' it."

"All these Rebel women likes it," the other soldier who,

along with Angus, was holding her, said. "They's all whores, the lot of 'em."

The first soldier finished with her. Liberty felt his semen running down her thigh. But there was no respite, for Angus was next, grunting and breathing heavily until he, too, was finished. Then he and the smiling soldier held her for the third. Mercifully, before the third had finished with her, Liberty passed out, and when she came to, how much later she didn't know, the three soldiers were gone.

She stood up, fighting the bile of nausea which tore at her throat. Her body was battered, and her mind assaulted, but she knew that if she let herself go, she would scream herself into insensibility. Slowly, deliberately, she got dressed. The dress was torn in several places, but, thankfully, it was basically in one piece and, with her cloak pulled around her, it was almost undiscernable.

Liberty pulled herself together. She would not let this stop her. She would see Blackie Beauregard, and she would beg him to release her father from the battle. If he wouldn't do it, then she would go to General Bragg, and if she got little satisfaction there, she would go to General Beauregard, or Johnston himself if need be.

After she finished making what repairs she could on the dress, Liberty continued on her quest. She reached the place where Colonel Blackie Beauregard had been, only to discover from the handful of rear echelon soldiers that Beauregard's division, along with Bragg's entire corps, had already moved out.

"I'm not defeated," Liberty said aloud. "I'll follow them into the line of battle if need be." With determination and courage, Liberty returned to Trailback, there to prepare for the trip up to the front lines. Whatever it took to get her father out of there, she would do.

Chapter 23

"WATCH YOUR HEAD, cap'n, caisson comin' down!" a gruff voice shouted. Dan looked up to see the caisson being swung off the steamer with a rope and tackle. He ducked, then watched it move over to willing hands on shore.

Dan had just arrived at Pittsburgh Landing. He'd made the trip from Island Number Ten in just two days. It was the night of April fourth, and though the air was cool, it was not brutally cold, a fair departure from the month of privation he had put up with at New Madrid.

"Lieutenant," Dan called to one of the officers supervising the unloading of the steamer.

"Yes, sir."

"Where can I find General Grant?"

"Captain, his headquarters is up at Savannah," the lieutenant said. "But he's been spending every day down here, and far into the night as well. Like as not, he's around somewhere."

"Thanks," Dan replied, and he started through the hustle and bustle of the troops to look for the short, bewhiskered commander.

Everywhere Dan looked there was activity, and the sight of so many men and so much materiel was a thrilling one. But, and this nagged at him a little, it was also a frightening sight, for he saw no signs of defense. Few men that he saw were even carrying arms. Rifles were stacked. Even the cannons which were being unloaded had not yet been assembled. Dan couldn't help but think what a fine target they would make should the rebels decide to launch an attack.

He climbed up the rather steep riverbank and saw what appeared to be a thousand campfires scattered out through the fields and hills, stretching nearly as far as the eye could see. Now he breathed easier, for who could dare attack an army this large, this grand?

There, not fifty feet in front of him, Dan saw General Grant. The general was sitting on a fallen tree trunk, listening to the reports of a couple of cavalry officers. Dan started toward them.

"Well, Captain O'Lee," Grant said, smiling at his approach. "It's good to see you here."

"It's good to be here, general," Dan said, pleased that Grant had recognized him so quickly.

"Gentlemen," General Grant said to the two officers who were with him, "this is Captain Dan O'Lee. Regardless of what you might hear from General Pope or Commodore Foote, this man is the true hero of Island Number Ten."

"I'd hardly say that, sir," Dan said, laughing self-consciously under the unexpected praise.

"But I would say it," Grant replied. "I believe that that canal you dug is going to go down as one of the engineering feats of genius of this or any other war. Our great grandchildren will tell of it," he added. "I just wish I had assigned you to General Buell."

"General Buell?"

"Yes," Grant said. "It has taken his engineers twelve days to build just one bridge. Twelve days he's been sitting up there, ninety miles from this very spot, waiting to ford one river. God's whiskers, I never saw a slower or more cautious man in my life! He should have been here by now."

"Are we badly exposed here, sir?" Dan asked. Grant smiled. "Exposed? Of course we are exposed. But I have scarcely the faintest idea of a general attack being made upon us. No, I think they'll be spending their time erecting defenses around Corinth, and while they are occupied doing that, we'll be growing stronger and stronger."

"What is the size of the Confederate army now?" Dan asked.

"Who can say?" Grant replied. "We've had estimates of everything from twenty thousand to seventy thousand. These gentlemen have just returned from a scouting expedition and are in the process of giving me a report. This is Colonel Morris and Colonel Thomas." Grant pointed to the two officers. They were both younger than Dan, and Dan was struck with the fact that both were lieutenant colonels. They had obviously proven their worth in battles before now, to have obtained so high a rank at such a young age.

"General," Colonel Morris said, "I ranged nearly nine miles, and I encountered a pretty large body of cavalry. We skirmished somewhat, killed a few of them, and lost two of our own. They broke off after about half an hour."

"How large a body was it?" Grant asked.

"I'd say battalion size," Colonel Morris said. "I'd agree, sir," Colonel Thomas put in. "And maybe even regimental size, as they had a battery of artillery with them."

"Any infantry?"

"None that we could see."

"Hmm," Grant mused. "I'd say it was just a nuisance raid. More than likely they were going to unlimber the artillery pieces, throw a little iron our way just to keep us on our toes, then skedaddle on back to Corinth. Nevertheless, advise Generals Sherman and McClemand to be especially watchful."

"Yes, sir," the two colonels said as one, and they rendered a sharp salute before retiring.

Grant returned the salute almost halfheartedly, as if

bemused by the whole thing. After they left, Grant pointed to the tree trunk.

"Have a seat," he invited. "Are you hungry? I have some hardtack and jerky here."

"No, sir," Dan said. "I had supper on the boat."

"You don't mind if I have a bite?" Grant asked. He opened his haversack. As he rummaged through it, Dan saw the unmistakable glint of a bottle of whiskey.

"Maybe you'd like a little drink instead?" Grant offered, making no effort to hide the bottle but handing it directly to Dan.

"Don't mind if I do," Dan said. He uncapped the bottle, turned it up for a generous drink, then returned the bottle to Grant. Grant held it up and examined the remaining liquid. "Not much sense in saving that," he said offhandedly, and he turned the bottle up, draining the rest in one long draught. When he finished he wiped his mouth with the back of his hand, then tossed the bottle aside. Dan heard it break with a tinny crash.

"I'm technically in command of Buell," Grant said, bringing that general's name up again. Dan could see from Grant's behavior that Buell was more or less steadily on his mind. "But he's been senior to me until just a couple of weeks ago, and to tell the truth, I'm a little hesitant to make an issue of it. But here it is, the fourth of April, and he was supposed to be here no later than the twenty-fifth of March. If he hasn't shown by the morning of the sixth, I want you, personally, to go up there and take charge of that outfit he calls his engineers. I want you to get them across that damned river."

"Yes, sir," Dan said.

"You know what the problem is, don't you?"

"No, sir."

"Halleck is supposed to arrive next week to take overall command. I think Buell wants to wait for that moment, rather than put his army under my command. I've still got a cloud over my name. Halleck even relieved me once, did you know that?" Grant asked.

Dan did know of it, but he knew that Grant wanted to talk, needed someone to hear him out, so he said nothing.

"Halleck sits up there in the Federal Building in St. Louis, giving fancy dinner parties and entertaining politicians, and he gets upset if I don't tell him everytime I blow my nose. Then he got the idea that I left my command without proper authority, and he decided to relieve me. So he relieved me and appointed General Smith in my stead. Within a week Smith had so botched up everything that Halleck gave me my job back. Politics, captain. I hate politics."

"General, the steamer is ready to return to Savannah," someone said, coming upon the two men.

"Thank you," Grant replied. He stood up, brushed the back of his pants, and smiled. "One of your duties, captain, is not to pay too much attention to what I say at times like this. It's just like a safety valve on a steam engine. I need to let a little of it out every now and then."

"I understand, general," Dan said.

"I thought you would, captain, or I would have never said a word. Oh, find yourself a billet down here somewhere, would you? I think it would be good for me to have someone from my staff stay here all the time."

"Yes, sir," Dan said.

After General Grant left, Dan stopped a passing soldier.

"Where can I find your commanding officer, soldier?"

"He's got him a tent pitched just t'other side o' that ridge, sir," the soldier said.

"What's his name?"

"Savage, sir. Cap'n Bill Savage."

Savage, Dan thought. That's a good name for a warrior, but he hoped it didn't fit the captain's personality, because if there was room for him, he intended to throw his bedroll in with him for the night.

Dan finally reached the tent, then called from outside. Savage? Captain Savage?

"Yes," the voice answered from the dark interior of the tent.

"I'm Captain Dan O'Lee of General Grant's staff. I need a place to throw my roll for the night. Can I come in with you?"

There was a long pause. Finally a muffled voice answered. "Yes. Throw it over in the corner."

Dan opened the tent flap and stepped inside. It was pitch-black. "Do you mind if I light a candle?" he asked.

"You can't throw a bedroll in the dark?"

"Well, I suppose so, but . . ."

"Then do it," the voice answered. "I have an early patrol."

There was something about the voice-which Dan found intriguingly familiar. But he couldn't quite put his finger on it.

"Do I know you, Savage?" he asked hesitantly?

"Who'd you say you were?"

"O'Lee. Dan O'Lee."

"I never heard of you," Savage said. The voice, coming from down in the sleeping bag, seemed even more muffled than before. "Will you for chrissake shut up and let me get a little sleep?"

"Sure," Dan said. "I'm sorry I disturbed you."

In her sleeping bag, Tamara scarcely dared to breathe. Of all the luck! To have Dan O'Lee, of all the men in Grant's command, come into her tent! Fortunately it was pitch-black, and she would be leaving before first light. She would have to be on guard now, for she knew he would recognize her the moment he saw her. Tamara would just have to make sure that Dan O'Lee never got a good look at Captain Bill Savage.

Chapter 24

THE NIGHT PASSED slowly, almost reluctantly from the earth. When the darkness lifted, the slanting bars of morning sunlight revealed an army of gray, stretched out in a line three miles long. The line was composed of soldiers who made up the corps of Hardee, Bragg, Polk and Breckenridge, and the soldier who had been bloodied in previous battles stood side by side with the man who but two weeks earlier held not a musket but a plow.

"Now, listen to me, men," one senior officer was saying, marching back and forth behind the line. "When you aim, aim low. You do nobody any good by getting in so much of a hurry that you discharge your weapon into the trees."

"And you greenuns, be suren prime the pan," one old veteran called, and the other veterans guffawed. Truth was, there were few of them who had not, in the heat of battle and pitch of excitement, poured in powder, wad, and shell, then snapped the trigger uselessly against a firing pan which was not primed, and thus would not discharge.

"Don't get afraid," the senior officer went on. "Just keep it in mind that there's more than forty thousand of us. Forty thousand brave and true, and there's no army in the world that can stand up against us."

The soldiers were growing restless now. Why didn't the generals begin the attack? They had been in battle line since before sunup, and now the sun was rising higher. Didn't the generals know that the more time you had to think about it, the harder it became? There were a few with watches, and they passed the word down the line that it was nearly eight o'clock.

"Eight o'clock is when our attack begins," one of the soldiers said. "I heard the officers talkin' about it."

The soldier's rumor spread through the line. As the seconds ticked off toward eight, nervous hands began to squeeze the muskets, and itching fingers to caress the triggers, waiting for the word to move out.

"Why doesn't it come?" the soldiers asked, over and over again. "Don't them damn generals know that the hardest thing is the wait- m?

"Yeah," another would answer, and then, as if he had just made the observation for the first time: "Don't they know that the hardest part is the waitin'?"

The same question was asked many more times by many more soldiers, each certain that he was expressing an original thought. Slowly, relentlessly, the time passed until the magic hour of eight came and went, and the sun clicked higher in the eastern sky. But, still the long gray lines waited, and now it was nearly nine. As yet, no order to attack had come.

Five hundred yards behind the line, General Johnston was holding a meeting in an open space beneath some trees. There were ten or twelve generals present, and they listened as Beauregard addressed them. He walked about gesticulating rapidly, jerking out his sentences. General Johnston stood apart from the rest, with his tall, straight form standing out like a specter against the sky. The illusion was sustained by the military cloak which he held folded around him. Finally he walked to the middle of the group and spoke.

"Gentlemen, I fear we have now lost the advantage. We were unable to launch our attack on schedule, because of a misunderstanding." "Misunderstanding?" Beauregard said. "It is more than a misunderstanding, general, it is pure dereliction of duty. And I hold myself responsible for it, as I was the fool who gave him the division."

"What is the difficulty?" Breckinridge asked, arriving at that moment. "Why have we not begun the attack? My men are growing nervous.

"We have a large gap in the line," one of the other generals explained. "Colonel Beauregard's division didn't arrive on time."

"Well, how late were they?"

The general who had explained the difficulty coughed, then looked up at General Beauregard. "Actually, he's not there yet," the general said.

"Gus, see here, what's this all about?" Breckinridge asked.

"Believe me, I wish I knew," General Beauregard answered. "But I shall relieve him immediately he shows up."

"No," General Johnston said. "I feel you are being too harsh on him because he is a kinsman. Would you similarly relieve any other officer, without giving him a chance to present his reason?"

"General, as he is assigned to my corps, I feel I should come to his defense," General Bragg said.

"What defense can there be? By his failure to carry out his command he has cost us many precious hours," Beauregard said.

"Be fair," Bragg interceded. "After all, he was only given the command two days ago, and it is at best a bastard element, never before on the march. Believe me, we experienced some difficulty in getting into line on time with seasoned troops."

"General Bragg is right," Johnston said. "There is, no doubt, a very good reason for your nephew's tardiness. At any rate, it will do no good to remorse over it now. We must make new plans."

"I say we go ahead and hit them," Bragg said.

"Without Beauregard's division?" Breckinridge replied. "That will leave my flank unprotected."

"I think we have completely lost the opportunity to strike today," General Polk said. "We must wait, and strike at dawn tomorrow."

"The Bishop is right," General Johnston said, referring to the fact that General Leonodis Polk was a Bishop of the Episcopal Church. "We have only one recourse now, and that is to reschedule our attack for tomorrow."

"General Johnston, that will give Buell twenty-four hours more to close ranks with Grant," Beauregard argued.

"We have no choice," Johnston said. "We've lost the element of surprise we could have realized by hitting them early this morning. We can only wait and regain it at dawn tomorrow."

"We could also return to Corinth and move into our fortifications there," Beauregard suggested.

"No," Johnston said. "We must hit them while we still have something close to numerical parity. Gentlemen, return to your units. Put them into bivouac, and prepare them for an attack at dawn tomorrow. Oh, and light no campfires tonight. I don't want to alert the Yankees that we are this close, in this great a number."

"What about Beauregard's division?" Bragg asked.

"If Colonel Beauregard hasn't shown up by six o'clock tonight, replace his position on the line with a brigade from Polk's reserves."

"Replace an entire division with a brigade?" Bragg asked, astonished.

"I'll give you my best brigade," Polk offered. "They're proven men, and that should more than make up for an untested division."

"You have a point," Bragg agreed.

General Johnston returned the salute of the assembled generals, then walked over to stand alone, beneath a tree. The bars of sunlight, much higher now, cut through the limbs to highlight the general in a single spot. It gave him the appearance of standing in a cathedral, washed in some holy light

Beauregard looked at him for a moment, then walked out onto a small hill to gaze back down the Corinth road. Where was his nephew?

"Colonel, I'm sure it wasn't anything more than an advanced patrol," a colonel was saying.

His name was Kelly, and he was commanding officer of the First Alabama volunteers. It had been Kelly's regiment, along with Colonel Welles' home guards, which had helped to form Beauregard's new division. Unlike Welles' group, Kelly's regiment had seen action. More action even than the Second Mississippi Horse.

"Suppose it wasn't merely a patrol?" Blackie Beauregard said. "Suppose it was a reconnaissance in force? Or suppose it is the advance element of the Yankee positions?"

"We know it couldn't be that," Colonel Kelly said. "We've had patrols through this whole area every day for a month. There's no way the Yankees could have adjusted their lines that far without our knowing."

"But if they have and we blunder into them, then we would be chewed to pieces," Blackie mused. "How would that be, our one division launching an attack against the entire Yankee army?"

"We could move in column," Colonel Kelly suggested. "If we encounter stiff resistance, we could pull back to the tree line and send for help."

"No," Blackie said. He rubbed his hands together nervously, then pulled on his Vandyke beard. "Let's fall into fortified positions here, then I'll send out scouts."

"There are no fortified positions here, colonel," Kelly explained patiently.

"Then have the men dig them," Blackie ordered.

"But, colonel, that would take hours. We couldn't possibly make it to the line of attack in time."

"Mind my orders, colonel," Blackie said sharply. "I'll not lead my division one more step, unless I know where the hell

I'm going!" "Yes, sir," Kelly said dejectedly. He started back to his regiment.

"Colonel Kelly may have a point, Blackie," Colonel Welles said. "After all, he's fought the Yankees before."

"I'm not exactly a green soldier myself," Blackie snapped. "I have a few campaigns under my belt. And I led my men through the Reelfoot Swamp, while being pursued by the whole of Pope's army."

"I'm not questioning your experience or your ability," Colonel Welles said hastily. "Heaven knows, I can't offer any of my own. I was just hoping to be of some use as a mediator."

"There's no mediating to be done," Blackie said simply. "I'm the commander, and that's that. Now, you get back to your regiment and tell them to dig in. After we've prepared for a possible Yankee attack, we'll send out a scouting party."

Blackie took out a pair of field glasses and climbed up on a large rock. He looked north, searching the tree lines for any telltale sign of the enemy, but he saw nothing. The fact that he saw nothing didn't mean they weren't there, he knew. He had learned from his experience at New Madrid. They could be right out there, and he'd never know it unless he looked for them.

Blackie did look for them, sending out three separate patrols and getting an all-clear report from each, before he regrouped his men on the road and continued his march toward the position he was supposed to occupy. He finally arrived at three o'clock in the afternoon, seven hours late.

"Where have you been?" General Bragg asked, not raising his voice, though showing his displeasure in his eyes.

"We encountered a Yankee reconnaissance in force," Blackie said. "I was afraid that to fight my way through would compromise the element of surprise General Johnston is trying to achieve."

"Colonel, there have been daily skirmishes for weeks," Bragg pointed out. "One more skirmish wouldn't have caused any problem."

"Perhaps you're right, sir," Blackie said. "I desperately wanted to engage them, but I felt to do so would have been construed as an act of glory-seeking, perhaps at the expense of the overall objective. It was a command decision I was forced into making. If I erred, I'm sorry."

General Bragg sighed. "Well, who knows?" he said. "You were in the best position to make the determination."

"Is the attack still on?"

"It is set for dawn tomorrow morning," Bragg said. "Cook all your rations during the daylight hours, using small campfires only. There will be no fires tonight."

"Yes, sir," Blackie replied.

"You'd better give your men some rest. Tomorrow will likely be a very long day," Bragg said.

"Tomorrow will be a day of glory, the likes of which the South has never seen," Blackie said.

"Save your speeches for your men, colonel," Bragg said dryly. "I know better."

"Captain Savage to see General Prentiss," Tamara said, swinging off her horse in front of General Prentiss's tent.

The adjutant showed Tamara in, and she looked at Prentiss. He was a veteran of the Mexican War and wore a sash which had been worn by General Hardin, his slain commander in that war. Prentiss was a politician turned general. He had been an unsuccessful candidate for Congress from the fifth district of Illinois. It was his hope that an inspiring military record would promote his post-war political ambitions.

"General, I think the Confederates may be planning to launch an all-out attack," Tamara reported.

"What gives you that opinion, Savage?"

"I led a patrol this morning, and I encountered a large group of them moving up Corinth road."

"We've had demonstrations on that road for nearly a

month," Prentiss said.

"This wasn't a demonstration, general. This was a march. I believe they were coming up to prepare for an attack."

Prentiss laughed. "Captain Savage, General Grant doesn't believe there will be an attack, General McClemand doesn't believe there will be an attack, General Sherman doesn't believe there will be an attack, and I don't believe there will be an attack. Now we can hardly change the entire conduct of this operation, merely because you have been frightened by the sight of a few of the enemy, can we?"

"No, sir," Tamara said. "But I don't believe any of you gentlemen have had the view I had." General Prentiss tore off a sheet of paper from a note pad and scribbled on it.

"Here," he said. "If this will make you feel any better, I've written a note to General Grant, telling him that one of my patrols spotted Rebel troops marching *en masse* up Corinth road. If there is a significance to that, I'm sure he will see it. Will that satisfy you?"

"Yes, sir," Tamara said.

"Give this note to Captain O'Lee."

"Give it to whom, sir?" Tamara asked, drawing a quick breath of surprise.

"Dan O'Lee. He's a captain on General Grant's staff. He's a tall, sandy-haired man, clean-shaven, about thirty or so. Ask around, someone will show him to you."

"Very good, sir, I shall," Tamara said.

She saluted General Prentiss, then stepped back outside the tent. So, now she was between the rock and the hard place. She wanted General Grant to have this message, but the only way she had of getting it to him was through Dan O'Lee. And if Dan saw her, he would recognize her, and she would be taken from the field before the battle even commenced.

Tamara thought about it for a long time. If she did give the note to Dan, and Prentiss was right and she was just overreacting, she would have compromised her identity for no good reason. On the other hand, if she was right, then General

Grant could at least prepare for an attack. But, as a general, wouldn't he have made preparations for the attack anyway? Not that she could see, she decided. But then, how did she know? After all, she was an amateur at this business. Grant, Sherman, McClemand, Prentiss . . . they were the experts. They certainly knew of the possibility, and yet they weren't concerned. So why should she be? And most of all, why should she expose herself just to give voice to that concern?

Tamara wadded the note into a tight ball and tossed it into Lick Creek, a stream which ran nearby. It floated a little ways downstream, became sodden, then sunk to the bottom. Tamara squared her shoulders and returned to her company, determined to avoid being exposed at all costs.

Chapter 25

THE CONFEDERATE ARMY was bivouacked in position to launch their attack early the next morning. They were stretched from Owl Creek on their extreme left to Lick Creek on the extreme right, in three parallel lines of battle, with General Breckenridge's corps poised at the center rear, ready to supply reinforcements wherever needed.

Though most of the army was in line, the necessary train of supplies was still in motion up the Corinth Road, and as Liberty moved toward the front, she was able to find General Johnston's headquarters simply by asking directions of the teamsters. She reached the area of General Johnston's encampment at about two o'clock in the afternoon. She approached silently, waiting for the opportunity to speak with Johnston or Beauregard regarding her father's regiment.

"Where is General Buell?" Johnston was asking, as he paced about nervously. "We must know when he is expected, for if he arrives during the night we'll be moving into a slaughterhouse."

"All we've been able to determine is that he isn't there yet," Beauregard said.

"I wish we had a balloon," Johnston said sourly. "Or failing that, a daring and accurate spy within their headquarters."

"I will be that spy, general," Liberty said. She stepped out of the trees and walked forward into the clearing in time to hear the generals' discussion.

"Miss Welles!" Johnston said, obviously shocked at seeing her here on the eve of the battle. "What are you doing here? You shouldn't be this close, you will be in danger."

"I've been in danger before," Liberty said simply. "And I would willingly place myself in danger again. I will locate General Buell for you.

"No," Johnston said. "I can't let you do that."

"Why not? Liberty asked. "I feel responsible for this battle. It was my information which has set it up, am I right?"

"Yes, but you've done enough. I'll not risk putting you in further danger."

"General, because of me, forty thousand of my countrymen are going to be placed in danger. If I can do anything which will lessen that danger—even by a small amount—then I will willingly do it. Now, please, allow me to steal into the Yankee camp and find out what you want to know."

"It would be of inestimable value to us," Beauregard said hesitantly.

"Yes, but such information would be better gathered by a man," Johnston said.

"Why?" Liberty wanted to know. "As a woman, I would have the advantage of placing the Yankees off-guard. And, as I am experienced in this endeavour, I will know what and how to gather the needed information." General Johnston ran his hand through his hair. Finally he sighed in resignation. "Very well, I shall allow you to go. But be very cautious, and return before darkfall."

"I shall," Liberty said.

"And again, may I say that the South owes you a debt they can never repay?" General Johnston said quietly.

"General, there is something you can do for me," Liberty

said. . .

"Name it, and it's yours."

"My father's regiment,' Liberty said. "It has been attached to Colonel Beauregard's division, and is now on the line of battle. I ask that you pull it out, and hold it in reserve."

"An entire regiment?" Johnston said slowly. "Miss Welles, you ask a great deal. But in deference to your past services, and in view of your father's age, I will concede to withdraw him. I will give command of his regiment to another."

"No," Liberty said. "My father would never forgive me if he alone were pulled from the ranks. It must be his entire regiment. Surely, you've a better regiment to put into the line than his home guards. They're nothing but old men and young boys, never before under fire."

"Home guards?" Johnston asked. "Are you serious?"

"Yes, sir," Liberty said.

General Johnston looked at Beauregard in astonishment. "How did we get a home guard regiment on the front lines? If they break under fire, the Federals could pour an entire division through the gap and turn our flank."

"General, I'm sorry," Beauregard said. "I just assigned the regiments to Blackie to make up the new division. I must confess that I paid no attention to their composition."

"Miss Welles, I thank you very much for calling this matter to my attention," General Johnston said. "And you can be sure that I shall replace the entire regiment. But please, don't think it is necessary for you to buy this consideration at the peril of your own life. I would replace that regiment anyway, given its composition, and my knowledge of the fact."

"I will locate General Buell for you," Liberty said, smiling.

"God be with you, girl," Beauregard said.

Liberty returned to the Corinth road. Twenty-two miles behind her was Corinth, issuing forth a steady stream of

Confederate soldiers. The road was absolutely deserted for half a mile in front of her, a no-man's-land, as it were. Then, for the final half mile, the road was in possession of the Union troops in and around Pittsburgh Landing.

Liberty squared her shoulders and started up the road. She'd gone less than one hundred yards when she was challenged by the advance pickets of the Confederate lines.

"I wish passage, sir," Liberty answered to the challenge.

"Ma'am, they ain't naught but Yanks up that road."

"I am not a combatant, sir. I do not feel any jeopardy."

"I don't know," the picket said. "Maybe I'd better see the cap'n."

Liberty felt a degree of frustration. She could have General Johnston clear it with the captain, who would then inform the pickets, but that would increase the number of people who would be aware of her mission. She had learned from experience that the fewer people who knew what you were about, the better the chances for success.

"Let er go, Clay," his companion said. "Like as not we go see that fool cap'n, he'll have dreamed up somethin' else for us to do."

"Yeah," the one called Clay said. He scratched his beard and looked at Liberty. "Ma'am, I don't know why you want to go up there, but if you' want to, go ahead. Only do me a favor, would you? If you get stopped by any of our rovin' patrol, don't tell 'em you come through here."

"I won't tell them," Liberty promised.

The Rebel soldier, a man in his mid-to-late thirties who sported a long red beard, waved her on with his rifle. Liberty thanked him, then started on up the road, headed for Pittsburgh Landing. She thought of the soldier who had stopped her. He certainly wasn't fighting this war to preserve slavery. She had known his kind all her life, and she could look at him and tell his entire history. He was no doubt a farmer, owning perhaps twenty acres or less. His only help in running the farm came from his wife and perhaps his oldest child. He had no slaves.

If he saw fit to fight in this war without a vested interest in slavery, then that should prove that this war wasn't to perpetuate slavery, as so many in the north believed. She could be a Confederate as well as an abolitionist. People like Clay proved it.

As Liberty continued to walk along the road, she was struck by its look of absolute peace. The sun was shining brightly, the temperature in the high sixties. In the woods to either side of the road, birds chirped gaily. A rabbit was frightened from a clump of weeds, and it darted in front of Liberty, leaving little puffs of dust as it ran. A peach orchard bloomed in colorful profusion, and the fragrance of its boughs was carried softly on a light spring breeze.

Why can't men learn from nature? Liberty thought. It was madness to think that by tomorrow, this very area would be the scene of death and destruction the likes of which had never been seen on this continent.

"Halt!" a loud voice called, and Liberty stopped at once. "Who is there?"

"I want to speak with your commanding general," Liberty called out.

"What?" the soldier replied. "Did you say you wanted to talk to the general?" The soldier stepped out from behind a bush. Liberty saw a clean-shaven, handsome young man, no older than she. She smiled at him.

"Yes," she said. "I have information I think he would like to have."

"Whyn't you just give it to me, ma'am?" the young soldier asked. "I'll take it to him."

"No," Liberty said. "I must be satisfied that it gets into the right hands."

"Well, now, ma'am, what general are you talking about? We've got lots of them here."

"General Grant," Liberty said.

The soldier laughed. "I'll tell you what I'll do. I'll take you to my captain, and he can take you to see the colonel, and the colonel can take you to see one of the generals, and maybe that general can take you to see General Grant. That's the best I can do, ma'am, bein' as I'm just a private myself."

"That will do fine. Thank you very much," Liberty said.

"And ma'am, if you do get to see General Grant, well, whyn't you just tell him that Private Frank Gilbert is due a pass? I'd appreciate it, ma'am."

"I'll try and remember that, Private Gilbert," Liberty said, liking the young man's easy sense of humor. She felt a sudden pang. For hard on the realization that she liked him came the further realization that she was even now bound on a mission that could mean his death.

True to his word, Gilbert passed Liberty on, through the captain, the colonel, then General Sherman, so that now she was being taken by one of Sherman's orderlies to see General Grant.

"General, a dispatch from General Buell," a rider said, pounding into the camp at that moment.

"Good, good," Grant said. "Has he crossed Buffalo River yet?"

Liberty strained to hear the dispatch rider's answer, but she was unable to after he and General Grant walked away several feet and stood under a tree and talked in a very low voice. She looked around, trying to see if there was any way she could get closer and thus hear the conversation without being obvious, but she saw no such way. A moment later, the dispatch rider saluted, returned to his horse and rode away, and the opportunity had passed without Liberty being able to take advantage of it.

"Now, madam, what can I do for you?" General Grant asked, returning to talk to the young woman who had entered his camp.

"I have some information for you, sir, concerning the disposition of the Confederate troops in the area."

"Oh? And what is this information?"

"Generals Johnston and Bragg have joined General

Beauregard," Liberty said. "I've seen and recognized both of them in Corinth."

Grant smiled. "Thank you very much, madam. I do appreciate that."

"But they are here, now," Liberty insisted, continuing to play the game. Then she stopped and put her hand to her mouth. "Oh, how foolish of me. But of course you must already know this."

"We've had reports," Grand admitted drily. "Your story does serve to verify it, however, and for this we are thankful."

"You must think I'm a silly, foolish girl, trying desperately to serve her country," Liberty said.

"Madam, I think you are a patriot," General Grant said magnanimously. "But you have placed yourself in some danger. Please, allow me to provide you with an escort to some safe area on the other side of the river."

"Oh, no," Liberty said. "I wouldn't dream of tying up one of your men for such a thing. I'll just return to Corinth."

"You mean via the Corinth road?" Grant asked, suddenly taking a greater interest in Liberty.

"Yes, of course."

"Madam, did you come by that road today?"

"Yes," Liberty answered. "Why? Did I do something wrong?"

"No, of course not. Tell me, madam, have you seen any particularly large concentration of Confederate troops along the road?"

"They are all around Corinth," Liberty said.

"But no closer?" Grant said. "You weren't challenged?"

"I was challenged by one of your soldiers, general, a nice young man named Frank Gilbert," Liberty said. "He asked me to give you a message."

"He wanted you to give a message to me?"

"Yes, sir," Liberty said. "He asked me to tell you that he was due a pass."

Grant threw his head back and laughed. "That is good,

Hearts Divided

madam, that is very good. It tells me that the morale of my men is still very high. Oh, here comes one of my aides. I shall have him escort you, at least back through our pickets."

Liberty looked in the direction indicated by General Grant, then felt a sudden sinking in the pit of her stomach. Her head began to spin, and she felt for a moment as if she would faint. For there, coming toward her in the uniform of a Union officer, was Dan O'Lee.

"Captain O'Lee," General yGrant said. "Allow me to introduce you to. . . . I'm sorry, madam, I didn't get your name," Grant said, looking at Liberty.

"My... uh ... name is Jane Roberts," Liberty said. She looked down at the ground, hoping the brim of her hat would shield her face.

"Good afternoon, Miss Roberts," Dan said easily.

"I would like you to escort Miss Roberts back through our pickets," General Grant said.

"It would be my pleasure," Dan replied. "Come along, Miss Roberts."

Liberty followed behind Dan, still keeping her head tilted down. Praise be to God, could it be possible that he hadn't recognized her?

But then Dan spoke, and in so doing shattered all her illusions.

"Liberty, I didn't think you'd have the nerve to ever show your face again," he said stonily.

Liberty gasped. "You recognized me?"

"Of course I did. Do you think I could ever forget you?"

"But why? I mean, you said nothing to General Grant. Why didn't you turn me in?"

"I don't know," Dan said. "I truly don't know. Maybe it's just my way of trying to repay my brother for all the hurt I caused him."

"Have you heard from Burke?" Liberty asked.

"Burke is dead," Dan said simply.

They walked on in silence, Dan leading the way, Liberty

walking behind him. After a few moments, Dan heard a quiet sobbing, and he turned around to see Liberty crying.

"You're crying?" he asked.

"Is that so hard to believe?"

"But surely Burke meant nothing to you," Dan said. "I mean, wasn't he just one of the many? As Lieutenant Ward was? As I was?"

"What does it matter to you?" Liberty asked, dabbing at her eyes with a handkerchief. "You're going to believe what you wish to believe, no matter what I say."

They had left the road, and were now walking through a ravine. Dan stopped and turned around. "You tell me what I should believe," he said. "You tell me that I wasn't betrayed."

"I tried to warn you," Liberty said. "I told you that I was honor-bound to abide by my convictions."

"And did your convictions include making love with me, and with anyone else who would aid you in your cause?" Dan asked caustically.

"I made love with you, Dan, because I was in love with you. And, despite everything, I still am," she said.

"Liberty, don't," Dan said sharply. "You have no need for subterfuge now. I'm going to set you safely free, regardless of what your mission was here. You needn't toy with me any longer. You've no idea how I've suffered from the heartache you caused."

"I am not toying with you, sir," Liberty said. "And you've not suffered alone. Dan, can't you recognize an honest declaration of love when it's made?" Her voice came out in a sob.

"And did you make that same declaration of love to Lieutenant Ward? And to my brother?"

"I was very fond of your brother," Liberty said. "I may have even loved him, and I did tell him so. But I've never spoken those words to any other man, except you and your brother. Nor have I made love with anyone else."

"Liberty, why torment me with your lies? Captain Todd

told me of seeing you entering room 408 with Lieutenant Ward."

"Yes," Liberty said. "I went to his room, but we did nothing except eat dinner together. This is all that happened, I swear!"

"And you swear that no other man has ever known you?"

Liberty looked at the ground again. This time the tears began sliding down in even greater profusion. "No," she said. "I didn't say that. I said I have never made love with anyone except you and Burke. But there have been others who have known me."

"Just as I thought, madam," Dan said in bitter triumph. "No doubt, as a part of you spying activity?"

"I was raped, sir!" Liberty cried out. "I was raped not two days ago by three Yankee soldiers. They are the only others to know me!" Liberty began crying aloud, and the sobs racked her body so that she shook as with a chill.

"Liberty . . . I . . . I'm sorry," Dan said. At the sight of her genuine despair, he moved quickly and put his arms around her.

Liberty, feeling his arms about her, feeling comfort at long last, leaned into him. The hurt and bitterness fell away as she turned her trembling lips up to receive his kiss. There was a rushing sound in her ears, as a wind whispering through tall pines, and against her breast she could feel the pounding of his heart. Her body seemed to melt against his, and for a brief moment in the continuum of eternity, they were one, fused together, lip to lip, body to body, heart to heart.

"You do love me, Dan," Liberty said, when finally their lips parted. "Say it!"

"Yes," Dan admitted. "I do love you. I've loved you from the first moment I saw you. I've tried in every way possible to get you out of my mind, Liberty, but I can't do it."

Still he held her to him, trembling, as he spoke, with the fervor of the moment! And he looked at her with eyes tormented with struggle.

"Oh," she said. "Oh, if only we could leave this place now, and run away together, back to California."

"And forsake honor?" Dan asked.

"Yes!" Liberty said. "Oh, Dan, I've been so foolish, so self-righteous! I know now that there is only one honor, and that is to oneself. I love you, Dan, and nothing else matters but that love. Come, let's go away."

"No," Dan said. "In a curious way, Liberty, I've just come to see what you've said all along. I can't run away and you can't either. Don't you see? There would always be this between us. It would never let us go, and eventually it would consume us."

He let go of her and walked a few paces away, then turned to look back. Liberty felt for a moment as if she couldn't stand alone. She gripped a tree limb for support. Then she gathered herself, and looked at him with slow, sad eyes.

"I envy you, that you have found what I seem to have lost," she said finally. "Now, if you will be so kind as to guide me through the pickets, I'll be on my way. I won't bother you again."

"Liberty, no, don't say that," Dan said. "I love you, When this war has ended, I want to marry you."

"This war!" Liberty said, with a hollow mocking laugh. "We are on opposite sides, Dan, and yet we speak of love. Sometimes when I think of it, I think we've gone mad!"

"No, we're sane, Liberty," Dan replied. "It's just that in a world gone mad, sanity is no virtue."

Chapter 26

THE SUN WAS LOW but hadn't set yet when Liberty returned through the forward pickets of the Confederate lines. She managed to get through with no trouble, and she proceeded directly to General Johnston's headquarters.

"Miss Welles," General Johnston said, greeting her. "You've no idea how happy I am to see that you've returned safely. I've scolded myself continually ever since you left for authorizing such a foolhardy errand."

"I experienced no difficulty," Liberty said.

"Did you locate General Buell?" Beauregard asked.

"Yes. That is to say, I know where he is. But I do not know when he will join General Grant"

"Where is he?"

"He is at Duck River," Liberty said.

"Duck River? That's only ninety miles away!" Beauregard said. "General, we must call this attack off! If he marches all night and gets here before we have established our objectives, we'll be swept from the field!"

"On which side of Duck River is he?" General Johnston asked Liberty.

"I don't know," Liberty answered. "I heard a rider report to General Grant that he had a dispatch from Buell. Grant asked, 'Is he still at Duck River?' The dispatch rider answered in the affirmative but then they moved out of hearing range."

"General, we've got to call this attack off before it's too late," Beauregard urged. "Let's withdraw now to Corinth."

Johnston crossed his arms over his chest and pondered the situation for a few moments before he answered. "Gus, I know Duck River. It is in freshet stage now, flooded with the thaws and the spring rains. If he's on the other side, he could well be stuck there for a week, trying to cross."

"But we don't know how long he's been there, or even if he's on the other side." "Think carefully, Miss Welles," Johnston said. "Did Grant ask if Buell was *still* at Duck River?"

"Yes," Liberty replied.

"That means he's been there a long time," Beauregard said. "He may have already been there for a week."

"It could also mean that he's trapped on the other side," Johnston replied. "Gus, I feel we have no choice. We must make the attack tomorrow."

"Very well, general," Beauregard replied. "I will support in whatever way I can."

"You must promise me one thing," Johnston said.

"Of course, general."

"If ... if I am not around tomorrow night, and we have seized the advantage, you must press it hard. Drive the Yankees to the other side of the Tennessee and hold them there. If you control this side of the river they will have little chance of recrossing it."

"I promise, general," Beauregard said. "But you will lead us, not I."

"We shall see," Johnston replied. "And now, Miss Welles, I would feel much better if you retired from this area. You've exposed yourself to enough danger without adding to it by being on a battlefield dining an engagement."

"My father," Liberty said. "Where is he?"

"Your father's regiment has been taken from the line and

placed into Breckinridge's reserves," Johnston said. He laughed. "He wasn't very happy about it."

"No," Liberty replied, sighing with relief. "I'm sure he wasn't."

Liberty left the area where Johnston and Beauregard had pitched their tents, and started toward the area where she knew the reserves would be encamped. As she walked, she could sense the various moods of the Confederate soldiers on the eve of the battle. Some were almost melancholy, as if resigned to dying on the morrow. Others were excited, looking forward to the battle with eager anticipation. Most seemed unaffected, sitting or lying about with faces devoid of any expression save that which could be seen on any soldier s face in any bivouac: They ate their cold rations, or talked of home, or told jokes. Some were singing. Liberty could hear snatches of songs coming from different parts of the campground. The most popular one seemed to be *Home Sweet Home.*

"Miss," one of the soldiers called. "Miss, would you write a letter for me?"

Liberty stopped and looked at the man who called. He was about forty, with a long black beard and close-set coal-black eyes. He was holding a piece of paper and a pencil out toward her. "I got me these writin' implements, 'n I ain't all that good at my letterin'. I was a hopin' you'd help me out."

Liberty smiled at him. "Certainly I'll help you," she said.

"Thankee, ma'am," the soldier said, smiling broadly. "These here other fellers helps me sometimes, but they got their own letters to write, 'n it ain't fittin' of me to be beggin' off them all the time."

The soldier folded his poncho double, then put it on a log, making an elaborate show of preparing for Liberty a place to sit. She accepted the seat, then the pencil and paper, and prepared to take his dictation. She looked around and saw that several other soldiers had drawn close to listen to the letter as well.

"Would you rather go some place where you can dictate

privately?" Liberty inquired of the soldier.

"Oh, no, ma'am. All the boys, they like to listen to the letters I write to Marthy, 'n then they like to listen to the letters Marthy writes me back, 'cause the truth is, I got to have them read to me, same as I got to have them writ fer me.

"Very well," Liberty said. "I'm ready if you are.

"Dear wife," the soldier began. "I take this opportunity to write you again, having as my pen this time a lovely fair young belle of the South, but don't be jealous none, as my love is only for you, as you know. I am well, and I hope these few lines may come safe to hand and find you enjoying the same blessing.

"We are going to fight a big battle tomorrow, and with God's blessing, throw the Yankees back across the river and whip them good. Maybe that will make them think again before they come down here to raid us in our own homes.

"Tell mother I am well and I would like to see her very soon. Tell her to write to me as soon as you get my letter, dear wife. Tell our son Mark that it is up to him to get the crops in now, and you tell him I don't want to hear any more about his signing up to fight. I'm doing the fighting for both of us, and he has to do all the farming, but as he is fourteen now, he's big enough.

"Kiss little Anne and tell her that her daddy loves her very much. Martha, if you could get into Jackson and have your likeness made at that place that takes the likenesses and send it to me, I would carry it next to my heart forever.

"I must close now, and remain your husband until death. Direct your letters to Hosea's Infantry, D Company. Signed, T.J. Cole."

"Here it is," Liberty said, as she finished the letter and handed it back to Cole.

"Thankee, ma'am. I thankee kindly," Cole said, taking the precious missive from her.

"Miss, would you do one for me too, please?" another soldier asked, and Liberty took a pen and paper from him to write his letter. After his, there was another, and then another, and Liberty wrote letters until the failing light made it impossible to write any longer. Finally, she begged off, explaining that she couldn't see, and explaining that she was looking for her father's regiment.

"I'll take you there, ma'am," Cole offered, and Cole had plenty of volunteers to help him, so that when Liberty did enter her father's encampment a while later, she was escorted by four of the soldiers from D company of Hosea's Infantry.

"Daughter," Colonel Welles said, when he saw her. "What are you doing here?"

"I wanted to see you," Liberty said, going to him and accepting his affectionate embrace.

"Well, you've got your wish, daughter," Colonel Welles said dejectedly. "I've been pulled off the line of battle."

"I'm glad, father."

"They've pulled my entire regiment," Welles said. He hit his fist into the palm of his hand. "Damn it all, tomorrow is going to be the battle that brings victory to the South and ends this war, and I'm not going to be a part of it." "We'll be in reserve, colonel," one of his staff officers said.

"Reserve! What does that mean? It means nothing, that's what it means," Colonel Welles said.

"Papa, at least you're here," Liberty said. "If I had my way, you would still be at home, in Corinth."

Colonel Welles looked at his daughter, and the dejection left his eyes. He smiled at her. "You're right, Liberty. I could be at that. I guess we'll both have to settle for this. But if I didn't know better, I'd say you had something to do with getting my regiment pulled off line"

"Why, papa, whatever gave you that idea?"

"Because you're an independent girl, Liberty, and you don't give up easily. You're well-called, daughter, for liberty is your nature as well as your name."

"Colonel Welles, General Johnston has called a meeting for all officers, down to regimental commanders."

"This is it, daughter!" Welles said. Even in the darkness, his eyes shone with excitement. "I'm going now to get the battle plan for tomorrow's operation. I may get into this fight yet!"

Colonel Welles followed the staff officer who had delivered the message to him, and Liberty, quietly and unobserved, followed a short distance behind. If there had been any change in the plans, and her father was going to be used tomorrow, she wanted to know about it now.

It was a little after eight o'clock by the time the officers had all gathered in the clearing near Johnston's tent. In the middle of the clearing was a visible symbol of the adage "rank hath its privileges," for there burned a small campfire. The smell of bacon permeated the area, so that Liberty knew that the generals, at least, had enjoyed a hot meal on this night.

Nearly sixty officers were assembled, all with the rank of colonel or higher. They were talking quietly among themselves, but grew silent when General Beauregard appeared, stepping out of a tent at the far end of the clearing.

"Gentlemen," Beauregard said. "In a few moments, General Johnston will have a few words to say to you. Before he arrives, I have one thing I would like to say."

There was absolute silence, save the crackling of the fire. All the officers strained to hear Beauregard's one remark.

Beauregard pointed toward the river. "Tomorrow night, we sleep in the enemy's camp!" There was a round of cheers. Then Beauregard held his hand up, calling for quiet. "Gentlemen, our commanding general!"

General Johnston stepped out of the tent then and walked to the middle of the clearing to address his officers. His face had a hawkish appearance, dominated by a handlebar mustache. He had piercing black eyes beneath heavy dark eyebrows, and when he fixed his gaze upon a person, it seemed to penetrate to that person's very soul. Command set well with him. He was well-experienced, having served as a general in the armies of three countries: the United States, the Republic of Texas, and the Confederate States of America.

Johnston enjoyed the absolute confidence of Jefferson Davis and the Confederate government. When, after an earlier setback, there was some outcry for his removal, it was Davis who responded by saying: "If Johnston isn't a general, then we have no generals in the Confederate army, and had best give up this war." The Union thought highly of General Johnston as well. After their unsuccessful attempt to recruit him, they had made an equally unsuccessful attempt to kidnap him as he journeyed east from California to accept his Confederate command.

Now Johnston looked over the assemblage before him, then spoke in a clear, easily understood voice:

"I have put you in motion to offer battle to the invaders of your country. With resolution and disciplined valor, becoming men fighting as you are for all that is worth living or dying for, you can but march to decisive victory over the mercenaries who have been sent to despoil you of your liberties, your property, and your honor. The eyes and hopes of eight million people are resting upon you, and I assure you that I will lead you to victory!" He ended in a shout.

There was a rousing cheer from the officers. Johnston stood there, looking at them for a moment longer, with an expression on his face which Liberty couldn't fathom. It wasn't excitement, or anticipation, or even fear. It was more like sorrow. She stood back in the shadows and studied Johnston's face for several seconds, until the general turned and walked back into his tent.

Liberty breathed a sigh of relief. Nothing had been changed. Her father s regiment was still in reserve. But even with her relief, she realized the grim facts. Tomorrow, nearly one hundred thousand men would be locked in mortal combat.

Dan couldn't get Liberty from his mind. Should he have let her go? Surely her presence in camp, especially as it had been under an assumed name, bespoke of some nefarious activity. And yet, even as he asked himself the question, he knew there could be but one answer.

He'd let Liberty go because he was hopelessly in love with her. Verity Eternal, Tamara Calvert—they had been, at best, surrogates for the woman he truly loved. And, he had to admit, Liberty had been honest with him. She had tried to warn him during their time together in St. Louis that she might have to do something which would make him feel betrayed.

What a fool he was. She'd offered to deny the Confederacy, to deny everything, so they could be together. She wanted to run away to California with him, and he had spurned her offer. Why? He asked himself that over and over again. Why did he reject her? She was willing to admit that there was no honor, save the honor they felt for each other. Why couldn't he say the same? Why must they be caught up in the insanity of this war?

"Captain O'Lee," General Grant called, and the general's summons interrupted Dan's reverie.

"Yes, sir."

"I'm going back to Savannah to spend the night. General Buell's army has finally crossed Duck Creek, and they should be arriving at about dusk tomorrow evening. At that time, I shall move my headquarters here. I'd like you to scout around tonight, and find a suitable place to establish our field headquarters."

"Very well, sir," Dan agreed.

Grant started to leave, then scratched his beard and turned back to Dan. "Oh, while you're at it, you might scout around for a suitable place for General Halleck too, as he will be arriving soon."

"Yes, sir," Dan agreed.

Grant looked back at the river, then over toward Lick Creek. "You know, I haven't fortified our position against an attack, I've had no instructions from Halleck to do so, and besides—I speak frankly—I have so many untried men that I fear fortifying the camp will just make them fearful of an attack. I don't believe we will be attacked, I really don't. But if we are, this position is naturally strong. We have Snake Creek on our right, and Lick Creek here on our left. I don't see how an attack could come from anywhere except the area immediately to our front, and that would box them in."

"General, would you like me to give word to be especially watchful tonight?" Dan asked quietly.

"Yes. Tell Sherman to..." Grant paused. "No, you'd better not. The Rebels have been making constant demonstrations against us. If the men thought there was a real danger of an attack, they might give way at the first feint. I've seen how panic can rout an army. I'd like to put them on their guard, but I fear to."

"Well, there's just one more night, general, then we'll have Buell's troops and the Rebels would never attack," Dan said.

"I'm certain you're right," Grant said. "I'll bet the Rebels would like to know where Buell is. Well, goodnight to you. I'll be back by seven in the morning."

"Good night, general," Dan said.

Dan watched Grant walk down to the landing and step aboard the steamer which would take him the six miles upstream to his headquarters at Savannah. He knew the general was uneasy with good reason tonight. He wished that Buell had been more efficient in bridging Duck River. Grant was right. If the Confederates knew that this was the last night before Buell joined Grant, they would surely attack to maintain the advantage as long as . . . "Liberty!" Dan cried aloud. He snapped his fingers. "My God, that's why she was here! She was trying to find out about General Buell!"

Chapter 27

WHEN DAN REALIZED that the purpose of Liberty's visit had to be to gather information concerning General Buell's position, he went at once to see General Prentiss. Prentiss had already retired but agreed to see him, knowing him to be a member of Grant's staff. When Dan was escorted into the tent, Prentiss had put on his trousers, but nothing more. He sat on the edge of his bunk, running his hand through his tousled hair. The tent's interior was dimly lighted by a candle, and great shadows were projected on the canvas walls.

"What is it, captain?" Prentiss asked irritably. 'What is so important that it couldn't wait until morning?"

"General, I have strong reason to believe that the Confederates are going to attack us during the night," Dan said.

"What? Does that word come from General Grant?" Prentiss asked, showing more interest.

"No, sir," Dan admitted. "I have my own reasons for believing this."

"And what are those reasons, captain?"

Dan was stuck. He couldn't very well say that he had recognized a Rebel spy and then let her go without reporting her. He didn't know what to say.

"It's just a feeling I have, sir," he said wealy.

"A *feeling,* captain? You've awakened me because of a *feeling* you have?" General Prentiss said with illconcealed disgust.

"Well, it's more than a feeling, really," Dan tried to explain. "It's a combination of little things, which, taken by themselves, are insignificant, but in concert point very definitely, I think, to the possibility of an attack."

Prentiss stood up and walked over to the tent flap, then looked outside. A large, silver moon floated high in the night sky, and he looked at it for a moment before he turned around to face Dan. Now, Dan saw that Prentiss had a more thoughtful look on his face.

"Then the information Captain Savage gave you fits in with your other information?" General Prentiss asked.

"The information Captain Savage gave me?" Dan asked.

"Captain, are you going to tell me that Savage didn't come to you today with a note from me for General Grant?"

"No, general, Dan said. I haven t seen Captain Savage since a very brief meeting last night, when we shared a tent."

"That is most unusual," Prentiss said, frowning. "Savage seemed positive on his information, and wanted to transmit it to General Grant. I authorized the transmittal, and told him to have you take him to Grant."

"What information did he have?" Dan asked, puzzled.

"He said he spotted a large body of Confederate troops moving up the Corinth road this morning."

"A patrol?"

"That's what I believed it to be," Prentiss said. "But Savage seemed to think differently. That was why I authorized him to proceed further with the information. I assumed he had already done so."

"He made no such report to me, sir."

"Hmm," Prentiss said, rubbing his chin. "It may be that Savage had second thoughts. But, as you now have the same degree of jitters, why don't you speak to him yourself about what he saw?"

"I will, sir, and thank you."

"Don't thank me," Prentiss said. "If an attack is imminent, then we should thank you and Savage for warning us. Savage is in Colonel Peabody's brigade. Tell Colonel Peabody that if he deems it appropriate, he may send out a scouting party. But be careful not to bring on any unwanted engagements."

"Yes, sir," Dan said. He saluted, then left the tent and walked across the damp, rolling ground, looking for the tent he knew to belong to Captain Savage.

"Cap'n, I moved your gear outa Cap'n Savage's tent, and pitched one for you over by that oak tree," a private said, as Dan approached the bivouac area of Company G.

"Thank you, soldier," Dan answered. "Is Captain Savage in his tent?"

"Yes, sir. I think he went to bed 'bout half an hour ago."

"Captain Savage," Dan called, just outside the tent.

"Yes, who is it?" a voice answered.

"It's me, Captain O'Lee."

"You've got your own tent now, O'Lee. Let me sleep in peace."

"No, that's not it," Dan said. "I have a message for you from General Prentiss."

"What's the message?"

"He wants you to . . . why the hell am I standing here talking to a tent, Savage? Come on out here."

There was a rustle, and a moment later the small figure of Captain Savage stepped outside. The captain had his hat pulled low, and he had a scarf wrapped around his mouth and nose, so that only his eyes showed, and they were covered by the shadow of the brim of the hat.

"I think I'm coming down with the ague," Savage said, his voice muffled. "Excuse the scarf, but I'm trying to keep away the humors of this damp air.'"

"The chill and damp can make it worse," Dan agreed. He chuckled.

"What's so funny?"

"It has just come to me that I have known you for twenty-four hours now, and yet I wouldn't recognize you in the light of day."

"If I see you, I'll tell you who I am," Savage replied. "Now, what is this important message?"

"General Prentiss says you were to deliver a message to me for General Grant," Dan said. "But I never received the message."

"It had to do with an idea I had," Savage said. "I decided that my idea wasn't a very good one.

"It may have been better than you thought," Dan suggested.

"Why?"

"Captain Savage, I have every reason to believe that the Confederates are planning an attack on our position this very night."

"Then you mean I did see an army moving *en masse"* Savage said.

"I think you did."

"If Prentiss is concerned, why have we not gone into defensive positions?"

"Prentiss wants Colonel Peabody to send out a patrol," Dan said.

"Very well, I'll pass the word on to Colonel Peabody, then move my company out in force."

"I'm going with you, captain."

"No, you aren't," Savage said.

"Why not?"

"Because I'm going to have enough on my mind without having to play nursemaid to one of Grant's staff officers. I'll handle it, captain."

"I'm a staff officer," Dan admitted. "But I've had a fair measure of exposure to battle."

"You will not ride out with me," Savage said again, resolutely.

"Very well, captain, I won't press the issue," Dan said. "But I must insist that we inform Colonel Peabody at once of General Prentiss's wishes."

Dan followed the feisty little captain over to Colonel Peabody's tent, wondering why he and Savage had become such instant enemies. He couldn't think of anything he had said or done to incur such hostility. But, then, the captain had been exposed to daily patrols and harassing raids by the Rebels, and was no doubt under a great deal of pressure, so Dan made allowances for his behavior. Still, there was something about Captain Savage which haunted Dan. Why did it seem to him that recognition was there ... just beyond grasp, dangling tauntingly before him like a half-remembered melody?

As Tamara led Dan to see Colonel Peabody, she toyed with the idea of telling him who she was. Surely, now on the eve of battle, he wouldn't expose her! But even as the idea surfaced in her mind, she knew that now, more than ever, he *would* expose her. It would be his idea of chivalry, she knew, to try and protect her from the battle that was to come.

Oh, how she wanted to tell him! If only he could understand her reasons for doing this and could accept her for them! They could have comforted each other now, taking love where they found it.

Love? Tamara thought. No, not really, not in the girlish, romantic sense that she had once imagined love to be. Not even in the true sense of a man and woman, cleaving only unto each other until death do them part, she decided. For the truth was Tamara had abandoned those female concepts when she had abandoned the dress of a woman. The need she felt for Dan now was a physical need. No, it was more than just physical, she decided. It was an emotional need, greater than physical, though less than romantic.

Why couldn't Dan accept that? Why couldn't he fill the need she had, and allow her to do what she must do? But the question, unasked except in Tamara's mind, needed no answer. Things were as they were because of an inviolable law of society, and there was nothing Tamara could do about it.

Colonel Peabody was standing outside his tent when Tamara and Dan reached his headquarters.

"Hello, Captain Savage," Peabody said in greeting. "Captain O'Lee, isn't it?"

"Yes, colonel," Dan replied.

"What brings you two over here?"

"Colonel, General Prentiss requests that you send out a patrol tonight," Tamara said. "I would like to lead the patrol."

"I send out a patrol every night," Peabody replied gruffly.

"Colonel, I have reason to believe that an attack is probable, tonight or early in the morning," Dan said.

"I agree," Tamara put in. "Do you recall that in my patrol today I encountered a rather large body of men moving up the Corinth road?"

"Yes, but when I spoke to you later, you said that you had changed your mind about its significance."

"I've since spoken to Captain O'Lee, and feel that I was right the first time. So, in addition to the regular patrol you intend to send out, I should like to take one of nay own, my entire company."

"All right." Peabody nodded. "If you really feel there is something to it, I'll attach two other companies to you, and you can go out in strength."

"Thank you, colonel."

"Colonel I would like to accompany Captain Savage," Dan put in quickly.

"I don't have any objections," Colonel Peabody replied.

"No!" Tamara said quickly. "Colonel, forgive me, sir, but this is a very important patrol, and I would rather not have an interloper along."

Peabody raised an eyebrow, then shrugged. "Very well, captain, it's your command," he agreed. "I'm sorry, O'Lee, but I have to honor Captain Savage's wishes on this."

"As you wish, sir," Dan said dejectedly. Tamara turned to

Colonel Peabody's orderly. "Would you pass the word to the other two companies that I shall be ready to proceed in half an hour?"

"Yes, sir," the orderly replied, saluting, then hurried off on his mission.

"And, if you will excuse me, colonel, I've my own company to prepare," Tamara said.

"Good luck to you, captain," Colonel Peabody answered.

"I wish you good luck as well," Dan said.

"I'm sorry I couldn't overrule Captain Savage," Colonel Peabody told Dan after Tamara had left. "But as long as my officers serve me well, and faithfully, I make it a point to back them up."

"I understand, sir," Dan said. "What I don't understand is why Captain Savage was so adamant against my coming along. That puzzles me."

"Perhaps it is just as he said. He feels that a stranger along would make his job more difficult."

"I wish I could believe that," Dan said.

"You mean you don't?"

"No, sir. I've known Captain Savage from somewhere else, but for the life of me I can't place where. Wherever it was, though, I must have done something to incur his dislike, for he has barely said a civil word to me since we met".

"I'll admit he's a strange one," Colonel Peabody said. "He's very quiet, and he stays to himself all the time. But he's a courageous officer who never shirks his duty. I wish I had an entire brigade just like him."

"Has he been long in your brigade?"

"He joined us just before we left Cairo. 'Bout the seventeenth of last month, I guess. But he's found a home with me, I'll tell you that."

Colonel Peabody offered Dan a cup of coffee. They drank and talked as they waited for the patrol to depart. Colonel Peabody had heard of the canal Dan had built at New Madrid, and he asked many questions about it.

"Have you ever been to Vicksburg?" Colonel Peabody asked.

"No, sir."

"You mark my words, the battle at Vicksburg is going to be even harder than the one at New Madrid. Vicksburg is the next major fortress on the river. It sits on a big bend, too. Could be that a canal will be needed there."

"I don't know the terrain around Vicksburg," Dan said. "But if it isn't as swampy as the area around New Madrid, I doubt that a canal could be built."

Colonel Peabody chuckled. "I don't think there's any place that can compare with the swamps around New Madrid, except maybe the Okeefenokee in Georgia, or the Everglades in Florida. Besides, the land around Vicksburg is all good, rich farmland."

"Calvert Hills," Dan said.

"I beg your pardon?"

"I know someone whose father owned a plantation near Vicksburg. It was called Calvert Hills," Dan said, thinking of Tamara.

At that moment, the three companies started out on their patrol, and leading them was Captain Savage. The horse he was riding reared once in the excitement, and Savage had to grab the reins to calm the animal. At that moment, Dan got his first clear look at the captain's face, lighted as it was from the nearby campfire.

"Tamara!" Dan shouted, taking a step toward her.

Tamara spurred her horse and darted to the front of the column, quickly leading them away.

"What did you say?" Colonel Peabody asked, puzzled by Dan's strange behavior.

"Captain Savage, I know now who . . ." Dan started. He stopped. "I know where I've seen him," he finished lamely.

"I know you feel better about remembering," Peabody said. "Something like that can get in a man's craw and agitate him for a long time." He stretched. "Well, they should be out for a couple of hours. I think I'll grab a few winks of sleep. I'd advise you to do the same thing, captain. If we are about to be attacked, we need all the rest we can get."

"I agree, sir," Dan replied. "Good night, sir," he added, starting for his own tent.

But Dan knew he wouldn't sleep. He could think of nothing, except the fact that Tamara was out there leading a patrol.

Tamara had heard Dan's call just before she rode away. So. He recognized her—and was probably telling Colonel Peabody about it, even now. In all likelihood, that meant that this would be the last chance she would have at inflicting damage against the Confederacy. She hoped she would have the opportunity to fight. She smiled. She would create the opportunity. They were out there, she knew. She would just keep going down the Corinth road until she encountered them.

Tamara led the three-company-sized cavalry force down the road, going in a southwesterly direction, moving the animals at a brisk trot. The road lay out before her, dappled silver by the moonbeams which reached it through the spreading branches of the trees.

As they rode, they were not only advancing toward the Confederate lines but moving parallel with the front of the Federal lines. By now, they had moved into the area immediately in front of General Sherman's sector.

It was at that point that they rode right into Hardee's corps. The surprised Confederates, who were moving into a line of battle preparing for their own attack, opened fire at the Union troops.

Tamara heard the bullets humming about her. Then she saw a puff of dust rise from the tunic of the rider immediately to her left as one of the bullets buried itself into his chest.

"Return fire!" she ordered. "Skirmish line to the right!"

The Union troops moved out into a long skirmish line, exchanging fire briskly with the Confederate troops. The sound of the muskets fired by the Confederates, and the pistols and carbines fired by the Union cavalry, grew from rapid poppings to a low, sustained roar, and a huge cloud of smoke billowed over the battlefield.

General Johnston, at breakfast with his staff and hearing the fire of the encounter, turned to his son Preston and to his aide, Captain Munford. He directed them to note the hour in their log books. It was fourteen minutes after five o'clock in the morning.

"Gentlemen, our hand is played," Johnston said quietly. "Give the order all along the line. Attack at once."

Chapter 28

BY DAYBREAK, the wounded from Tamara's reconnaissance in force were returning to the camp, and Colonel Peabody, seeing that the Confederates had been engaged in strength, ordered the long roll beaten. A young drummer boy, perhaps fourteen years old, ran into the company street beating the call to battle on his drum. His call was taken up by other drummers in adjacent regiments, and shortly it began spreading down the line.

"What of Captain Savage?" Dan asked one of the wounded.

"When last I seen the fiery little devil, he was still mounted, leading a charge against a Rebel gun battery," the soldier said.

At that moment General Prentiss came riding rapidly down the line, looking for Peabody.

"Colonel, my orders to you were quite specific," Prentiss shouted angrily. "You were not to bring on a battle. I shall hold you personally responsible for this engagement."

"General, I am personally responsible for all my official acts," Colonel Peabody said.

"My God, colonel, look at that!" one of the nearby soldiers called, and Dan, along with Colonel Peabody and General

Prentiss, looked in the direction the soldier had pointed.

There, coming down a gentle slope just in front of them and already within easy musket range, were the Confederates. They were massed many lines deep. They were moving toward them like an ocean of gray, flowing down the hill, rolling over small shrubs and fence fines and crossing roads as if they were a mighty force of nature.

"What then?" Prentiss shouted, shocked at the sight.

The men of Peabody's brigade had fallen in with weapons at the ready. While Prentiss was staring in open-mouthed shock, the colonel had assessed the situation and now acted quickly.

"Attention, men," he shouted. "Ready, aim, fire!"

The muskets of Peabody's brigade sounded as one. But, though Dan saw a score of the gray-clad warriors go down, the Confederate army continued to move forward, and now they were answering the fire.

Dan carried only a pistol as a weapon. He pulled it from his holster and answered the Rebel shot. Bullets whizzed around him like angry bees, and he could feel the shock waves of those which passed very close.

"Hurrah, boys!" one of the officers shouted. "Here comes a battery up. We'll give them hell now!"

Dan answered the shout with a cheer, as did most of the men. But the cheers soon turned to exclamations of surprise and horror, as they realized that the gun was not Union, but Confederate. Within seconds after it was in position, it opened up on Dan and the others with grape and canister.

"Fall back!" General Prentiss started shouting. "Fall back!"

Dan looked around for Colonel Peabody. He saw his horse running by, riderless, the stirrups flapping in the air. He looked in the direction from which the horse had come and saw the colonel lying on the ground, face up to the sky, eyes and mouth wide open.

"Colonel!" Dan shouted, running to the fallen officer. But

as soon as he got there he knew that it was too late to help the colonel.

"Fall back, men," Prentiss shouted again. "Captain O'Lee, assume command of the left flank, sir!"

"Yes, sir," Dan shouted. He ran at a crouch to the left flank, where the shot and shell had already decimated the ranks.

Slowly Peabody's brigade retired from one defensible position after another until they finally reached a roadway termed Sunken Road, for it was cut for some distance through a low hill. Here, nature had provided what General Grant had hesitated to dig, a fortified position.

"Hold at this road!" Dan shouted to his men. He stood behind them, himself exposed to fire, and shoved and cajoled them back into position on the parapet of the road. "Stand here and fight, men!" he shouted.

Several of the officers, themselves as green and new to battle as the men they commanded, sought the cover of the embankment. They lay there as low as they could press their bodies, covering their heads with their arms and hands. But a few of the officers joined Dan in helping to squash the retreat. They forced the men back to the line to take up firing positions against the enemy. Finally, the men heeded Dan's entreaties. The retreat stopped at Sunken Road.

"Cap'n!" one of the men shouted. "Here comes that damned battery again!"

Dan looked toward a cannon being pulled rapidly behind galloping horses. Suddenly he recognized one of the outriders as Tamara!

"Don't fire on the battery, men, it's Captain Savage!" Dan shouted, and as the battery roared into position on Sunken Road, Tamara and the handful of men who were with her were given a rousing cheer.

"Where is Colonel Peabody?" Tamara asked, out of breath from the mad dash.

"Killed," Dan said. He looked up and saw a handful of

men coming in on horseback, swinging out of the saddles as their horses hit Sunken Road, then driving for the parapet to add their firepower to that of the men already in position.

"Where are the rest of your men?" Dan asked.

"These are all I returned with," Tamara said. "The rest are dead, wounded or missing."

"My God, from three companies?"

"Yes," Tamara said.

"Cap'n, they're fixin' up for another charge!" someone shouted.

"Hold your places, men!" Dan responded. "Is there any ammunition in the caisson of that gun you stole?" Dan asked Tamara.

"Quite a bit."

"Then let's get it firing. You take command." Tamara, whose face, like everyone else's now, was black with powder and gunsmoke, smiled broadly. "I'll get right on it," she said. "And thanks for not giving me away."

"Tamara, I swear to God, if there was any way I could give you away now and get you out of here safely, I'd do it. But you, like the rest of us, are trapped."

Dan heard the loud shouts of the attacking soldiers, screaming in what was now known as the Rebel Yell. It was an unnerving sound, issuing from the throats of thousands of men.

"Hold your fire, men," Dan shouted. "Load your weapons and hold your fire!"

Dan heard the cannon go off and watched the canister shell rip into the attacking gray line, cutting down five men. Their places were immediately filled by five others, and Dan thought it was like taking your finger out of a bucket of water and leaving a hole. Nothing seemed to stop them.

"Hold your fire until my command," he said again, and all along the line he could see the men nervously holding their muskets, drawing long and careful aim, and waiting nervously for that command.

Still they came.

Now the Confederates were so close that Dan could see their features. He looked at them in amazement, wondering that they could continue on in such an unbroken line, knowing that they were marching right into musketry fire.

One of the men in front of the advancing gray line held up a sword and shouted something to the others. Dan couldn't hear what he said, but he could hear the sound of his voice, small and tinny over the distance, carried to him because, except for the firing of the cannon, there was a temporary lull in the shooting.

The man was obviously an officer. He had obviously given the command to advance on the double, because the advancing army suddenly broke into a run. Again Dan heard the Rebel yell.

"Now, men, fire now!" he yelled, and his order was answered with the sustained roar of rifle fire.

Four more cannons moved into Sunken Road. They were from the famous Waterhouse battery, specially designed guns bought with private funds by a Chicago millionaire. They opened up on the Rebel lines almost as soon as they were in position. The cannonading, along with the crunching effect of the rifle fire, finally caused the Rebel lines to falter, hesitate, then break and withdraw.

"We whipped 'em, boys, we whipped 'em!" a jubilant soldier shouted, and the others cheered lustily.

But Dan, though he joined in the cheer, wasn't convinced that the tide had been turned. He walked back and forth behind the line of his men, feeling the sweat pour down his back, aware that a muscle in his leg was jumping uncontrollably, sucking in air in audible gasps.

"Do you reckon they'll come ag'in?" one of the men asked.

"Naw, we whipped them seven ways from Sunday," another said.

"I don't know. I never seen nothin' like it. I mean they

just kept on comin' at us, even though we was firin' at them somethin' fierce."

"They ain't comin' ag'in," another said. "They's no way on God's earth they could come ag'in."

"Lis'sen to that," somebody else said. From some distance away they could hear the crashing thunder of artillery and the roar of musketry.

"My God, they're attackin' all along our line! There must be a million of 'em!"

"What'll we do, cap'n? We can't stay here an' fight a million of 'em!" another cried.

"There are as many boys in blue as there are in gray," Dan said. "You just do your part and hold back the Rebs that are coming after us. We'll let the generals worry about the others."

"That's what I'm afraid of," one of the soldiers called back. "I'm not sure the generals know what the hell they're doin',"

"We know, soldier," Prentiss said at that moment. He'd come up Sunken Road from Dan's right.

"General Prentiss. How is it over on your side?"

"We've taken quite a few casualties," Prentiss said. "But we're still holding on. How is it with you?"

"About the same." Dan said. He reached for his canteen, then noticed with some consternation that it was only about one-third full. He normally filled it daily, but the events of last night and this morning had caused him to forget about it.

"I'm afraid the lack of water may give us quite a few problems," Prentiss said, noticing Dan's predicament. "Most of the men are in the same situation you are. Little or no water."

"Son-of-a-bitch, here they come again!" one of the men yelled.

General Prentiss looked toward the line of woods into which the enemy had disappeared on the last assault. He saw that they were, indeed, forming for another attack.

"I have to get back to my position," the general said,

starting at a crouching run for the right side of the road. "Give 'em hell, men!" he shouted.

"We will, general."

"Get ready, men, here they come," Dan said. The warning was hardly necessary. There wasn't a man in the whole of Sunken Road, now being called by some the Hornet's Nest, who didn't know another attack was shaping up.

This attack began just as the other one had. First came the slow, steady advance of the men in gray, then the ear-piercing Rebel yell, and finally the onslaught of firing.

The yells of the men in gray were answered by cheers of the boys in blue, and these yells and cheers rose and fell with the varying tide of battle. Those sounds, along with the hoarse and scarcely distinguishable orders of the officers, the screaming and bursting of shells, the swishing sounds of canister, the roaring of volley firing, the death screams of the stricken and struggling horses and the cries and groans of the wounded, formed an indescribable impression which Dan knew he would never erase from his memory.

Dan could hear the orders of the Waterhouse battery commander, sharp and clear, above all other noise: "Shrapnel," "Two seconds," "One second," "Canister." And then, as the Rebels reached the closest point: "Double canister!"

Vainly, courageous Confederate leaders attempted to rally their forces in the face of the devastating fire. But their lines wavered, halted, then finally made a mad rush for cover, leaving each cannon's line of fire marked by rows of dead and dying.

But with each advance the Confederates came closer. The defending fire lessened as the ranks were thinned and the ammunition expended. The day wore on, and Dan could see his lines gradually melting away. Then he saw Rebel troops crossing the peach orchard in the rear, threatening to surround what was left of General Prentiss's division.

Dan moved quickly down the line to tell Prentiss of the

Hearts Divided

new danger.

"We've got to get out of here," Dan said tersely.

"There's no way we can make it," General Prentiss replied. "Our only recourse is to surrender."

"Surrender? Never!" Dan said. "General, we can get out of here. I know we can."

"We'll be cut down like wheat," Prentiss insisted.

"Then at least give permission to any who wish to try and escape capture to do so," Dan begged.

"Very well," Prentiss said. "You have my permission. But if you intend to try that, do so at once, before your action places the rest of us in greater danger."

"Yes, sir," Dan said. He moved quickly back to his position along the line. "Men, listen to me," he called. "General Prentiss intends to surrender, but he has given me permission to try and escape, and to take as many of you as want to go. It will be dangerous, but I've no wish to become a prisoner of war. Now, who is with me?"

There were scarcely a handful of men who took advantage of Dan's offer. One who did was Tamara.

"I think we should try and get the batteries out of here," Tamara said. "I don't want them to fall into Rebel hands."

"Good idea," Dan said. "Are your horses hurt?"

"I've only one left without a wound," Tamara said. "But I think I can get them to pull the gun."

"Then let's get going," Dan said.

Tamara returned to the cannon she had stolen from the Confederates. Within moments she had it ready to leave. But when Dan looked back toward the Waterhouse cannons, he saw, amazingly, that they were not preparing to leave.

"We've got to get these guns out of here!" Dan shouted to the battery commander.

"No, sir," the battery commander answered, his eyes reflecting his fright. "I'm not going anywhere. If General Prentiss is about to surrender, I'm not going to take a chance on getting killed trying to escape. I'd rather be captured and accept a parole, or sit out the war safe in some Rebel prison camp."

"But the guns!" Dan shouted. "The Rebels will get the guns!"

"I don't care," the battery commander said.

"Dan, we've got to go now or it'll be too late," Tamara called desperately.

Dan gave an exasperated sigh. The Waterhouse commander would not even try! Then he looked at the ones who had indicated they would leave with him. "All right, those of you who are going, let's go now!" he shouted. A half-dozen brave men started down the road with him. Tamara, riding one of the horses that was pulling the gun, led the way. Because she was mounted and up front, she became the target for the Rebel muskets drawing fire away from the others so that they could make it.

"Cap'n, look at Cap'n Savage!" one of the men shouted breathlessly. "Every Rebel in Mississippi is shootin' at him."

Tamara, urging her horse on with whip and spur, finally rode behind a small hill which offered cover from the fire. She turned them and quickly put the gun into position to fire one covering charge of canister. It held the Rebels back just enough to allow Dan and his men to effect their escape.

Man or woman, Dan knew he had never been witness to a more courageous act. He doubted that he would ever see such bravery topped. He vowed to himself at that moment never to betray Tamara's secret. For surely, he thought, she had earned her right to fight her war.

Chapter 29

THE BRAVE STAND made by Dan and the men of General Prentiss's division in the Hornet's Nest was, for a time, the only thing which checked the Confederate advance. When Prentiss finally surrendered, the men in gray surged on through, cheering and yelling, and pushed toward the bank of the Tennessee River.

Then, unexpectedly, the right side of the advance faltered as the Federal soldiers took a stand and began fighting back. General Johnston, told of the stiffened resistance, ordered that an attack be launched against the Federal position. A few moments later, the messenger returned with a note from the Confederate commander who had been ordered into the assault.

"General," the note read. "I fear an assault of the kind you have ordered is not possible without first halting and regrouping my men. Also, I shall require the support of at least two additional regiments in order to ensure the success of the attack. Your obedient servant, B. Beauregard, Colonel, Commanding."

"I will not commit my reserves now," Johnston thundered. 'There is no reason Beauregard cannot begin his assault immediately. In fact, he should have already done so!"

"I expressed your wishes to the colonel, general," the messenger said. "But he refused to comply."

General Johnston slapped his reins against his horse and raced behind his attacking army until he arrived at the position occupied by Beauregard's division. There, he was amazed to see that the advance had not only been stopped but that the Confederates' positions were in danger of being abandoned. Colonel Beauregard was even then shouting orders to fall back to the tree line.

"Hold it, men," General Johnston shouted, reaching them at that moment. "Hold your position!" Johnston swung off his lathered horse and walked quickly to Colonel Beauregard, whose personal position was some twenty-five yards behind his men.

"Colonel, what's the meaning of this?" he asked. Even as he spoke, the whine of Union bullets could be heard around them.

Blackie looked at General Johnston, and Johnston could see that his eyes were opened wide with fear, his pupils dilated. He was ashen-faced and sweating, and he could talk only with difficulty.

"Ge . . . ge . . . general," Blackie said. "Th . .. the . . . the Yankees have reinforced their position, and they are turning us back."

"Nonsense, colonel," Johnston answered. "You are turning your own men back through your cowardice. Now you get in front of your men, and you lead them to the attack!"

"I ... I ... I can't," Blackie said.

"You are a coward, sir, and I shall deal with you later!" Johnston replied angrily. The general whirled around returned to his horse, then leaped into the saddle. He rode to the front of the lines, exposing himself to galling fire, then, moving slowly back and forth in front of the troops, began speaking words of encouragement to them, urging them to pull themselves together, to fight back.

"My God, look at the general!" one of the men shouted.

Hearts Divided

"I'll follow a general like that anywhere!" another said, and within moments, a cheer of defiance went along the Confederate fines.

"Let's go, men!" General Johnston shouted, and he led the charge.

The fine surged forward. The Union soldiers, seeing the Rebels suddenly rise up and charge, gave way, so that the rout became complete, and victory seemed at hand for General Johnston and the Confederate army.

Blackie, now given confidence by the success of General Johnston, rode quickly to the head of his troops. The conversation with General Johnston, and his charges of cowardice, had taken place out of the range of hearing of his troops, so Blackie knew that if he could re-establish himself, he had not yet lost face. Provided, of course, that General Johnston didn't press charges of cowardice against him after the battle was completed.

He had started toward Johnston to plead with him to give him another chance when he saw the general suddenly slump in his saddle. Blackie reached him just before he fell off his horse.

"General, are you wounded?"

"Yes," Johnston replied.

"I will get you to an aid station," Blackie said. Johnston shook his head. "The bleeding," he said. "I am growing weak from the bleeding. You must stop it at once."

Blackie led General Johnston on his horse to a shallow depression about one hundred yards behind the line of battle. There, he dismounted and took the general off his own horse. He lay him down.

"The bleeding," Johnston said again, his voice very weakened.

Blackie looked at General Johnston's leg. It was soaked with blood now, though the wound itself had not appeared to be too severe. An errant piece of shrapnel had evidently severed an artery.

"General, you won't press charges of cowardice, will you?" Blackie asked.

Johnston opened his eyes and looked into Blackie's face. He licked his lips and tried to say something, but now he was too weak to speak.

"It would be bad for morale," Blackie said. "I mean, how would it look if my men thought I was a coward? And me the nephew of General Beauregard. I think it would be best for all concerned if we just forgot all about that charge, don't you?"

Johnston was unable to answer. He had passed out.

Blackie stood there and looked down at the still form of the general for a moment. Suddenly he heard hoofbeats behind him, and he turned to see Captain Mumford, General Johnston's aide.

"How is the general?" Mumford asked anxiously.

"He has a leg wound," Blackie answered' easily. "He's resting now. Perhaps you'd better get a surgeon to look at him."

"Yes, sir," Mumford replied quickly. He didn't leave his horse to check on General Johnston's condition. Instead, he whirled the horse about and went for the surgeon at a gallop.

After Captain Mumford had pounded off on his errand, Blackie strode slowly and nonchalantly to his horse. As if mounting for a leisurely ride, he swung into the saddle. Once mounted, he rode a few steps toward the general, then looked down at the prostrate man.

General Johnson was absolutely still. There was a widening pool of blood below his leg. The pumping, gushing action had stopped.

The pounding of hooves reached Blackie again. He turned to see Captain Mumford returning, this time with the division surgeon in tow.

"I'm glad you're here," Blackie shouted. "He seemed to take a turn for the worse, and I thought I'd better summon you quickly."

"My God, man!" the surgeon said, swinging off his horse

and hurrying toward General Johnston. He knelt beside the stricken general, put his fingers on his neck, then opened Johnston's eyes and peered into them. He put his ear on Johnston's chest and listened for a moment. Then he straightened up and looked at Blackie and Captain Mumford with a look of surprise on his face.

"I thought you said the General wasn't badly hurt," the surgeon said to Mumford.

"Well, is he?" Mumford asked, clearly puzzled by the surgeon's reaction.

"He's dead, captain."

Captain Mumford looked at Blackie with an expression of shock and disbelief. "Sir, th impression you gave me was that the general was suffering from a slight leg wound only."

"I did not use the word 'slight,' captain," Blackie said easily. "And I did summon a surgeon, did I not? With the many other wounded soldiers, I would scarcely have summoned him had the need not been urgent."

"My God," Captain Mumford said, in anguished tones. "If the general has died due to my inattention, I shall never forgive myself."

"There, captain," Blackie said generously. "You mustn't blame yourself. It is an act of war. Now, if you gentlemen will excuse me, I must get back to my command. Captain Mumford, you'd best inform my uncle at once. He will have to assume command now."

"Yes, sir," Mumford said sadly. He looked at the dead general for a moment longer, then, with a tear sliding down his powder-blackened cheek, turned to deliver the sad message to General Beauregard.

There were more than two hours of sunshine remaining when Beauregard assumed command. At that moment the Confederate army was drawn up in a magnificent line of battle, extending up and down the river bottom to the right and left as far as the eye could see. The Union army, backed up to the banks of the Tennessee, was awaiting the final push and the summons to surrender.

"General, we've got them where we want them," Beauregard's aide said.

"Exactly," Beauregard replied.

"Shall I pass the message to commence the final advance?"

"No," Beauregard said. "We shall stay right here."

"But, general, we have them!" the captain said, not understanding Beauregard's reluctance to attack.

"They will be there tomorrow," Beauregard said.

"Tomorrow? Why wait until tomorrow?"

Beauregard looked at his aide and smiled. "Because if we continue the attack now, I will have to share the victory with General Johnston. If we attack tomorrow, the triumph will be mine alone."

The word was passed to hold positions and continue to fire at the Union lines. By now the enemy was obscured by the battlefield smoke, which lay over everything like a thick fog, so that the firing was without aim or order.

Over on the Union side, General Grant, who had arrived early in the morning when he heard the intense shelling, had formed a last stand on the ridge which commanded the bank of the river. Grant and Sherman were seemingly everywhere at the same moment, staying the retreat and reforming the fines, directing the artillery fire, urging the men to stand fast. The drama of this day was drawing to a close. Grant had been beaten along his entire front, and he knew it.

Then, just before sundown, a breathless messenger arrived and handed a note to Grant. Grant read it, then smiled broadly.

"What is it, general?" Dan asked anxiously. Dan had returned to General Grant's staff after his narrow escape from the Hornet's Nest.

"General Buell has arrived," Grant said. "The tide of battle has turned."

Chapter 30

BECAUSE OF THE EBB and flow of the battle, there were dead and wounded scattered over an area of ten square miles. The first day's fighting had left a total of nearly ten thousand, counting the casualties of both sides, and as night fell, the sound of their groans and moans were piteous to even the most hardened ears.

One who could not bear the sounds of the suffering without making some effort to provide aid was the small captain whom most knew as Bill Savage, but who was in reality Tamara Calvert. A couple of hours after sundown, Tamara, without telling anyone what she intended to do, picked up as many canteens as she could carry and started out to help the wounded.

The night was dark and overcast, without moon or stars to light the way. A breeze came up, carrying on it a damp chill. Tamara pulled her coat about her and continued on, picking her way across roads and fields now littered with the discarded materiels of war: weapons, equipment, and the dead and dying.

"Water," a weak voice called, and Tamara halted. "I beg of you sir, be you Union or Confederate, if you re a Christian man, you'll give me water."

"Yes," Tamara said. "I have water." She moved quickly

to the soldier, a young Union private wearing the insignia of the 14th Illinois on his collar, and held a canteen to his lips. The boy began to drink deeply.

"No," Tamara said, pulling the canteen back.

"You mustn't drink too deeply. It isn't good for you.

"I'm dying anyway," the boy said matter-of-factly. "I'd rather die with my thirst quenched."

Tamara gave him the canteen and let him drink his fill. Finally he gave it back to her, then thanked her.

"I'll tell a surgeon where you are," she said.

"Don't bother none, cap'n," the boy said. "There's others out here need'n a drink too. You carry the water to 'em, 'n when you come back this way, why if I happen to still be alive, I might just want another, if you don't mind."

"I promise to do that," Tamara said, choking back the lump in her throat. She stood up, looked down at the wounded soldier, then went to the next one and gave him water as well.

Tamara passed no one, giving water and comfort to Union and Confederate alike. It was in this way that she recognized one of the Confederate soldiers as a young man who had grown up on a plantation adjacent to her father's. She had known him her entire life, and when she bent to give him water and looked into his face, she gasped.

"Jimmy?" she said. "Is that you?"

The wounded man opened his eyes. Even in the dim light she could see the agony in them. "Do you know me, sir?" the soldier asked.

"Are you Jimmy Wix of Fairhope Acres?"

"Yes, sir," the soldier said. "Who are you? Why, you're a Yankee. I don't know any Yankees."

Tamara tipped the canteen up and let him drink. She put her hand on his forehead. It was burning hot, and she knew a fever had set in, compounding the wound.

"Do you want me to make you a pillow from your knapsack?" Tamara asked.

"Yes, sir," the boy said. He continued to look at Tamara

with intense curiosity. Finally, he spoke again. "I do know you, don't I? But you aren't a Yankee. What are you doing in a Yankee uniform?"

"I'm Tamara Calvert," Tamara finally said.

"I swan, you are!" the soldier said. "But . . , but what are you doing here, Miss Tamara?"

"Surely, you've heard the story by now," Tamara said.

"Oh," the boy said. "Yes, yes I suppose I have. You were to marry Colonel Beauregard, but... uh ..." He stopped in embarrassment.

"I see you've heard it," Tamara said.

"Colonel Beauregard is here," the boy said. "He's commandin' the Second Mississippi Horse. My regiment," the boy added proudly.

"Blackie is here?" Tamara asked, with quickened interest.

"Yes, ma'am," the boy went on. "He was a hero this afternoon, you know that? The whole Second Mississippi Horse was heroes. We made a charge that pushed the Yankees all the way back to the river."

"Where is Blackie now?" Tamara asked.

"Oh, I 'spects he's with General Beauregard. They'll be plannin' what to do tomorra'. Miss Tamara, do you reckon you could see fit to leave me have another drink of water?"

"Certainly," Tamara said, holding the canteen to the boy's lips.

After making Jimmy Wix comfortable, Tamara went on, picking her way through the battlefield, providing what aid she could. But even as she did so, her mind was now racing ahead, concentrating on what she knew she must do.

There were others out aiding the wounded. Confederate and Union soldiers alike worked together to comfort the fallen, without regard as to the victim's side. Because of that it was not unusual to see northern and southern soldiers walking around in the dark, unarmed, sometimes talking to each other.

That was when Tamara realized that her plan would work.

The battlefield was strewn with bodies, and Tamara began

to take a special interest in the Confederate dead. Finally, she found a soldier of about her size. Quickly, she stripped him of his uniform. A few moments later, dressed in the gray of a Confederate private, she started walking toward the Confederate lines. She had no particular plan of action, just a purpose. It was to kill Blackie Beauregard.

Because the Confederate army had carried the battle on the first day's fighting, they were better organized in handling their casualties than the Union army was. The Confederate fines were advanced nearly to the river, so much of the battlefield had been within their control during the day. That meant that though thousands of dead and dying Confederate soldiers were still lying out in the dark, many hundreds had been brought back to the rear areas, where a hospital was functioning.

The wounded were lying shoulder to shoulder, stretched out in rows of fifty to sixty men. Some lay stiff and quiet, but many were writhing in pain, moaning and groaning, occasionally screaming out a curse, or a prayer, screaming it in such a way that one couldn't be sure which it was.

Everywhere there was blood, dirty bandages, the smell of unwashed bodies, purged bowels and emptied bladders. Added to this was a vicious swarm of mosquitoes, gorging themselves upon the pitiful victims.

Volunteers and nurses worked feverishly, and in most cases, futilely, to alleviate some of the suffering of the soldiers. One of the volunteers was Liberty Welles.

When Liberty first arrived, she took, one look and one smell, then shrank back in horror. She had to fight against throwing up, so overwhelming was the odor, so terrible was the sight. She had never seen anything like this in her life, nor dreamed it, even in her most horrible nightmare. But this was no nightmare .. . this was real. And buried deep in her mind was the knowledge that she was the cause of this battle. *She* was the cause of all this pain and death. But Liberty allowed that thought to surface for an instant only, then buried it with a will, for to dwell on it, she knew, could drive her insane with remorse.

"Miss," one of the soldiers called, as Liberty stood there, looking out at the mass of suffering humanity.

Liberty put all her queasiness aside, pasted on a smile, and moved quickly to the soldier. "Yes?" she answered.

"Miss, would you see to Tim? He's been sufferin' somethin' fierce, though he's quiet now, 'n I'm worried about him."

"Which one is Tim? Liberty asked.

"He's the feller over to the fence there," the soldier said, raising himself with effort and pointing to a prostrate figure.

"I see him," Liberty said. "I'll see how he is for you."

"Thankee, ma'am," the soldier said, lying back down.

Liberty picked her way through the men, passing those who lay dull-eyed, with hands clutched to wounds, glued there now by coagulated blood, until she reached the soldier named Tim.

Liberty gasped. It was T.J. Cole, the soldier whose letter she had written earlier in the day. She bent down to look at him, but even as she did, she knew that T.J. Cole would never need another letter written, or get back to his farm, or kiss his little Anne, or see the likeness of his wife, Martha. For T.J. Cole was dead.

Liberty couldn't face it any more. She stood up quickly, with tears burning her eyes. She had only one thing on her mind now, and that was to run away.

"How is he?" the soldier who had sent her to check called. *"How is he, miss? How is old Tim? Tell me, miss, me'. Tim, we're good friends, how is he?"*

Feverish hands reached for her, grabbed at her skirt. Though they may have been asking for water, or a blanket, in Liberty's troubled mind they were shouting accusations at her.

"You did this!" they seemed to shout. *"It is all your doing. You, you, you, you!"*

"How is he? How is he, miss? How is old Tim? How is

he? How is he?"

"You killed us! You killed us! Murderer! MURDERER! MURDERER! Liberty screamed, then ran as fast as her legs could carry her, past the surprised surgeons and officers and muses who looked at her with shock, until finally, she was far enough away that she couldn't smell the stench, or hear the groans, or feel the accusing eyes. And there, she threw herself to the ground, where, no longer able to hold it back, she vomited in the damp, dark dirt.

Less than one hundred yards from where Liberty lay retching on the ground, a jubilant group of Confederate officers celebrated the day's triumph and contemplated the next day's final victory.

"I must confess, Blackie," General Beauregard said proudly, "I had some reservations about giving you a division of your own. But your inspired leadership, coupled with that of our fallen commander, carried the day for us.

I have mentioned you in the dispatches, and I shall petition Congress to appoint you a brigadier general."

Blackie beamed under his uncle's compliments and proudly accepted the congratulations of the other officers. "I just wish General Johnston could be here with us to accept the just fruits of his efforts today," Blackie said.

"Hear, hear," one of the other officers responded.

"Gentlemen, if you would, lets have a moment of silent prayer for our fallen leader," General Polk recommended.

The officers all bowed their heads in silent reverence, and Blackie could scarcely contain his glee. He was going to be a general! And Johnston wasn't around to stop it.

There was a soldier, just outside the circle of light created by the campfire, who was staring at them. In fact, he seemed to be staring directly at Blackie, and it was making Blackie nervous. Who was he? Was he someone who may have overheard General Johnston s accusations of cowardice? Was he about to say something now?

The soldier started toward the group of generals, and

Blackie felt a strange sense of foreboding. Somehow, he sensed, this soldier represented a danger to him.

"Blackie," the soldier called.

The fact that a common soldier would address a general-designate by his first name startled the other generals, and they looked up in surprise. They were also annoyed that the soldier had interrupted their moment of silent meditation. Curious, General Polk asked Blackie who the soldier was.

"I don't know, general," Blackie said, starting toward the soldier. "But I shall soon find out."

The soldier took his hat off, then shook his long hair free.

"You know who I am, Blackie, for you were to have married me," Tamara said.

"Tamara, what the hell? What are you doing here?"

"I think you can guess at that," Tamara said. She drew her pistol and pointed it at Blackie. "Draw your gun, Blackie," she said.

"What? Tamara, don't be crazy!"

"Young lady, I don't know who you are, but I'm ordering you to put that pistol down," General Beauregard said.

"I'm sorry, general," Tamara said. "But I don't take orders from you. My commanding general is General Grant."

There was a gasp from those assembled.

Tamara's pistol was steady and unwavering. "I said draw your gun," she said again.

"Don't be a fool, young lady. You'll never get away with this!" General Beauregard said.

"I don't intend to," Tamara replied. "But I do intend to kill Blackie first. For the last time, Blackie, draw your gun, or I'll shoot you where you stand."

"You'll shoot me as I start to draw," Blackie protested.

"No, I won't do that," Tamara said. "I'll give you the benefit of an affair of honor." She laughed. "How does it feel to be fighting a duel with a Negress?"

"Tamara, I never meant anything by that," Blackie pleaded. "I was going to get it all straightened out, and then ."

"Pull your gun!" Tamara said again, interrupting him.

Resignedly, cautiously, Blackie pulled at his gun, fully expecting a ball to crash into his brain at any moment. He was relieved, and somewhat surprised, when he was able to draw the gun free and raise it into position.

"General Beauregard, would you count to three, please?" Tamara asked.

"I will not sanction a duel," General Beauregard said.

"If you don't count to three, I will," Tamara said. "That would give me un unfair advantage. Do you want that?"

"I will not count the numbers," General Beauregard said again. "To do so would give the illusion of my approval, and I heartily disapprove."

"Then I'll have to count," Tamara said.

"No ... I'll count," one of the general's aides, a captain, said.

"Thank you," Tamara said.

"Tamara, please, you've gone mad," Blackie said desperately. His tongue had thickened, and his throat was dry. From the corner of his eye he could see the others standing around in horror, helpless witnesses to this bizarre encounter.

"Quiet," Tamara said. "Begin counting, please."

"One," the captain said.

Blackie could feel his heart beating wildly.

"Two."

Blackie, cheating by one count, pulled the trigger. With a sudden surge of joy, he saw that his bullet had struck Tamara in the chest. Tamara was knocked down by the impact. Blackie started to shout in triumph, but Tamara forced herself into a sitting position, raised her gun, and fired once before falling back.

The bullet struck Blackie between the eyes. He spun around, then crumpled to the ground, dead.

"Arrest that woman!" General Beauregard shouted, pointing at Tamara. Two of the officers hurried to where she lay.

"Why did you do such a thing?" one asked.

"It was something that had to be done. And it had to be done by me." Tamara tried to sit up again, but when she did blood gushed from her wound.

"You'd best lie still, miss."

Others came to stand over her. They spoke in hushed tones. To Tamara, it sounded as if the words were coming from deep in a cave. She felt a spreading coldness invading her body, and by degrees, began to lose feeling. She knew without being told that she was dying.

"Send for the surgeon," someone said, as if speaking from a great, great distance.

"It's too late," another replied. "She's already dead."

Tamara wanted to tell them that she wasn't dead. She wanted to shout that she still lived. But even as the words formed in her brain, she knew they were false. She felt herself slipping away, as if sliding head-first down a long, long hill. She knew she couldn't hold onto life, and she wasn't sure she even wanted to.

Chapter 31

COMPLETE PHYSICAL, COMPLETE PHYSICAL, mental, and emotional exhaustion took command of Liberty. She lay where she'd fallen for twelve hours. So she was unaware of the drama which had been played out in General Beauregard's headquarters, in which Tamara and Blackie Beauregard had died at each other's hand. And she was equally unaware of the drama which was being played out right now, as General Beauregard saw his lines being steadily rolled back by the Union troops, now reinforced by General Buell.

In the distance she could hear thunder. In the deep recesses of her mind, she wondered, if her window was closed. She knew she should get up and check, but she was just too tired ... and the bed felt too good.

"Get those damn guns up on the road. You there ... what are you doing?"

"Colonel, I've got six guns and teams to pull only three."

"Then select the best three guns and spike the others, but get moving!"

"You heard the man, get moving," the second voice called.

At first, Liberty was confused as to why those men were

in her bedroom. She lay there, fighting consciousness, until finally, slowly, she awakened.

She was not in bed.

Opening her eyes, she saw that she was lying in the dirt beneath a tree. She could hear voices, just from the other side of a small rise, and she raised up and looked toward them. There, men were working feverishly, hitching teams to cannons.

Liberty had a foul taste in her mouth and very much wanted to wash her face and hands. She knew where she was now. She knew also that a stream ran close by. So she gathered the strength to walk to the stream, where she fell on her hands and knees, drank deeply, then splashed the cool water on her face and hands.

She heard the pounding of hooves and looked up just as the cannons, which had been harnessed, came speeding through the stream. The spokes of the wheels were a blur and the horses sent up silver droplets of water as their pumping legs danced and splashed through the creek in their hasty retreat.

Liberty, somewhat refreshed from the water and the impromptu bath, walked back to the road and stood there, looking on in confusion as the army moved out.

"What are you doing here, miss?" an officer called to her. "General Beauregard sent all the civilians out of here this morning."

"What's going on?" Liberty asked. "Where is everyone going?"

"We're movin' back to Corinth, ma'am," the officer said.

"Moving back? But why? I thought we had the Yankees beaten!"

"Buell's army reinforced Grant," the officer said. He touched the brim of his hat. "You'll excuse me, ma'am, but I've got work to do."

"Where is Beauregard's headquarters?" Liberty asked.

"He's been set up over to the meetin' house, ma'am. It's

called Shiloh."

Liberty thanked the officer and watched as he left, spurring his horse into a gallop. Once again, she found herself going one way on a road that was filled with soldiers going in the opposite direction. But this time the soldiers were retreating. . . . And whereas two days ago they had been full of bravado and jokes, today they were solemn, if not dispirited.

When Liberty reached General Beauregard's headquarters at Shiloh, she found it a beehive of activity. Mounted officers were arriving with messages and just as rapidly departing with them.

"Colonel Welles is in position, sir," one of the officers said.

"Good," Beauregard replied. "Tell him to commence his attack at three o'clock."

"Colonel Welles? Attack? What are you talking about?" Liberty shouted, running over to General Beauregard.

"Miss Welles, what are you doing here?" General Beauregard asked, surprised at Liberty's outburst.

"Never mind what I'm doing here. The question is, what is my father doing leading an attack? I thought he was in reserve!"

"That's precisely why he's leading the attack, Miss Welles," General Beauregard said. "I've ordered a general retreat of the entire army, but first, I intend to take the offensive again with vigor and drive back the enemy as far as possible. Your father will lead that attack, then hold his position, while the army withdraws to Corinth."

"But . . . but that's insane! That's a suicide mission!"

"Your father is aware of that. But he has assumed command of the division, and ..."

"He's commanding the division? What happened to Colonel Beauregard?"

"He's dead," the general said simply. "As is Colonel Kelly. That leaves your father in command."

"No," Liberty said. "I won't allow it. General Johnston

promised me ..."

"General Johnston is dead too, Miss Welles," Beauregard explained. "Now, if you will, please retire from the battlefield. You aren't safe here." Another rider came pounding into the headquarters area. "General Beauregard, Colonel Welles's compliments, sir, and he says to tell you that he has already been engaged by the enemy. He's been forced to start his attack now."

"No!" Liberty said. She started running toward the sound of battle.

"Lady, wait, there's fighting going on there," the dispatch rider called to her.

"Let her go," Beauregard said. "Deliver the message to all commanders. Fall back to the works around Corinth."

"Yes, sir," the rider said.

It was not difficult for Liberty to find her father's division, for she had only to go to the sound of crashing musketry. She ran, blinded by tears of rage and frustration, and finally burst forth from the woods to find herself in an open field. There, on that field, a long line of gray was advancing steadily against a long, low rock wall. There were cannon set up behind the wall, sprouting flame and death, and every foot of the fence line was occupied by a Union soldier, who held his musket at the ready, waiting for the Confederates to come.

"Oh, God, no!" Liberty said, breathing a prayer. "What are they doing?"

The line of gray continued on a slow, steady, unwavering march toward the rock fence. Even from where she stood, she could hear the roll of the drum as they moved out as on the parade field. In front of the line, regimental colors and the Stars and Bars of the Confederacy snapped in the breeze.

Liberty started running across the field. She was nearly even with the left flank of the attacking army when the Union soldiers opened fire. Fully one third of the advancing Confederates were cut down by the opening volley, yet still they continued, still at a slow, stately march.

It was nearly twenty seconds before the majority of the soldiers who had fired the first volley were reloaded, and though they were now firing without command, the natural timing of the action created a second volley nearly as devastating as the first. Nearly one third of the remaining Confederates went down.

Liberty saw her father, now holding a sword aloft with one arm while the other dangled uselessly at his side. He was covered with blood from a Minie ball. She gave a cry and started running to him, but at that moment a third sustained volley erupted from the Union position, and this time her father, along with half of the remaining attacking force, fell.

Seeing their leader down, the remaining soldiers turned and ran, chased across the field by the cheers of victory of the men in blue.

Liberty reached her father, then fell on her knees beside him. Tears were streaming down her face as she called out to him, beggingly.

"Please, don't die," she cried. "Please, don't die. Just don't die!"

But it was too late. Even as she held him, Colonel Welles breathed his last.

Liberty cradled his head in her lap and looked at him. Then she looked at the others, strewn dead and wounded for as far as she could see. At that moment, she knew she was getting a glimpse of hell. And, she realized, it was a hell of her own making.

"Miss," a Union officer called to her from behind the stone wall. "Miss, you'd best get off the field of battle before they come back and there's more shooting."

Liberty didn't move.

"Miss," the officer called again. As yet he had not left the relative safety of the stone fence. "Miss, you'd better get out of there."

Liberty felt defeated. It was as if she carried the weight of every casualty on her shoulders ... now more than sixteen thousand. She stood up and walked toward the stone wall. "Here, miss, come through right here," the officer invited, holding his hand out to help her.

"I want to surrender," Liberty said.

"Surrender? Miss, we don't take civilians as prisoners," the Union officer, who was a captain, said.

"I'm not just any civilian," Liberty said. "I'm a spy. Take me to General Grant. He knows of me. My name is Liberty Welles."

"I don't know," the captain said, scratching his head.

"Cap'n, it looks like the Rebs is about to come back," one of the soldiers called.

"Let's get ready for them," the captain said. "You," he called to a private who was standing near by. "Take this woman to General Grant's headquarters. I don't know what he'll do with her, but I'll not have her on my battlefield."

"Yes, sir," the soldier answered, more than willing to leave before another attack.

Liberty walked along quietly. Even when the soldier offered to make friendly conversation, she remained closed-mouthed. She imagined she would be shot . . . perhaps executed this very day. That was normally what they did with spies, she knew.

At his moment, the prospect wasn't all that unpleasant.

Chapter 32

GENERAL BEAUREGARD had ordered that a heavy artillery barrage be sustained just before the attack of Colonel Welles' division. The purpose of the barrage was twofold. It was, of course, to provide Colonel Welles with as much support as possible, but it was also to mask Beauregard's true intention of withdrawing from the battlefield once he had learned of the arrival of Buell's reinforcements.

The mules of the Union army which had packed the supplies in for General Buell were caught in this last great barrage. Many were killed and many more were wounded. Their screams continued on until after the barrage had finished and then they stopped. Finally, even the quiet moans of the wounded men ended.

The heavy bombardment which had gone on for two hours was reduced now to an occasional bursting shell. One would come in, swooshing like distant, rolling thunder, then detonate in a fiery rose, sending deadly missiles of shrapnel whistling through the forest. After each explosion a plume of smoke would drift lazily up through the early morning bars of sunlight, which were just beginning to slash down through the trees.

Dan, who had been exposed to the intense fighting of the

Hornets' Nest on the day before, then the heavy artillery bombardment earlier this morning, was able to view the occasional shell with a sort of detached interest. He had come through several engagements without a scratch, and was beginning to believe the myth of personal invincibility. Then, while attempting to move some of the uninjured mules out of the way, one lone shell burst nearby, sending a smoking, jagged piece of shrapnel at him, which tore a large chunk of flesh out of his leg. He let out a sharp cry of pain and surprise, then passed out.

When he woke again he was lying outside a field aid station, very near Grant's headquarters. His leg hurt badly, and in a war in which amputation was nearly always the accepted treatment of injured limbs, he feared that he would lose it. He had been put aside, along with the wounded who could wait and the dead. On both sides of him he saw men with lifeless, open eyes and spilled insides.

"Well, how're we doing?" someone asked. He was a tall man, and he scratched at his face as he looked down at Dan. He had been working with the dead and the wounded and the blood was on his hand so that he left a smear on his cheek when he scratched.

"My leg hurts," Dan said.

"I imagine that it does," the tall soldier said. He smiled. "But you've a few things to be cheered about."

"Tell me," Dan said. "I would like to be cheered."

"Well, one is, you won't be losing the leg. It's an ugly, painful wound, and it cut away some of your muscle so that you'll be walking with a limp for the rest of your life. But you'll keep the legs God gave you."

Dan breathed a deep sigh of relief. "Thanks," he said. "I don't mind telling you that I was worried about that."

"I don't blame you," the tall soldier said. "Oh, the other good thing is, you'll be getting a surgeon's ticket out of the war. You're being evacuated tonight, with the other wounded." Dan suddenly realized that the sound of battle was further away, and much less intense than it had been earlier.

"The Rebels?" Dan asked. "Have we-beaten them?"

The tall soldier laughed. "I'd say they've hightailed it all the way back to Corinth by now.

They tried one final charge down at the stone wall, but we stopped them good and we've not heard from them since then."

"Good," Dan said. "That is good."

"Oh, and did you hear about the spy?"

"The spy? What spy?"

"A lady spy. They tell me she's as beautiful as a spring flower. A girl by the name of . . . let's see, what was it?"

"Liberty?" Dan shouted anxiously. "Was it Liberty Welles?"

"Yep," the tall soldier said. "Now that you mention it, I mind that that was the name I heard. Why, have you heard of her?"

Dan sat up quickly, but when he did a wave of pain struck his leg, then swept over him so acutely as to bring on instant nausea and dizziness.

"Easy," the tall soldier said. "You shouldn't try to move."

"I've got to," Dan said. "Where did they take the girl? The spy? Where is she?"

"I just saw her go into General Grant's tent about ten minutes ago," the tall soldier said. "Get me a crutch," Dan ordered.

"Captain, you're in no condition to . . ."

"I said get me a crutch!" Dan ordered again, this time more forcefully than before.

The tall soldier shrugged his shoulders, as if washing his hands of it, then went over to a cache of supplies to get one. It was only then that Dan noticed that the tall soldier was himself wounded, his left arm wrapped in bandages.

Dan took the crutch from him, then, steeling himself against the pain, half-hopped and half limped across the open space to General Grant's tent. There were two guards outside, but, they recognized Dan as a member of Grant's staff and made no attempt to keep him from pushing on inside.

There, sitting on a chair near General Grant's bunk, Dan saw Liberty Welles. She looked small and helpless, and his heart went out to her then as it had never before.

"Oh, Liberty, no," he finally said. "What are you doing here?"

"No," Grant said sourly. "The question is, what are *you* doing here? Captain O'Lee, it wasn't thirty minutes ago that they were debating whether or not to take off your leg, and here you are walking around on it."

"My leg is fine, sir," Dan said offhandedly. "General, how serious is it? What did she do?"

"I don't know," Grant replied. "I might ask you that same question."

"Ask me?" Dan said, looking at Grant in some surprise.

"This is the same girl who came to see me Saturday night, isn't it? The one who identified herself as Miss Roberts?"

Dan felt his face flushing red. Of course the general would put two and two together and realize that he had recognized her but hadn't turned her in.

"I ... I couldn't turn her in, General," Dan said.

"As it turns out, you didn't have to. The girl turned herself in."

"You ... you turned yourself in?" Dan asked. "But why?"

"Do you have to ask that question, Dan O'Lee?" Liberty asked. "Have you any idea how many are dead because of me? Have you any idea how many are laying out there in unspeakable agony, because of me?" Liberty pointed at Dan's wound. "You are crippled, because of me, and yet you ask why I turned myself in."

"Why do you say it's because of you?" Dan asked. "Liberty, you didn't bring on this war."

"No, but I brought on this terrible battle," Liberty said, her voice cut with self-loathing. "I'm the one who transmitted the information to General Beauregard that the Union Army intended to strike at Corinth."

"Of course you did," Dan said easily. "That's just what you were supposed to do."

"You mean I was honor bound to do it? God, spare the dying from my honor."

"No," Dan said. "I don't mean that at all. I mean it was planned for you to carry the word to Johnston and Beauregard. Don't you see?"

"Don't I see?" Liberty asked, clearly puzzled by Dan's remarks. "No, I don't see. I don't see at all. What are you getting at?"

"He means you were set up, Miss Welles," General Grant said evenly.

"Setup?"

"General Halleck knew you were a spy. He gave you just the information he wanted to give you, hoping you would carry it to Johnston and thus bring on this battle."

"You mean ... you wanted this terrible battle to take place?" Liberty asked in a small voice.

"Yes."

"But . . . but the casualties. Surely, general, your side suffered as many casualties as the South?"

"Oh, I wouldn't be surprised if we didn't suffer more," Grant replied. "But we could have lost two times as many men and would still have won the battle, Miss Welles. It's all a matter of arithmetic."

"A matter of arithmetic? No, general, it's a matter of blood. Blood. Blood that's on these hands." Liberty held her hands out and looked at them. Then, suddenly, she realized what General Grant had said. She got a look of horror on her face, then turned on Dan. "You!" she shouted. "You did this! You brought on this battle, and then you let me suffer with the thought that I did it!"

"Liberty, believe me, I didn't..." Dan started, but before he could finish his statement, Liberty, in a move of incredible speed, grabbed General Grant's pistol and swung it toward him. She pulled the trigger, and the roar of the handgun was deafening inside the tent.

Dan could feel the hot air and hear the angry buzz of the bullet as it whizzed by his head and punched through the side of the tent. He looked at Liberty in shock and fear, then saw with relief that she wasn't going to shoot at him again. She lowered the gun until her arm was hanging straight by her side. She hung her head and cried.

The guards from outside came running in with their rifles at the high port, but General Grant stopped them with a wave of his hand. Quietly and gently, he reached for his pistol, then gingerly pulled it from Liberty's unprotesting grip.

As soon as she was disarmed, General Grant motioned for the guards to take her away.

General Grant and Dan were alone in the tent for a few minutes after Liberty had gone. "Where will they take her, general?"

"To the gunboat *Lexington*," General Grant said. "There is a brig on board. We'll confine her there."

"Is she to be shot?"

"That will depend on the court-martial," General Grant replied.

"General, does she have to be court-martialed? Couldn't you just let her go?"

"Are you in love with her?" General Grant asked quietly.

"Very much in love with her," Dan replied.

"Even though she tried to kill you?"

"If she had really tried, general, I'd be dead now," Dan said.

"Yes," Grant said, "I suppose you would at that." Grant walked over to the door of the tent and looked outside, standing in pensive silence for a moment or two. Then he turned back to look at Dan. "General Halleck is coming down here soon. Did I tell you that?"

"Yes, sir," Dan replied.

"If he gets here and the girl is still in the brig, it will be he who convenes the court-martial. I fear he will not be of a generous nature."

"I'm afraid you are right."

"On the other hand," Grant mused, "if the girl was gone before he got here, there would be no prisoner to court-martial."

"Gone?" Dan asked.

"I do have the authority to parole her into the custody of an officer," General Grant said.

"General, you would do that?"

"I would, yes," General Grant said. "I would parole her to you."

Dan hobbled out of the tent and looked down toward the river at the gunboat *Lexington*. In the west the sun was sinking in a large crimson ball, as if that heavenly body had been it self bloodied by the terrible strife which had taken place on the battlefield for the last two days. Dan studied it quietly for a moment. Finally he turned to Grant.

"I appreciate it, general, but, perhaps you'd better parole her to another. It would not be honorable of me to leave here with the task as yet undone."

Grant put his hand on Dan's shoulders. "Dan, how many of the dead boys lying out there would have gone to Congress had they lived? How many would be doctors, schoolteachers, writers, farmers, carpenters, architects and bridge-builders? Those are men whose skills will never aid the rebuilding of our nation once this war is over. As a commander, I know the folly of squandering all one's resources, and I say that our nation cannot survive if all our resources are wasted in battle. The surgeon has certified your wound of sufficient seriousness to warrant sending you away from the battlefield, and that's just what I'm doing. You will be needed after this war, Dan, and I want to make sure you are still around. You are one of them."

"One of them?"

"One of the builders," General Grant said. The whistle blew three times, and Dan looked toward the boat.

"I've already had your things loaded aboard," Grant said. "I did that as soon as the surgeon gave me the warrant on your condition." Dan sighed. "Then I guess I'll be going."

"Have a good trip," Grant invited.

"Thank you, general. Thank you very much," Dan said.

Dan started toward the boat. Just before he stepped aboard, he looked back at the short, stocky general. He had never known anyone quite like General Grant. He was a common man, who, in an uncommon situation, had risen to greatness.

Dan was helped aboard and shown to a cabin, which had been prepared for him. He sat, gratefully, on his bunk, then raised his throbbing leg up to give it a rest. He was massaging it gently when he heard a light knock on his door.

"Come in," he called.

The door opened and closed, and Liberty stepped in. She was looking at him with a puzzled expression on her face.

"I'm told I've been paroled to you."

"That's right."

"And what do you intend to do with me?" Liberty asked.

"I don't know," Dan replied. "That all depends."

"Depends on what?"

"On whether or not you still wish to kill me," Dan said, looking up at her.

Liberty hung her head. "I'm sorry," she said. "It was a foolish thing. I guess I was just upset that you succeeded in turning the tables on me."

"But I didn't," Dan said.

"What do you mean?"

"Liberty, I tried to tell you. I had nothing to do with that. I didn't know you were set up until later. In fact, we were both set up."

"Oh," Liberty said, putting her hand to her mouth. "And to think that I almost killed you."

Dan smiled, a slow, knowing smile. "No," he said. "You didn't even come close."

"What do you mean?"

"You didn't really want to kill me," Dan said. "If you had wanted to, you would have."

"You're right," Liberty admitted. "I didn't want to. I mean, I did want to, but I just couldn't do it."

"Why couldn't you?"

"You know why."

"Yes, I know why," Dan said. "But I want to hear it." He smiled again. "Or, perhaps you'd rather be returned to the brig?"

"No, I ... I don't want to go back there," Liberty said. She looked at Dan, then realized that he was teasing her. "Oh . . . you weren't serious."

"About as serious as your attempt to kill me," Dan said. He swung his leg off the bed, intending to stand up, but when he did the pain hit again, and he winced against it.

"Dan, oh, darling," Liberty said, seeing his pain. "How awful of me. Here you are suffering so, and I've been so cruel to you." She crossed the cabin in three quick steps, then, gently, lay him back on the bed. "Are you all right?"

"Liberty, I . . . I . . ." Dan gasped. He breathed hard, as if groping for breath.

"Dan . . . Dan . . . what is it? Is there anything I can do?"

Dan opened one mischievous eye and smiled up at her. "Yeah," he said. "You could give me a kiss."

"Well, I don't know, if you're going to act that way, I might just..."

Dan pulled her to him and kissed her with lips which promised much more. Then, after breaking once, he kissed her again before she could regain her breath. Finally, when she was totally breathless, he broke off the kiss the second time.

"Say it," he demanded.

"Say what?" she replied, now teasing him.

"Say it, damn it!" Dan demanded.

Liberty smiled. She put her finger on his lips. "I love you," she said.

"That's more like it. I like the sound of it, Liberty, and you'll be saying it often."

"Whenever you wish, my love," Liberty said, kissing his lips quiet.

The End

A look at Long Road to Abilene by Robert Vaughan

LONG ROAD TO ABILENE, is a classic hero's journey, a western adventure that exemplifies the struggles, the defeats, and the victories that personify the history of the American West. After surviving the bloody battle of Franklin and the hell of a Yankee prison camp, Cade McCall comes home to the woman he loves only to find that she, believing him dead, has married his brother. With nothing left to keep him in Tennessee, Cade journeys to New Orleans where an encounter with a beautiful woman leads to being shanghaied for an unexpected adventure at sea. Returning to Texas, he signs on to drive a herd of cattle to Abilene, where he is drawn into a classic showdown of good versus evil, and a surprising reunion with an old enemy.

About the Author

Robert Vaughan sold his first book when he was 19. That was 57 years and nearly 500 books ago. He wrote the novelization for the mini series *Andersonville*. Vaughan wrote, produced, and appeared in the History Channel documentary Vietnam Homecoming. His books have hit the NYT bestseller list seven times. He has won the Spur Award, the PORGIE Award (Best Paperback Original), the Western Fictioneers Lifetime Achievement Award, received the Readwest President's Award for Excellence in Western Fiction, is a member of the American Writers Hall of Fame and is a Pulitzer Prize nominee. Vaughn is also a retired army officer, helicopter pilot with three tours in Vietnam. And received the Distinguished Flying Cross, the Purple Heart, The Bronze Star with three oak leaf clusters, the Air Medal for valor with 35 oak leaf clusters, the Army Commendation Medal, the Meritorious Service Medal, and the Vietnamese Cross of Gallantry.

Find more great titles by Robert Vaughan and Wolfpack Publishing at http://wolfpackpublishing.com/robert-vaughan/

Made in the USA
Middletown, DE
17 August 2023